Starting Over at Starlight Cottage

Debbie Viggiano

Starting Over at Starlight Cottage © Debbie Viggiano 2024

Published worldwide 2024 © Debbie Viggiano

All rights reserved in all media. No part of this book may be reproduced or transmitted in any form by any means, electronic or mechanical (including but not limited to: the Internet, photocopying, recording or by any information storage and retrieval system), without prior permission in writing from the author.

The moral right of Debbie Viggiano as the author of the work has been asserted by her in accordance with the Copyright, Designs and Patents Act 1988.

This e-book is licensed for your personal enjoyment only. This e-book may not be re-sold or given away to other people. If you would like to share this book with another person, please purchase an additional copy for each recipient. Thank you for respecting the hard work of this author.

ISBN: 9798300894733

For all my lovely readers!

Chapter One

'Oh, bog off!' I shrieked down the phone.

The air quivered with the force of my tone.

'Tut, tut, Tilly. Always such unimaginative and limiting vocabulary,' drawled my husband.

Robin had played his usual trick on me. The goading game. He'd pressed all my buttons. Wound me up. And any other expression one cared to sling into the wordy equation.

I'm not usually a pink-cheeked, bosom-heaving harridan. Certainly not at nine o'clock on a Sunday morning when about to don my sou'wester and take my dog for a walk. Outside, November rain was downpouring like a carwash in full flow. Inside, my soon-to-be ex-spouse had yet again brought out the worst in me.

Robin, now firmly in the thrall – and under the thumb – of a very pushy mistress, wanted me to leave the marital home and make way for him and Sexy Samantha. Well, fine. But not until I was good and ready. And right now, I wasn't.

I needed to detach emotionally from this house. It had been my home for all our married life. Twenty years. A lot of love had gone into its bricks and mortar, not to mention a major refurbishment. What a shame one couldn't refurb one's marriage.

Angrily, I tucked a strand of long blonde hair behind one ear. I needed fresh air. Now. With Cindy. And where *was* Cindy?

I took a step back. Bent my knees. Tipped my head sideways and peered under the kitchen table. A brown-and-white furry body was wedged between the legs of one chair. A long stringy tail wagged cautiously as a pair of chocolate-brown eyes regarded me anxiously. In that moment I felt like the worst doggy mummy on the planet.

'Sorry,' I crooned. 'Sorry, sorry, *sorryyy*. I love you.'

'Apology accepted,' said Robin crisply. 'As for the love bit, Tilly, it's too late for that.'

The line went dead before I could deliver a crushing reply.

I abandoned the mobile as Cindy crept out from under the table.

'That was Robin,' I said. 'The man who once promised to love and cherish me until death do us part. As you know, I am now legally extricating myself from him at considerable expense.'

Indeed, Mum, I imagined her to reply.

Such was my life these days. The only conversation within these walls was of the make-believe kind between me and my four-legged friend. Naturally Cindy understood my every word. And it went without saying that she was on my side.

Your ex is a prat.

See?

'Absolutely,' I agreed. 'Sorry you've got caught up in it

all. It's not what I wanted for you. Not when you've already come from one broken home.'

It's fine, Mum. As long as I'm with you, then that's all that matters.

'You are such a darling.'

Mum?

'Yes?'

Do you ever worry about the conversations that you and I have?

'I know what you're hinting at,' I said carefully. 'You're suggesting I'm having a spot of bother with my mental health. That it's a bit wobbly.'

More like kaput.

I ignored the dig and headed off to the coat cupboard with Cindy at my heel. In this weather she'd need to wear her waterproof coat. She wasn't a fan of rain at the best of times.

'And also' – I prattled – 'you think I'm lonely. But I'm not. I have you, so how can I ever be lonely?'

You know what I mean. I think you should get out more.

'I don't want to get out more,' I said, strapping her into the waterproof and clipping the lead to her collar. I shrugged on my own waterproof, then grabbed my wellies. 'I'm not even sure I want to go out in this weather,' I declared, opening the front door.

For a moment, the two of us regarded the rainstorm, then Cindy looked up at me in consternation.

I'm not sure I want to go out in it either.

'C'mon,' I sighed, pulling on my boots. 'Let's do this.'

Together, the two of us stepped out into the deluge.

We walked along the pavement, hugging the fences and garden walls of the executive houses in my street. This was Meopham's most prestigious tree-lined road. Occasionally Cindy and I would pause and cower, anxious to avoid a fountain of puddle-splash from passing cars.

Getting into stride, I reflected on the chit-chat that had just taken place between me and my dog. Well, okay, if you want to be picky, the conversation between me... and me. I didn't doubt for one second that Cindy had her own thoughts and that she tried to telepathically convey them, but her vocab was probably more along the lines of:

Food... now! Treat... now! Wee... now!

But like most dog owners – and maybe cat owners too – I had entire conversations with my pooch, and I liked to believe that she reciprocated. Cindy was privy to all the details of my upcoming divorce from Robin.

I'd also entrusted some of it to Lisa, my colleague and bestie. She'd listened in wide eyed horror when I'd revealed the reason for me and Robin abruptly separating.

My husband had been staying increasingly late at the office, apparently chasing an elusive account. The whole *working late* thing might have continued forever if I hadn't surprised Robin and unexpectedly turned up at his office.

Protheroe & Jameson Accountants were situated near Sevenoaks' Stag Theatre. I'd anticipated that Robin – the *Jameson* part of the business – would be amazed by my off-the-cuff gesture to see a comedy act followed by a late-night candlelit dinner at a trendy bistro. However, the surprise had been on me.

I'd walked purposefully through the main open-plan office area. Usually heaving with activity, at this later hour it had been empty. I'd then paused to give a light tap on the door to Robin's private office. Without bothering to wait for a reply, I'd gone through – straight into a nightmare.

For there, skirt rucked up around her thighs, was my husband's PA. Samantha was sprawled across Robin's desk, legs in the air. Her bare backside had been positioned over the ink blotter. I'd vaguely wondered if the Montblanc I'd gifted Robin last Christmas had been wedged up her arse. But all thoughts about fountain pens had fragmented as my brain struggled to process my husband giving not dictation, but *dick*tation.

It was one of those moments where the three of us had all reacted with split-second precision, causing us to bellow, squawk and shriek in perfect synchronicity.

In hindsight, it would have been most satisfying to have grabbed the waste bin and rammed it over Samantha's head, before tugging hard on Robin's balls. Unfortunately, I'd been ambushed by a tidal wave of tears. The weeping had been so copious as to be semi-blinding. I'd hardly been able to see. In fact, the flow from my tear ducts had not been dissimilar to the deluge I was now walking in with Cindy.

Certainly, my exit from Robin's office had been horribly undignified. Desperate to flee, I'd spun on my heel, crashed into the doorframe, cannoned into a desk, bounced off the photocopier, then tripped over a typing chair before finally making my getaway.

'Wait, Tilly,' Robin had called after me. 'Come back. I've made a stupid mistake.'

'You WHAT?' Samantha had screeched. 'You told me you were leaving her!'

Their subsequent row had been drowned out by my strangled sobs and the roar of my heartbeat thanks to my aortic valves seemingly relocating to my eardrums.

Rather than head home, I'd bobbed down a side street. Retrieving my mobile from my handbag, I'd switched off the Locator app, then ducked inside the Stag Theatre.

Finding my seat, I'd been acutely aware of the empty space beside me. I'd quietly sobbed along to the comedian's banter, while the audience had split their sides. To this day I have no idea what the guy's name was. Nor could I repeat any of the jokes he told. But I do remember the man sitting in front of me. As I'd worked my way through a packet of Kleenex, he'd repeatedly turned to glare at me.

'Are you aware that you sound like a trumpeting elephant?' he'd hissed.

I'd regarded him through puffy eyes.

'And are you aware' – I'd snorted attractively – 'that somewhere you're depriving a village of an idiot?'

Chapter Two

I'd left the theatre with swollen sinuses and eyes that resembled jam doughnuts. How could I not have known that Robin had been having an affair? And how long had it been going on?

A range of emotions had ripped through me. Disbelief and sorrow. Disbelief and incredulity. Disbelief and heartbreak. Disbelief and rage. By the time I'd reached the carpark, the rage had been in full throttle. Snarling like a rabid dog, I'd located Octavia, my bright orange Fiat 500.

Lip curled, I'd practically thrown myself into the vehicle. Ramming Octavia's gear into reverse, I'd failed to check the rearview mirror. The car had shot backwards and nearly flattened a man. There had been a horrible thud – like that of a body bouncing off the boot end – followed by the screech of swiftly applied brakes.

Flinging open the driver's door, I'd made to leap out, and nearly garrotted myself on the seatbelt. Frantically unbuckling, I'd fought my way out of Octavia to find a very good-looking man apoplectic with anger.

'Oh thank God, you're alive,' I breathed.

'No thanks to you,' he roared.

In the carpark's dim light I could make out dark hair and

matching eyes. He reminded me of Antonio Banderas in his heyday. In fact, I could imagine this man, right now, in one of those domino masks. An instant metamorphosis. From mere mortal to superhero. Any man could wear one and be changed for the better. Even my postman – who was a dead ringer for Nigel Farage. Suddenly my postie would become *Superrr Postie*. Perhaps I should buy a few of those masks. Send them off to Parliament. Never mind Reform. There could be a whole new party. *Transform* spearheaded by *Super Nige*.

I shook my head. Evidently this latest shock was interfering with my ability to be clearheaded.

'Did I hit you?' I quavered.

'No,' the stranger growled. 'But if I hadn't slapped my hand against your rear window to warn you of my presence, it might have been a different story.'

'So… are you okay?'

'Funnily enough' – he glared at me furiously – 'I am *not* okay. That was a close call, and I feel somewhat shaken up. Women like you…'

Uh-oh. A rant was imminent.

'Let me stop you right there.' I stuck one hand in the air like a traffic cop. 'Never mind women like me. It's *men* like *you* who need to take a good long look at your own actions. Walking through a dark carpark in black clothes and getting in the way of a reversing vehicle is nobody's fault but your own.'

'Are you having a laugh?' the man spluttered.

I gaped at him.

'Do I look like I'm splitting my sides?'

'You are insane,' he declared.

It was too much. First, the discovery that my husband was an adulterous git. Now a judgemental one-liner from this sanctimonious prat. I had a feeling my emotions were about to get the better of me.

'Apologise right now,' I barked.

'Excuse me?' he said incredulously.

I shook my head in a parody of sadness.

'Ah, of *course* you're not going to apologise.' I put my hands on my hips. Planted my feet wide. 'And do you know HOW I know?'

'Because you're a psychic madwoman?' he ventured.

I stuck my chin in the air. Gave him a thin smile.

'Nope. It's because you're not *man* enough. Not *man* enough to say sorry.'

'You really are something else,' he mused.

'Thank you.' I inclined my head. 'I would challenge you to a battle of wits, but I see you are unarmed. Now, if you'll excuse me.' I headed back to the still open driver's door, hopped behind the wheel, then buzzed down Octavia's window. 'Meanwhile, try not to get run over by any other innocent drivers.'

The man gawped at me, then found his voice.

'Tell me, is being stupid a profession, or are you just gifted?'

Me? Stupid? I hit the brakes. Leant out the window.

'If I could transplant your brain into a bird' – I snapped – 'it would probably fly backwards.'

He narrowed his eyes.

'I heard that scientists are trying to figure out how long a person can live without a brain. Do be sure to tell them your age.'

'Ha! Well, you're the reason scientists decided we descended from apes.'

'Oh grow up,' he snarled.

'No, *you* grow up.'

Damn. Not the greatest riposte. One nil to Antonio Banderas. Suddenly, all my pent up hurt and angst about Robin and Samantha rushed to the surface.

'How DARE you play verbal gymnastics with me and cause emotional mayhem when I was happily minding my own business and replaying the moment I discovered my husband shagging his secretary in full technical glory. Oh yes, that's got your attention, hasn't it?' His expression was now startled. 'Have you any idea how I feel right now, hm? Well, I'll tell you. I'm in unspeakable agony. My heart feels like smashed avocado. So take your self-righteous insufferable arrogance and MOVE OUT OF MY SODDING WAY.'

And with that, Octavia once again sprang backwards, this time nearly taking out a loved-up couple strolling towards their parking bay.

Shaking like an aspen tree in a storm, I then smartly drove off before anyone else came dangerously close to ending their days under the wheels of a bright orange car.

As I'd roared off, my inner voice had cautioned me to slow down. Equally, another voice – a truly nasty one – had encouraged me to go faster. To imagine that instead of

Antonio Banderas being squashed flat by Octavia's tyres, rather it was Robin. Or, more precisely, Robin's penis. And then for me to screech to a halt, exit Octavia, and bend over my gasping husband and say, "Don't panic. I know a cure for a flat penis. You simply tickle it. It's called a *test tickle*."

As I'd finally driven into Meopham, I'd presumed to find Robin at home. Maybe holed up in the spare room. Or perhaps in the marital bedroom, keeping my side of the bed warm while he worked out a plausible explanation for his shattered wife. That he might come up with a half-decent excuse. *It's not your fault, it's mine.*

Or would he instead blame me?

You neglected me, Tilly…

Never paid me any compliments…

Didn't cook yummy dinners to keep me by your side…

Almost immediately my inner voice rose to the surface, urgently reminding me not to fall for any sexist tripe.

Woman up, Tilly! Tear him off a strip. When was the last time Robin bothered about romance? Took YOU out for the evening? Wasn't that the whole point of you purchasing those theatre tickets? To inject some va-va-voom into your marriage? To have a flirty drink in a nearby bar… then hold his hand as you sat side by side in the stalls? To later tell him that he was not just your world but also your moon and stars. And this is how he repays you?

'Too bloody right,' I snarled, accidentally jumping a red traffic light.

My inner voice had urged me to calm down. To calm down and *slow* down. It was one thing to have your marriage unexpectedly come to an abrupt full stop. It was quite another to end the evening in a police cell for reckless driving.

Trembling, I'd eased my foot off the accelerator, attempted to stem a fresh outbreak of tears, and mentally tried to press the pause button on the image that would not stop playing in my head. Robin and Samantha shagging. That and Samantha's hairless vagina.

Had Samantha lasered off her pubic hair? Or gone mad with the wax strips? Or even bought a razor and shaved the whole lot off? I'd once done the latter and ended up looking like a plucked chicken with folliculitis.

No, she must have had it all lasered off. How else could a woman achieve a fanny smoother than an Elgin marble? And why was I even thinking about Samantha's privates when my world had imploded? It was a question I would repeatedly ask myself over the days and weeks to come.

By the time I'd parked Octavia on our driveway, I'd been in a state of high anxiety and anticipation. What would Robin say to me?

But when I'd let myself into the house, there'd been no sign of him.

Chapter Three

That night, I'd tossed and turned in bed believing I'd never get to sleep. Much to my surprise, I'd eventually fallen into a dreamless slumber.

What had seemed like seconds later, the alarm clock had awoken me. Its shrill call had catapulted me out of black nothingness. I'd lain there, back in the real world, contemplating whether to message my boss and throw a sickie.

After a couple of minutes, I'd rejected the idea. There was a need to offload. And who better to do that with than with my bestie and fellow colleague at Home and Hearth Estate Agents.

I'd met Lisa some ten years earlier when I'd first started working for the agency. She was basically the sister I'd never had. Lisa always listened to problems and gave sound advice. And, yes, I could have also confided in my parents who were – it went without saying – wonderful at sharing their wisdom and guidance. However, telling them about Robin's thrusting hips and Samantha's lack of pubes was one step too far. On the other hand, Lisa could be given a full account of the previous night's debacle, right down to me nearly flattening Antonio Banderas.

Throughout our friendship, whenever life had thrown a curveball, Lisa had been a tower of strength. Obviously, I reciprocated when she encountered challenges. Over the years we'd worked our way through hundreds of tissues and thousands of chocolate biscuits. Naturally, when I'd told Lisa about walking in on Robin and Samantha, she'd been appalled.

Robin had contacted me later that day. He'd made sure that he was in his office in Sevenoaks while I was at work in Meopham and seated at my desk. Several miles were between us. Sensible man. By not coming into my office, he'd avoided me whacking him in the face with a property file. Equally, there was no risk of me picking up a ruler and poking out his eyeballs. Although, right now, a different pair of balls figured in my revenge fantasies. Samantha wasn't exempt either. My mouth twisted at the thought of pinning her down and giving her new pubes – in blue biro.

Robin's telephone conversation was businesslike.

'Listen, Tilly. It takes two to tango.'

'Meaning?'

'I made a mistake, but the blame is with you.'

'Eh?'

'If you didn't nag me so much, then I wouldn't have strayed.'

'Nag you?' I hissed down the line. 'As in *please pick up your socks, please hang up your clothes, please* – when you've used the loo – *swizz the toilet bowl with the loo brush.* Is that what you're referring to?'

'Spot on,' he said, oblivious to my sarcasm. 'So, if you

could just see your way to stopping the nags, we can be reconciled in a heartbeat. Let's start again in our marriage. I'll book a nice holiday, eh? A getaway. Romantic, obviously. And look, Tilly. I know it hit you hard never having kids.' His voice dropped an octave. Became persuasive. 'But I'm willing to negotiate.'

I froze. My hand gripped the phone tightly. Lisa was staring at me, desperately trying to work out what Robin was saying at the other end of the line.

'What do you mean?' I whispered. 'Negotiate as in… IVF?'

Lisa now looked like she'd swallowed a gobstopper.

Robin had played his trump card. A family. But, at forty-nine, surely I was too old to be considered for fertility treatment? But, then again, I'd never fully explored this avenue. Robin had always been dead against it. He'd made his feelings known on the subject long ago.

It's God's way, or no way…
Leave it to Mother Nature…
If it's meant to be, it will be…

And all those other crappy phrases.

But now, Robin had my full attention. After all, these days, plenty of women were older mums. And where there was a will, there was a way. I was still having periods. Albeit a little spluttery of late. And – now I came to think about it – only last week there'd been an article in a woman's magazine about a fifty-six-year-old female who'd given birth to her own grandson.

Omigod! Was *this* what Robin was suggesting? That we

find a surrogate? I mentally shook my head. Cleared away the crowded thoughts.

'Well?' I prompted. 'Are you talking about fertility treatment, or what?'

Lisa was now gaping at me, mouth open, but I ignored her. I was desperately trying to stay grounded. To not let my mind rush off to another place. A place I'd never dared go. But... too late.

There I was, patting my swollen tummy. A protective hand over my abdomen as I attended a prenatal appointment. A scan. The sonographer saying, "Congratulations, Mrs Jameson. You're expecting a little girl." A mini-Tilly. A tiny replica of me. Blonde. Blue-eyed.

Or maybe the sonographer would instead tell me a baby boy was on the way. A mini-Robin with chestnut hair, brown eyes – but more fun looking than my husband. Yes, *this* mini-Robin would have a Just William impish grin and a face full of freckles. Adorable. Too late I realised that my mind had taken me on a wild ride down Happy Ever After Street.

'No, Tilly,' said Robin, bringing me abruptly back to the present. 'IVF is way too stressful. I'm talking about adoption.'

I froze. For a moment, I couldn't speak. Adoption? I wasn't sure I could go there. What... take some distraught new mother's precious newborn? Wonder if she'd ever emotionally recover from giving up a piece of herself? Forever wonder what the story was behind her tears? Like... had she been abandoned by the child's father? Left unsupported? Financially not been able to cobble together the money for a loaf of bread, never mind nappies and formula milk?

And then my mind jumped on a plane. Headed overseas. To orphanages. Babies and tots with tearstained cheeks, holding out their little arms as we approached their cots.

Will you be my new mummy and daddy? Mine were killed in war.

Robin and I scooping up two children. Four. No, six. Ten! Emulating Angelina Jolie and coming home with our very own rainbow family.

Ah, yes. There were we all were. Our readymade family walking hand in hand, once again in Happy Ever After Street.

'Okay,' I said tentatively. 'You have my full attention. If you're truly serious, then I'm open to the idea of starting again.'

Lisa now appeared to be choking on her own tongue.

'Good,' said Robin sounding relieved.

'Have you an agency in mind?' I ventured.

'Agency?' queried Robin in surprise. 'I don't think we need go through anything like that.'

Oh no. Not a black-market baby. I couldn't do anything illegal.

'I want everything above board, Robin,' I asserted.

'For what?' he said in confusion.

'The adoption, of course,' I cried.

Had sex with Samantha addled his brain? And that was another thing. That woman would have to go. Robin must employ someone else. Preferably an old boot. A matronly female on the cusp of retirement. Preferably one with a whiskery chin. I could see such a person now. A Mrs Doubtfire type with spectacles. Iron grey hair. A penchant for bobbly cardigans. Long skirts to cover her varicose veins.

It wasn't lost on me that Samantha looked something like me. We both had long blonde hair and blue eyes. However, I was a jaded version of her. These days there was a puffiness to my eyes and the start of a sag to the jawline. The major difference, of course, was the age gap. Samantha was twenty-nine to my forty-nine. Bitch.

But for now I'd have to park my issues over Sexy Samantha. Mrs Doubtfire could be employed in due course. All in good time. Currently there were more pressing matters to discuss. Like that of our future child.

'Tilly,' said Robin cautiously. 'I think we're at cross purposes.'

My brow furrowed. What could I possibly have misunderstood?

'You said no to IVF, but yes to adoption,' I pointed out.

Lisa was now heaving gusty sighs. She threw me a look that translated as *this is going to end in tears.*

Robin cleared his throat.

'I'm talking about us adopting a dog.'

'A dog?' I repeated stupidly.

'Yes,' said Robin, his tone indicating he was currently talking to someone educationally challenged. 'A dog. I thought we could start with a trip to Battersea.'

'But… I thought you meant a *child*,' I croaked, my eyes brimming.

Lisa flashed me another look. One that said *I knew it*. She stood up. Made her way to the small staff kitchen at the rear of the office. In crisis, resort to biscuits and a brew.

'No, Tilly,' Robin tutted. 'I'm not talking about a child. There's been a misunderstanding.'

'You can say that again,' I snarled furiously, blinking away the tears.

'So, are we both now on the same page?'

'Yes, we're talking about dogs.'

'We are.'

'In which case' – I growled – 'IF we get back together, I assume you'll be getting rid of Samantha?'

'Don't be ridiculous,' Robin spluttered. 'Samantha is an excellent PA. Secretaries like her are scarcer than gold dust.'

For a moment I was too upset to speak. For one second there, I'd allowed myself to go down a path of new beginnings. Starting over with Robin. A later-in-life family. There had been no trust issues because Samantha hadn't figured in this new future. Instead, I'd been offered a four-legged companion to keep me company while Robin continued to work late at the office alongside an attractive woman who had a bald vagina.

'Thanks, Robin,' I said, as Lisa returned. She set down a mug of steaming tea and a plate of bickies.

'I'm glad you've seen sense,' said Robin smugly. As well he might. It wasn't every day a husband got away with porking his PA, telling the wife it was all her fault and that she should spend her evenings with a dog.

'Rest assured that I've seen sense,' I declared. I picked up a biscuit and took a savage bite. 'This marriage' – I announced, spraying crumbs across my keyboard – 'is officially over.'

Chapter Four

After making a pre-booked appointment, in due course I'd travelled to Battersea Dogs Home.

The misunderstanding with Robin over adoption had stirred up something deep in my soul. I'd left the dogs' home with Cindy.

My *baby* was a one-year-old brown-and-white mongrel. Like all new parents, I adored her, and my love was unconditional.

I'd also made a second appointment, this time with a law firm, and filed for divorce. Since then, I'd reverted to my maiden name. After twenty years of being Mrs Jameson, it felt strange to suddenly be Miss Thomas. That said, it was also very liberating.

Robin had been livid at my rejecting his offer of reconciliation. I didn't think he was particularly upset about losing me. More likely devastated at the prospect of losing half his assets. This included our marital home at the affluent end of Meopham, along with his considerable savings. These I'd contributed to. Regrettably the account was solely in his name. However, the solicitor had said she'd sort it out – along with Robin's million-pound pension pot.

My husband had since been relentless in his attempt at

persuading me to vacate the marital home. His plan was to have Samantha move in, then rent out her flat for extra income. He'd offered to buy me out – at a pittance.

So far, I'd been awkward and refused to comply. My solicitor had written a snotty letter to Robin on my behalf, then charged like a wounded rhino. My takeaway had been that I was perfectly capable of writing my own snotty letters if I chucked in a few *whereins* and *heretofores* and put *Without Prejudice* in the reference line.

'I don't understand why you're being so uncooperative,' Robin ranted in his latest phone call. 'Why can't you move in with your parents?'

'You know full well they live in Cornwall,' I said crisply. 'How am I meant to commute to work?'

'On your turbo-charged broomstick,' he said snidely.

I ignored the insinuation that I was a witch.

'Anyway' – I sniffed – 'it's not as if you're homeless. You are living with Samantha and have a roof over your head.'

'It's a two-bedroomed flat,' he blustered. 'It's about the size of a supermarket food freezer. I have nowhere to hang my suits and other clothes.'

'Put them in her second bedroom,' I suggested.

'I can't,' he wailed. 'She's had it converted into a dressing room. It's rammed with her own stuff. I mean, how many shelves of shoes and handbags can one woman have? It's obscene.'

'Sorry,' I said, sounding anything but. 'Not my problem.'

I was aware that Samantha had her eye on the marital prize. Not only becoming the second Mrs Jameson but also hanging up her keyboard and spending her days watching Loose Women in my front room.

Meanwhile, my parents calmly took the news of my marriage breakdown. They showed no surprise. They offered words of support and said a bed was always available with them.

Deep down, I knew they'd never cared for Robin. They thought him self-centred, materialistic and tight. I'd once accidentally overheard Dad talking to Mum. It had been when Robin and I had stayed a weekend with them in Falmouth. They'd been in the kitchen washing up after Sunday dinner. Robin had retired to the upstairs loo with the Sunday papers, and I'd nipped into the downstairs toilet to have a quick wee, before helping with the drying up. I'd paused outside the kitchen as Dad had confided in Mum.

'That fella has more padlocks on his wallet than all the love lock bridges around the world,' he declared. 'He never puts his hand in his pocket.'

'I know,' Mum quietly agreed. 'I hope he's not mean sharing his money with our Tilly.'

Dad had made a harrumphing sound.

'I wouldn't bet on it, Sylvia. Our girl goes out to work and earns her own living. However, I can't shake the feeling that what is Robin's is Robin's, and what is Tilly's might be Robin's too.'

Mum had tutted.

'I do hope you're wrong, Malcom.'

'Hm. Not sure about that. It's not as if he's penniless either. The man is an accountant. He has a partnership.'

'Perhaps he's careful because he's thinking of their future. Retirement. And he wants their Golden Years to be comfortable.'

'Maybe,' said Dad, not sounding convinced. 'Or perhaps he's like that nursery rhyme. You know the one. *The king was in his counting house counting all his money...*'

My parents weren't far wrong about Robin and his predilection towards money. He certainly didn't splash his cash on me. He liked to spend as little as possible. But then again, wining and dining a young mistress and buying a Mulberry handbag here and Prada sunglasses there – as I later discovered – isn't cheap.

I'd told my parents about there being another woman. Regarding Samantha, I'd been economical with the truth. There had been no mention of how I'd found out about the affair. That said, Dad was nobody's fool. He suspected I wasn't spilling all the beans because it was too traumatic to do so.

'Wretched man,' he declared upon hearing there was a love triangle. 'If I was a couple of decades younger, I'd get in my car, drive up to Kent, stomp into Robin's office, and bop him on the nose.'

'Thanks, Dad,' I said, smiling at the other end of the phone. It was touching that my darling father still wished to protect and defend his only child – even if that child was almost half a century old. 'But there's no need. It's fine. *I'm fine.*'

That much was true. Since Cindy's arrival in my life, I might not be dancing around my bedroom or singing into my hairbrush as the radio played, but I *was* doing okay. Better than I'd dared to hope, anyway.

It saddened me to be suddenly single at forty-nine. The next birthday – a big one – would be celebrated without a partner. But then again, was that so bad? I could pop down to Cornwall and see my parents. Take Cindy with me. And I had my bestie here, in Kent. Lisa would happily celebrate with me. She had an on-off relationship with a guy called Phil. Currently it was off. She said it didn't bother her at all.

'I have Ronald, my rabbit,' she happily informed me. 'He keeps me satisfied between relationships.'

It had taken me a moment to realise that Ronald didn't have long ears and a twitching nose.

Meanwhile the weeks had limped by. My new life had ebbed and flowed at much the same pace as previously. Despite the divorce being underway, nothing much was happening other than Robin's endless nagging about him and Samantha having the marital home, and suggesting I do some sofa surfing. And maybe that situation would have continued for a few more weeks if a Mr Albert Garroway hadn't telephoned Home and Hearth on a rather quiet Monday morning advising that he wished to put his house on the market.

Lisa took the call. Afterwards, she told me all about Starlight Cottage in the not-so-far-away village of Starlight Croft. Somehow, I knew, just *knew*, that this house was going to be pivotal in my new future.

Chapter Five

One of the benefits from working as an estate agent is getting inside info. Getting the *heads up* on property valuations. Knowing mortgage brokers. Having a working relationship with conveyancers. Also, identifying from our client database, who might be interested in a potential sale or purchase days ahead of a property's details being uploaded online. And right now, I fell into the latter category and wanted first dibs on Starlight Cottage.

'This property sounds perfect for you,' said Lisa cosily. 'It's certainly affordable. After all, you should achieve a good price for your place. You and Robin own an executive house with several empty bedrooms.' She caught my expression and swiftly moved the conversation forward. 'Your property is also perfectly placed for schools, bus routes, railways stations, shops and motorway links.'

Together we did the maths. If the sums were right, I'd just about have enough to buy Starlight Cottage with a manageable mortgage, but time was of the essence. I'd need to give in to Robin and let him and Samanatha buy me out.

That afternoon, the vendor came into the office. Lisa shook Albert Garroway's hand before going through the paperwork with him. After some chit-chat, Mr Garroway handed over a housekey. Now that his wife's funeral was out the way, he wanted to head off to Dorset and spend a week with family recharging his emotional batteries. Meanwhile, he was entrusting the agency to oversee the internal photographs and take care of any viewings.

When Mr Garroway left, Lisa turned to me.

'After work, why don't you drive over to Starlight Croft. Do a recce of the village. Have a peek at the outside of the cottage. You could also give Robin a call. Let him know that you've come round to his way of thinking and might even consider moving out immediately.'

'I can't vacate at the moment,' I protested. 'I have nowhere to go.'

'You can have my sofa until the conveyancing is done,' said Lisa generously.

'But what about you and Phil?' I asked.

Phil had been in touch again. He was badgering my bestie to pick up where they'd left off.

'What about him?' Lisa sniffed.

'I presumed you were thinking about getting back together.'

She shook her head.

'Nah. I blew him out.'

'Oh, I'm sorry to hear that. What did he do wrong this time?'

So she told me. Apparently, Phil, despite being a rather bland and non-descript fifty-five-year-old, was a fan of an app that promoted no-strings hookups for couples who wanted threesomes.

Lisa pursed her lips.

'Phil told me that life was short, and that I should be adventurous while I still had the chance. That I needed to let my hair down and' – she adopted a silly voice – '*be more fun.*' She rolled her eyes. 'The stupid prat. He also said that a threesome was every man's fantasy, and that it was now or never.'

'Bloody cheek,' I said, affronted on my friend's behalf.

'I said I'd think about it.'

'What?' I squawked.

She gave the ghost of a smile before continuing.

'Don't look so shocked. Phil was initially delighted. He said, "Oh, babe, that's amazing. I just know you're gonna love being sandwiched between me and another woman." Whereupon I retorted, "Who said anything about the third person being female?" Phil then got the right hump. He called me a pervert for even thinking he could get it on with another man. Pot, kettle, black,' she smirked.

'Oh,' I blinked. I gave Lisa a curious look. 'You wouldn't really be up for a threesome with two men, would you?'

'Of course not,' she snorted. 'I'm an old-fashioned girl who likes straightforward couplings. Anyway, Phil and I are now on an indefinite sabbatical. If he wants to do threesomes, foursomes, or even fivesomes, let him get on with it. But he can count me out. Currently there seems to be a lot of fifty-something men having some sort of sexual crisis. The amount of guys I've come across popping Viagra then going on weird websites to perk up their willies and fragile egos.' She looked pensive for a moment. 'Maybe I should chat up the vendor of Starlight Cottage.'

'Mr Garroway?' I said in surprise. 'He must be around seventy.'

'Mm,' she mused. 'The older man. Never had one before. And he's newly widowed. Ripe for consoling.'

'Lisa,' I tutted, shaking my head. 'Apart from anything else, that's a twenty-year age gap.'

In that moment, it came to me that if Robin and Sexy Samantha's relationship endured, then one day she'd be fifty to Robin's seventy.

'Think how grateful Mr Garroway would be' – Lisa interrupted my thoughts – 'to have a younger companion in his life.'

'I suppose,' I said uncertainly. 'But what about sex? I'm not sure I could do it with someone so much older than me.' Frankly, I had no idea what Sexy Samantha saw in Robin – other than his wallet. 'I mean, what about dentures?' I pulled a face.

The thought of a man popping his teeth into a glass before puckering up for a kiss didn't make my loins twang.

Lisa looked pensive for a moment.

'I'm fairly sure Albert has his own teeth. And anyway, why do you think God invented pink rabbits?'

'Right,' I said faintly.

'Meanwhile' – Lisa shifted in her chair – 'back to Starlight Cottage. Check the place out after work.'

'I will,' I assured. 'I'll have to go home first. Let Cindy out. In fact, she can come with me.'

Chapter Six

'Hello, baby girl,' I said, stepping into my hallway and returning Cindy's effusive greeting. Yes, she was my baby, and yes, she was my girl. 'Mummy wants to take you out.'

Walkies?

'Absolutely, but we're going in the car.'

How is it possible to go for a walk in the car?

'You'll see,' I said, finding her lead.

I led her outside to Octavia. The back of the car was swathed in a protective cover. It stopped dog hair embedding into the upholstery. Cindy jumped in.

Where are we going?

'To check out a village called Starlight Croft,' I said, as the engine turned over.

Have you taken me there before?

'No, but it's not far away. However, it's located at the top of a horrendously steep, winding hill that seems to go on forever. Up and up. Then up some more. Hence the village's name. Starlight Croft is one of the highest points in the south-east of England. Come winter, the village always gets a snow dump. Also, the hill is notorious for becoming an ice rink, which is especially iffy when the local council don't always remember to grit the road.

Sounds fun. We could buy ourselves a sledge and toboggan down the hill.

'We could, my darling.'

I wasn't quite sure what the locals might make of that. One woman and her dog who went, not to mow a meadow, but to mow down locals on a sledge. Especially when that woman was increasingly a few Bonios short of a full box.

I swung a left taking Octavia off the A227. The twisty climb began. As the road narrowed to a single-track country lane, the gradient became steeper. As Octavia's engine struggled, I shunted the gears from third to second. The car gave a high-pitched whine and lurched onward. There was no street lighting in this part of the world, and I toggled the headlights to full beam.

I couldn't remember the last time I'd visited Starlight Croft. It was one of those *satellite* villages – if you blinked, you missed it.

What with the hill and the narrow road, it wasn't a location for the fainthearted. I hoped I didn't meet a farm tractor coming along in the opposite direction. I didn't fancy reversing in this inky darkness while scanning the grassy banks for a handy layby and passing point.

Finally the hill flattened out and Octavia's headlamps lit up a sign peeking from an overgrown hedgerow.

Welcome to Starlight Croft

We were now on Starlight Street. We drove past a small church, a tiny pub by the name of The Starlight Arms, also a sizeable village hut called Starlight Hall, presumably for community gatherings.

Cindy had now abandoned the back seat and cheekily opted to join me in the front. Her body swayed as she sat bolt upright on the unprotected front seat, peering into the gloom. She was noting the new surroundings with interest. Her eyes were alert, and her wet nose quivered.

Why are we here?

'We're checking the place out.'

But why?

I sighed.

'Because, at some point, we need to move house. Lisa gave me a tip off about a cottage here. It's about to go on the market. She thinks it will be perfect for us. It's called Starlight Cottage.

Is everything in this village called Starlight Something-Or-Other?

'Not sure,' I said, as Octavia completed the road's final twisty turn. We were now driving past the local farmer's place.

'Oh, look!' I pointed. 'Over there. Fern Farm. The surrounding fields have a dairy herd and grazing sheep. Ooh, and there's the farm shop,' I said excitedly, peering myopically at an adjacent outbuilding. 'It's called The Strawberry Shed. How charming.'

I was now leaning over the steering wheel, foot lightly touching the accelerator as Octavia pootled along at fifteen miles per hour. Pretty pastel houses hugged the lane.

'And over there' – I indicated a property with a thatched roof – 'is Honeysuckle House, and the conversion next door is known as Bluebell Barn.' Octavia slowed to a snail's pace as

I picked out the various names etched on plaques made of slate, granite or wood.

'Lilac Lodge... Poppy Place... oh, and look at the size of that house.' I jabbed a finger. 'Moonlight Manor,' I sighed dreamily. 'They all have such gorgeous names.'

Which one is ours?

'It's not ours yet,' I reminded, as my eyes scanned the immediate vicinity. 'There!' I squeaked as Starlight Cottage came into view.

Beyond the cottage was a curved row of some twenty terraced properties. According to an ornate sign, they were collectively known as Jingle Bell Terrace.

That's a strange name for a row of houses.

'Mm,' I agreed. 'Very... Christmassy. Maybe it's because we're so high above sea level, we could almost be hugging Santa Claus territory.

I drove past Jingle Bell Terrace, which marked the end of the village. Seemingly the lane looped back on itself, with a sizeable duck pond acting as a roundabout. A visitor could then travel back along Starlight Street, then down... down... down, until – like an aeroplane coming into land – one's ears popped before alighting in Meopham.

I steered Octavia around the pond and doubled back, feeling my spirits lift as Starlight Cottage once again came into view.

Can we get out?

'Yes, of course. We'll walk back and forth. Stretch our legs. Have a good nosy at the property.'

Won't we look a bit suspicious?

'How do you mean?'

Well, if anyone sees us, they might think we're casing the joint.

'Hardly. There might be lights in the windows, but the curtains are drawn against the night. No one can see us,' I assured. Unbuckling, I opened the driver's door. 'Come on. Jump over my seat.'

Cindy didn't need telling twice. She sprang over the driver's seat with alacrity, her nose sniffing the night air. I quickly grabbed hold of her lead. I didn't want her spotting a wild hare and taking off into the dark.

Fumbling with my phone, I switched on the torch. The two of us then set off along Starlight Street. We went back and forth several times. Eventually the location of every house and outbuilding was imprinted upon my brain.

By now I was completely smitten with both the cottage and the village. It was so unlike Meopham with its residents on the right side of posh. Starlight Croft, with its potholes and puddles, was more… the Welly Brigade. Cindy would love it here. I could see her now, racing across the surrounding fields, following that public footpath that disappeared into dense woodland.

I didn't need to see the inside of the cottage to know that I wanted it. But as anyone who has embarked on a conveyancing journey will attest, moving house is stressful. It's not so much about the packing of boxes. More the red tape. The endless paperwork. Keeping fingers tightly crossed that *the chain* wouldn't break. That a coveted house didn't turn out to have galloping dry rot. Or that someone suddenly couldn't bear to leave their house after all, due to it being in the family for umpteen generations.

I paused in the chilly night air and feasted my eyes on the small standalone cottage. I mentally determined there and then that no conveyancing nightmare would happen to me. I would make sure of it.

How, Mum? After all, you don't have a magic wand.

I chewed my lip thoughtfully.

'Because… because' – I closed my eyes tightly – 'I'll *manifest* it. That's how.'

Eh?

'Watch. Listen. Learn.'

Okay.

'Oh, universe,' I intoned.

Why are you speaking to the universe?

'Shh. I'm concentrating.'

I see, Cindy sniffed. *Are you aware that one of us is barking? And it's not me.*

'Oh, universe,' I repeated, staring at the moon. My body vibrated slightly as I noted all the stars scattered across the sky. 'I don't care *how* you do it… or which *way* you do it… or what happens in the *process* of doing it… just give me Starlight Cottage.'

And as any seasoned manifester will tell you, sometimes you need to be careful not only what you wish for, but the way in which you do it.

Chapter Seven

On Tuesday morning I took Cindy into the office with me.

Leslie, the boss, was very relaxed that way. He didn't mind Cindy occasionally coming into work with me, especially if I had things to do in my lunch hour and didn't have time to nip home to let her out.

Today I most definitely had something to do in my lunch hour and didn't want to scrimp on time.

Thanks to Mr Garroway now well on his way to Dorset to be with family, the coast was clear to view the inside of Starlight Cottage in my lunchbreak.

'Here,' said Lisa, tossing me the key.

I snatched it up and, eyes shining, clasped it to my chest. Lisa caught my expression. She cleared her throat.

'Tilly?' she said cautiously.

'Yeah?'

'Look, there's something you need to know.'

I gripped the key as a frisson of alarm rippled through me.

'What? Oh, don't tell me. Mr Garroway's wife popped her clogs at Starlight Cottage and now her ghost haunts the place.'

'Er, no, it's—'

'The property is off mains drainage and has a kaput cesspit that will cost a fortune to replace?'

'Nothing like that, it's--'

'Omigod, don't tell me, Albert Garroway has upped his price and I can no longer afford it.'

'Will you stop,' said Lisa in exasperation. 'It was simply to say that if – when you return to the office – you decide you're serious about buying it, don't prevaricate.'

'Why?'

But I already knew what she was going to say.

'You have competition,' she said, her mouth drooping. 'Last night Leslie mailbombed the details of Starlight Cottage to prospective buyers. There's already been a flurry of phone calls which has resulted in a viewing this evening. Apparently, the person was blown away by Leslie's blurb and is very keen.'

'What?' I gasped. 'Who is this person and what are their circumstances?'

'Well, that's just it.' Lisa pulled a face. 'It's a chap called Milo Soren.'

'Details,' I said impatiently.

'He's divorced. Currently living in rented accommodation. No chain.'

'Flaming Nora,' I muttered. This wasn't good. 'Any family?'

Hopefully Milo Soren had a dozen kids that wouldn't fit into a tiddly cottage, not forgetting that Starlight Croft was miles from the nearest school.

Lisa was now making see-saw motions with one hand.

'Milo Soren has an adult son who is living with him temporarily. Therefore, our Mr Soren only needs two bedrooms.

'Absolutely bleeding marvelous,' I fumed. 'Right. Understood. So, if I like it, there's a need to act quickly.'

'That's it,' she chirped. 'Have you spoken to Robin yet about your change of heart and selling to him?'

'No,' I shook my head. 'But I will.' I pressed my fingers to my temples. This was not the time to get a migraine. I had as good a chance as Milo Soren of successfully buying Starlight Cottage. Oh, but wait.

'Does this guy need a mortgage?'

Lisa gave me a bleak look.

'He's a cash buyer, Tilly. Apparently, he sold the marital home ages ago when his divorce was finalised. He immediately banked his half of the spoils. Also, the mortgage on the marital home was paid off years ago.' Lisa gave me a moment to digest that. 'In other words, Milo Soren is sitting pretty. Don't waste a second.'

'On it,' I said, fishing in my handbag for Cindy's lead. 'Come on, girl. We have things to do. Places to go. A house to see.' Cindy leapt to her feet. 'There is one thing,' I said, pausing for a moment. My expression instantly gave me away.

'I have an inkling what you're about to say.' Lisa gave me a stern look. 'You know it's more than my job is worth.'

'Okay,' I said grimly. 'In which case, *I'll* do it.'

A quick phone call to Mr Soren. A few brief words delivered with fake sympathy.

'Hello, Mr Soren, or can I call you Milo? Home and Hearth here. Yes, fab thanks. You? Jolly good. I was just giving you a quick call with an update. Unfortunately, we need to cancel this evening's viewing. You see, Starlight Cottage has gone under offer. I know. Quite incredible. What's that? Offer more money? Ah, I don't think you'll be able to match this prospective buyer's offer. Well, I shouldn't divulge such information but… yes… yes… I understand you want to be in with a fighting chance so… can you exceed an offer of ten squillion pounds? I thought not. Well, quite. However, we've since been instructed on a very nice property in Cheyne Walk. Let me send over the details…'

'Tilly,' said Lisa mutinously. 'Don't do it. Leslie loves you to bits, but a quick sale is all. Apart from anything else, you need to sort out your divorce and the financials before being able to start the conveyancing process.'

'All right, all right,' I huffed.

'One thing at a time, eh?' she said gently. 'Go and look inside the property first. After all, you might hate it.'

'I won't,' I sulked.

'And then' – Lisa was not to be distracted – 'talk to Robin. Let him make you a revised offer on the marital home and then you can go from there. You never know, Mr Garroway might be sympathetic to your circumstances and tell Milo Soren to sod off.'

'Yes,' I said, although we both knew that scenario was highly unlikely.

I gripped the key to Starlight Cottage tightly, then headed out of the office with Cindy at my heels.

Chapter Eight

As I parked on the driveway of Starlight Cottage, I felt a rush of mixed emotions. Anticipation. Longing. But also fear.

Fear of the unknown. Of knowing that buying a house on my own really did mean my marriage was well and truly over. That there was no going back. Well, I'd known that for ages. Robin had replaced me with a younger model. Such a cliché.

A part of me wished I could do the same. Although, I couldn't quite see myself hooking up with a twenty-nine-year-old. In my book, that was a bit… *bleurgh*. Way too young. But if a nice forty-something guy were to enter my life – preferably with eyebags to match mine and a dash of grey hair – well, that might be rather splendid. And if he happened to be more attractive than Robin, with more hair than Robin, and less paunch than Robin, even better.

It would be so good to parade such a man in front of my ex, then toss him a defiant look. One that said, *Yeah, buddy, I'm not on the scrap heap yet!*

I took a shuddering breath and opened Octavia's door. Visits to divorce lawyers aside, this moment was a defining one. Another step in the direction of *Moving On*.

Cindy jumped out of the car and hugged my heels, just

as a knot of anxiety landed in my stomach. Perversely, a part of me was also bubbling with excitement. My heart was reflecting this unalignment of emotions. It was knocking hard on the underside of my ribcage, as if I'd exerted myself.

I gave myself a swift pep talk. Keep calm. Take some deep breaths. Stand still with Cindy and, for the next minute or two, just quietly observe Starlight Cottage.

What are we doing, Mum?

'Observing.'

Oooh, look! Cindy let out a squeak of excitement. *I observe a squirrel. Quick. Let's chase it!*

'Heel!' I squawked, as Cindy lunged forward, yanking my arm painfully. 'We're not chasing squirrels.'

'It's a good day for it,' said an amused voice.

I swung round to see a very striking lady. She was around eighty with piercing ice-blue eyes, a halo of white hair, and the aura of an angel. Her back was ramrod straight and her complexion bore testament to a strong relationship with the Great Outdoors.

Despite her age, she gave off a vibrant energy, and even though there were deep creases in her cheeks, she was still very attractive. It was obvious she'd once been a stunner.

'I'm Hetty Cartwright,' she said, coming towards me, one hand extended. 'I live at Fern Farm.'

'Tilly Thomas,' I said, shaking her hand. 'Pleased to meet you.'

Our dogs were now doing the canine equivalent of introducing themselves. Tail wagging and bum sniffing.

'Are you buying the cottage?' Hetty asked.

'Hoping to,' I said, giving her a nervous smile.

'What will be will be,' she nodded. 'But that said, I can see you here.' She put her head on one side, as if considering. 'Yes, definitely. One day it will be your home.'

'I hope you're right,' I said with feeling. 'So, if you live at Fern Farm, you must own all these cows and sheep.' I made a sweeping gesture with one hand, indicating the surrounding arable land.

'Once,' she smiled. 'Nowadays my son and daughter-in-law run the farm. You see, I lost my husband a couple of years ago and-'

'I'm so sorry,' I interjected.

She flapped a hand dismissively.

'George was eighty-five. Even so, it was time to let Hugo and Linda fully take over. They now live in the farmhouse with my grandchildren, while me and Shep' – she nodded at her collie – 'reside in the annexe. It's the perfect set up. My family keep an eye on me, but we're not in each other's pockets. And that's how it should be,' she declared. 'If there's anything you want to know about Starlight Cottage, do ask. I was born and bred at Fern Farm, as was my father.'

'How wonderful,' I said, genuinely enthralled by this lovely old lady.

'It was Linda who broke the mould,' Hetty declared. 'No home birth for her. She insisted on a hospital delivery. All mod cons around her. Just as well because she needed an emergency caesarean.' Hetty blew out her cheeks as she recalled a moment that had clearly been dramatic. 'And what about you, my dear? Do you have kiddies?'

For a moment my heart missed a beat, and my stomach contracted unpleasantly.

'No,' I said.

'Ah, I detect sadness,' said Hetty. 'I'm a bit of an intuitive,' she confided. 'You don't have to tell me your story, but I'm being shown some of it.'

'Shown?' I frowned.

'By my guides. Yours too.' She smiled mysteriously.

I wasn't a believer in mumbo jumbo, but it would have been rude to have said so. Instead, I cleared my throat, mentally preparing an explanation.

'I'm newly separated,' I explained. 'And my husband and I never had children – despite trying for years. And now it's too late.'

'Do you think?' she smiled.

'Oh, definitely,' I nodded. 'My next birthday is the Big Five Oh. I'll be a fully-fledged hot-flushing lunatic.'

'You don't look it,' she said.

'What, a lunatic?' I grinned. 'And before you answer that question, I will confide that me and Cindy here have whole conversations, which surely makes me ever-so-slightly certifiable.'

'I meant you don't look your age,' Hetty laughed. 'And as for talking to your dog, I believe that's perfectly normal. I've confided in Shep many a time.'

'That's good to know,' I said, feigning relief and giving a mini swoon. 'Same here. My girl knows all my darkest secrets.'

'Not so dark, surely, dear?'

I paused, momentarily taken aback.

'Dark in my books,' I said sadly.

'Well, you know what they say,' she said brightly. 'Dark clouds have silver linings. And I see lots of silver linings coming your way, Tilly. You mark my words.'

'That would be wonderful,' I said wistfully, deciding that Hetty was lovely but also a tiny bit bonkers.

'I'm always right, dear,' she said cosily. 'Although you'd do well to remember that secrets always out.'

I didn't tell Hetty that my secrets – well, it was just the one – would never out. Only my parents knew of it, and the three of us hadn't discussed it in decades. Figuratively speaking, it had been put in a box, tied up with string, and placed in the loft of our respective minds, never to be revisited. And unless some clever clog invented a translator app for dogs, then no way could Cindy ever spill the beans.

'Anyway' – Hetty patted my hand – 'there's not much I don't know about this place, or the people in it. Starlight Croft is in my DNA.'

'Ha!' I laughed. 'I once did one of those tests. My ex-husband bought me a kit as a gift. I was really hoping to see something exotic in my results. It was rather disappointing to discover I was ninety percent English with a bit of Celtic in the mix.'

'Likewise,' Hetty agreed. 'Although apparently one per cent of me is Chinese. Possibly my tastebuds. I do love a bit of sweet and sour,' she chuckled. 'As I said, feel free to look me up if you have any questions about the village.'

'Thanks,' I smiled. 'It's been lovely chatting, Hetty. And

who knows. Maybe I'll see you around.'

'Of that you will,' she assured, before setting off with a cheerful wave, Shep beside her.

I watched the old lady walk along the lane towards Fern Farm before disappearing out of sight. I turned to Cindy.

'Did you hear that? Hetty thinks we're going to live here.'

I hope she's right.

'Me too,' I said fervently.

And with hope in my heart and a spring in my step, I removed the cottage's housekey from my pocket. Seconds later, Cindy and I were inside Starlight Cottage.

Chapter Nine

'Oh, Cindy,' I breathed, as I paused in an attractive flagstone hallway.

This issued into a surprisingly spacious open-plan room. To the left was a cosy lounge area. To the right, a modern kitchen with mini-island and tall stools.

Mr Garroway might be an older gentleman, but he had very contemporary taste. I'd been expecting chintz sofas, twee curtains and gingham cushions. Instead, everything was in neutral tones of taupe, cream and the palest mushroom. It might have been bland had it not been for some bold abstracts on the walls, and colourful cushions that lined a squashy L-shaped sofa.

I took a closer look at the paintings. Originals. Wow, they were signed too. I peered at the artist's swirly signature. Audrey Garroway. Oh, blimey. They'd been painted by the vendor's deceased wife.

I quickly deduced that it might be the artist who'd had the impeccable taste in the cottage's modern décor. Certainly, the soft furnishings were worthy of an interior designer.

Moving around the kitchen, I admired the stainless-steel range with its shiny ceramic hob. Opening the door to the oven, I peered within. Spotless. Just like the cottage.

Gazing about, I noted the plentiful cupboard space, the fitted units in the lounge's alcoves, the handsome woodburning stove, the artfully stacked logs alongside, all set off by a large brightly jewelled rug.

Opening what appeared to be a cupboard door proved to be a well-kept secret. For beyond the door, was a cloakroom-cum-downstairs loo. Perfect.

'What do you think?' I said, turning to Cindy.

I think I'd like to curl up on that very cosy looking sofa.

'Mm,' I agreed.

I could easily visualise me and Cindy lolling around in its squashy depths. I'd also wiggle my toes in front of that wood burner. I could imagine it lit. Logs flaming. The comforting sound of crackles and pops.

The daydreaming continued. There I was again. This time flopped down on the rug. Guzzling a hot chocolate topped with marshmallows and whipped cream. Cindy warming her belly while contentedly chewing on one of my old slippers.

'Let's check out the upstairs,' I said eventually.

Cindy bounded ahead of me, nimbly whisking up a rather steep staircase.

A compact landing revealed just two doors. Beyond these were two generously sized double bedrooms. The front bedroom had picture windows that looked out across the fields. The rear bedroom overlooked a cottage garden that gave way to woodland.

Each room had its own ensuite. One contained an enormous copper bathtub shaped like a giant open egg. The second bathroom – a wet room with open shower – was generous enough to take two people.

I wondered if Albert and Audrey had ever showered together. Larked about. Thrown soapy sponges at each other. I instinctively felt there'd been a lot of laughter in this house. It had a happy vibe. I could almost hear its echoes as I moved around the upstairs rooms, pausing in front of the dressing table to look at an old photograph.

A young Albert Garroway looked back at me. His wedding day. The lovely bride on his arm beamed at the camera lens. I regarded the happy couple. Touched the frame. If Lisa had clapped eyes on Albert Garroway in his heyday, she'd have been smitten. He'd been quite a looker. And Audrey looked like a film star from a bygone Hollywood era.

I sighed and moved back to the landing, once again taking the door to the second bedroom. From here I could take a closer look at the spacious garden. At the rear was a large shed that looked like it had seen better days. When the cottage was mine, I'd probably remove it. Either that or replace it with one of those gorgeous gazebo thingies covered in climbing plants. Clematis and honeysuckle sprang to mind.

The flowerbeds were full of heavily pruned shrubs. Ornamental trees edged an immaculate lawn. In summer, lupins, foxgloves and roses would bloom and froth giving a riotous explosion of colour. How gorgeous. The whole property was delightful. My mind was made up. I wanted to buy Starlight Cottage.

'Oh, universe,' I intoned.

Oh, not again, my dog sighed.

'Hush,' I admonished. 'Do you want to live here or not?'

I suppose.

Cindy flopped down at my feet. Sighing heavily, she rested her nose on her paws. She knew when she had to be patient.

Shep was nice, she said. *I think he could become a mate. Especially if he likes chasing squirrels.*

I tutted.

'I don't know why you're so obsessed with squirrels.'

I don't know why you're so obsessed with checking out Samantha's social media.

That brought me up short.

'Shh,' I hissed, nervously glancing about, as if I'd been caught in the act. And yes, it was true. I often stalked Samantha's Instagram profile. Repeatedly curled my lip at her pics. Particularly the one that had showed off her figure in last summer's bikini.

She'd been somewhere hot and sunny with her gal pals. Samantha had been grinning at the camera, taut tummy on display, ample cleavage thrust forward. She'd been kitted out in the sort of skimpy beachwear I could only dream about.

After one evening of feeling particularly sorry for myself, I'd poured a large brandy, then duplicated one of Samantha's insta pics and sent it off to my printer. Armed with an A4 printout, I'd grabbed a black felt pen and had a lovely time making certain adjustments to Samantha's image.

I'd sniggered tipsily whilst drawing a handlebar moustache over her upper lip. A pair of blacked out teeth had followed. Moments later, Samantha had been the proud recipient of some Harry Potter specs. I'd then coloured in her torso so that she appeared to be wearing a staid one-piece swimsuit . I'd also added a generous spare tyre around her midriff. Perfect! Childish? Of course. But the exercise had been immensely satisfying.

'Oh, universe,' I intoned again. 'I've already asked for Starlight Cottage. Hetty Cartwright – one of the residents in this village – fancies herself as a bit of an intuitive. She thinks I'm going to live here. Anyway, I know you're currently busy making sure this happens – positive vibes etcetera. However, I'd like to add a footnote to my previous request. I miss Robin. No, scrap that. I don't miss *him*. What I mean is, I miss having a man in my life. Someone to love. And it would be so nice to have someone who loves *me* for being *me*. Do you understand? Can you find me a man who doesn't care that I'm a menopausal woman with a muffin over the waistband of her jeans? A man who doesn't give two hoots that I tweeze the odd hair from my chin. And if he could also be reasonably goodlooking and financially sound, that would also be most acceptable.'

I stared down at the little apple tree in one corner of the garden. Currently it was devoid of its leaves and fruit. Wouldn't it be wonderful if human beings could rejuvenate annually, just like nature did? If that were possible, then by next spring I'd have glowing skin, luscious hair and a toned figure.

Have you finished daydreaming? Cindy interrupted. *Because I'm mighty bored.*

'Yup,' I said, moving away from the window. 'Come on. Let's have a quick walk to the duck pond and back. Then, when I'm back at the office, I'm going to make a formal offer on Starlight Cottage.'

Together we headed back across the landing and down the stairs.

Chapter Ten

I returned to Home and Hearth in high spirits.

The key to Starlight Cottage was still in my handbag. I dumped the bag under my desk. Sitting down, I gave Lisa a quick shufty. She caught me looking. Noted the wide grin on my face. But she didn't return my smile. Instead, she gave me a troubled look.

'There's been developments,' she hissed.

'Developments indeed,' I beamed, ignoring her ominous tone. 'I'm well and truly smitten with Starlight Cottage.'

Lisa's mouth drooped. She jerked her head in the direction of our boss's office. Beyond, I could hear Leslie on the phone. Suddenly, I had a bad vibe.

'I'm talking *developments,*' she enunciated.

'Define *developments*,' I quavered.

'Two words. Milo Soren.'

'What about him?'

'He's viewing Starlight Cottage.'

'Yes, I know. You told me that earlier. He's going this evening.'

'Was.'

'You mean… he's cancelled the viewing?'

'No.' Lisa shook her head. 'On the contrary. He's so

keen, he telephoned while you were out. He asked if he could bring forward the viewing appointment.'

I paled.

'And?'

'And' – said Lisa patiently – 'Leslie is currently on the phone rearranging his diary so that he can accommodate Mr Soren and personally give him a guided tour of Starlight Cottage. Milo Soren is on his way to Starlight Cottage as we speak.' She gave a quick glance at her wristwatch. 'In fact, he's probably already there. It's a wonder you didn't bump into each other.' She held out her hand. 'You'd better give me the key.'

'No way.' I snatched up my handbag. Hugged it tightly to my chest. 'You can't have it.'

Lisa rolled her eyes.

'Don't be childish, Tilly.'

'I'm not being childish,' I argued. 'I'm intending to make an offer on the property.' My chin jutted. 'As of now.' I hugged my bag tighter. 'Starlight Cottage' – I informed my friend – 'is officially under offer.'

Lisa sighed.

'You know perfectly well that's not how things work and-'

'Full asking price,' I interrupted. 'No quibbles. And if Mr Garroway wishes to sell the cottage fully furnished, that's fine with me too. Tell him to name his price.'

'Tilly–'

'I mean it.' My chin jutted further.

Lisa knew this look. She'd seen it many times before.

Done it herself, too. *The chin of determination.* Both of us employed *the chin of determination* on certain occasions. Like the time we'd made a pact to diet together and to stop each other from cheating, no matter what. Then Leslie had brought into the office a vast chocolate cake to celebrate his birthday. Lisa had wanted to break the diet and indulge.

'But we're meant to stop each other,' I'd reminded her. 'No giving in to temptation.'

She'd responded with *the chin of determination.*

'I'll go back on the diet tomorrow.'

'No you won't,' I'd said, flashing my own *chin of determination.* 'Put your hands in the air, and move slowly away from the chocolate cake.'

We'd nearly come to blows over the photocopier.

Unfortunately, right now, my *chin of determination* was starting to wobble rather alarmingly. Uh-oh. It was rapidly turning into *the chin of jellification.* It was quivering all over the place. My eyes filled with tears.

'Phone Mr Garroway,' I croaked. 'Go on,' I urged Lisa. 'Do it. Now,' I pleaded.

'I can and will,' Lisa soothed. 'But you don't need me to remind you that – when the chips are down – you're not in a position to proceed.'

'But I will be,' I bleated, swiping at a tear that had escaped from one eyeball. 'I simply need to speak to Robin. I'll call him now,' I cried. 'He's been mithering me over the marital home. Well, he can have it. As of tonight!'

'Tilly, stop!' Lisa ordered. 'You can sort out your sale through the proper channels in due course. For now, give me the key.'

'Oh dear,' I said carelessly. My *chin of determination* had one last stab at defiance. 'I think I dropped it somewhere. You'll have to phone Mr Garroway and ask for another key. Meanwhile, I'll get hold of Mr Soren. Tell him to sling his… I mean… go home.'

'Ah, ladies.' Leslie stepped out from his office, beaming widely. 'I'm off to do a viewing.'

It was obvious from his smile that he thought business with Milo Soren was a done deal. As far as he was concerned, the guy had already made his offer and had it accepted. Maybe even now Leslie was, somewhere in his head, hitting the phone lines, urging solicitors to pull their fingers out and have contracts exchanged by five o'clock, thank you very much.

'Who has the key to Starlight Cottage?' he asked, looking from Lisa to me, then back to Lisa again.

'Tilly does,' she said.

Traitor.

I cleared my throat.

'The thing is, Leslie–'

'Yes?'

'*I* want to buy Starlight Cottage.'

My boss raised his eyebrows.

'Er, right. That's nice,' he said cautiously. 'I wasn't aware that your property was on the market.'

For a moment he looked faintly peeved, as well he might. Why wasn't his employee selling her abode via Home and Hearth Estate Agents?

'It was all very sudden,' I gabbled. 'Robin is buying me out.'

'Oh, really?' Leslie looked perplexed. 'I thought you were refusing to sell to him?'

'I was,' I admitted. 'But now I'm not. I've had a change of heart.'

'I see,' Lesie frowned. 'And your respective matrimonial solicitors are up to speed with this new situation? After all, you of all people know that financials need sorting before proceeding with an offer.'

I stared at Leslie helplessly.

'Please,' I whispered. 'Don't let Milo Soren buy Starlight Cottage.'

My boss gave me a kind look. When he next spoke, it was as if he were speaking to a six-year-old.

'Hey, it's just a viewing. There's no offer on the table.'

'Yet,' Lisa muttered.

'Mr Soren is keen to view,' Leslie admitted. 'But he might step inside and declare Starlight Cottage to be ghastly.'

'He won't,' I said miserably.

'Look, Tilly,' said Leslie gently. 'I think you're getting away ahead of yourself. Mr Soren might loathe the location. The road to Starlight Croft is a nightmare. But, even if he hates the place, I must warn you that I've had two further enquiries about the property. Both are chain free with mortgages in place. I'm afraid that even if Mr Soren gets run over by a tractor enroute to the village of Starlight Croft, there are two other potential buyers chomping at the bit.'

'Oh,' I said flatly.

It was obvious that I hadn't a snowball's chance in the fires of Hell to secure the purchase of Starlight Cottage.

'Can I suggest you sort out your divorce first,' said Leslie carefully. 'And then, when you know your financial position and the conveyancing is underway on the marital home, that will be the time for you to look at a property. That way you'll be in with a fighting chance on successfully purchasing whatever you've set your heart on.'

'Yes,' I said despondently.

'Meanwhile… the key? Please?' He held out his hand.

Miserably, I rummaged in my handbag. Found the key. Curled my fingers around it. Held it tightly. Briefly closed my eyes and wished with every fibre of my being that this key belonged to me.

And then I gave it up.

Chapter Eleven

'I've read your text,' snapped Robin. 'What's suddenly so urgent that I had to call you before – and I quote – *entering Samantha's supermarket freezer*?'

I was back home, a TV dinner on my lap, watching *Corrie* with a dribbling dog at my feet. Cindy's eyes were unblinking and firmly trained on my lasagne dinner-for-one.

I hastily muted the volume at a rather crucial point in my telly viewing. Would Rowan Cunliffe continue to successfully woo the naïve and vulnerable Leanne Battersby?

'Hey, Robin,' I said, attempting as much friendliness as I could muster. 'How *are* you?'

'No better for your asking,' he said tetchily.

Excellent news. I took a huge breath.

'I wanted to speak to you because I've had a rethink. I'm happy for you and Samantha to buy me out.'

There was a stunned pause.

'Forgive me for being rendered speechless,' said Robin eventually. 'It's just that the last time I asked you to sell you said – and I quote – *over my dead body and Samantha's bald vagina.*'

'Yes, yes, I know,' I blustered. 'But it's time to put the past behind us.'

'Is that so?' said Robin caustically.

'Indeed. And perhaps, when this is all over, Samantha and I might even one day become friends.' The idea sounded preposterous even to my ears, but I ploughed on. 'We could start off by exchanging Christmas cards. Maybe even a small gift. Obviously, I'd buy her something she needed. Like a merkin.'

'A what?'

'A pubic wig. But anyway' – don't bitch, Tilly, keep the conversation moving in the right direction – 'the thing is, I've seen the light.'

No need to mention that it had been *star* light.

'Have you gone all religious?' Robin demanded. 'Only I can't quite believe what I'm hearing.'

Me neither. I adopted a meek tone.

'I simply think it's better to be friendly, so that we can get this situation resolved. After all, it's been mentally ex*haust*ing,' I said wearily – as if I'd been browbeaten into giving up the marital home.

'Hm,' said Robin. 'I smell a rat.'

'No rat,' I said quickly. 'So, what do you say? Move in tomorrow?'

'Tomorrow?' Robin gasped. 'Tilly, are you feeling okay?'

'Never better,' I assured. 'Would you like to buy the house fully furnished?'

'Forgive me,' said Robin faintly. 'But I'm struggling to get to grips with your change of heart.'

'Believe it,' I said firmly. 'So, what's your preference?'

'Look,' said Robin, rallying. 'There needs to be some compromises between the two of us. That and a few promises.'

Oh-God-oh-God-oh-God! Was Robin revving up to do a deal?

'I'm all ears,' I said eagerly.

'Right,' he said, warming to his task. 'I will buy the marital home at the full asking price-'

'Ye*sss*,' I breathed, mentally punching the air.

'And you will leave the contents within out of the goodness of your heart-'

'Yes, yes, yes,' I gibbered.

'*Provided* you accept my offer as a clean break settlement and don't go after my pension pot.'

'Done,' I shouted.

If I'd been at an auction house, this would have been the moment the hammer had fallen with a crash.

Sold to the smirk at the back!

From the other end of the line was a bemused silence. I sensed Robin scratching his head. Well, it was either that or his balls. He'd often done the latter when negotiating.

'Tell me,' he said curiously. 'Have you met someone else?'

'Nope.'

'Then why all this sudden urgency?'

'Because,' I said mysteriously.

'Because what?'

'Just because,' I said, refusing to elaborate.

'Right,' said Robin after another pause. 'Obviously I'm

buying the house with Samanatha.'

'Obviously,' I said, as my lip involuntarily curled.

'And it's only fair that she has a proper look at the place.'

'Has she not already seen it?' I said, fishing.

I wasn't convinced that Robin hadn't smuggled Samantha in on at least one occasion. Like the time I'd gone to Cornwall to see Mum and Dad. Alone. Robin had cited pressing work issues for not coming along too.

'Samantha hasn't seen the house,' he said quickly. 'So, as you're now keen to be besties with my girlfriend, I'd appreciate you letting her look around one evening fairly soon.'

'Not a problem,' I assured. 'I'll even offer her a cup of tea and a biscuit. I have a feeling she might be partial to Gari*baldi*.'

'Tilly,' said Robin in a pained voice. 'You may be forty-nine years of age, but sometimes you are incredibly immature.'

'And sometimes' – I said sweetly – 'you are an incredible knob.'

'Okay,' Robin sighed. 'I guess that's our daily dose of amicability over and done with. Meanwhile, we will speak to our respective solicitors tomorrow morning, yes?'

'Yes,' I replied crisply.

'And I'll let you know when Samantha will be popping over.'

'That would be most' – I gritted my teeth – 'agreeable.'

If being pleasant to Sexy Samantha meant securing Starlight Cottage before anyone else got off the conveyancing starting block, then so be it.

I ended the call and grinned at my still slavering dog.

'Starlight Cottage, here we come,' I trilled, resisting the urge to upend my plate and jump for joy. 'Milo Soren, eat your heart out.'

Amazing, drawled Cindy. *Meanwhile, do you need some help with that lasagne?*

'No, thanks,' I said, hugging the plate possessively.

Unmuting the volume on the television, the lounge was filled with the wail of an ambulance siren. Leanne's sister was being rushed off to hospital.

Blimey, it was all happening – and not just in *Corrie*.

Chapter Twelve

The following morning, I fairly bounced into work.

'Aye, aye,' said Lisa, noting the spring in my step. 'Either you've received some good news, or you've had a one-night stand and released some sexual frustration.'

'I am *not* sexually frustrated,' I said, just as our boss stepped out of his office. He gave me a wary look while scooping up some paperwork from the printer. 'Morning, Leslie,' I chirped. 'Er, I was just telling Lisa that I'm not *extra* frustrated.'

'*Extra* frustrated?'

'Yes, as opposed to… ordinarily frustrated,' I said lamely.

'Right,' he said beadily. 'I know a good cure for that.'

'Hands off Ronald,' Lisa muttered.

'Get logged on and do some work,' said Leslie firmly.

Ouch.

'On it,' I said brightly as my boss made for his office.

I dumped my handbag and hastily switched on the computer.

'Oh, and Leslie?' I called after his rigid back. 'How did yesterday's viewing go?' My boss turned and regarded me blankly. 'Mr Soren?' I prompted.

Leslie's face cleared.

'Ah, yes. Milo. He liked it. He's going to discuss the matter with his son. Apparently, the son recently bust up with his girlfriend and has returned home to Dad.'

I wasn't interested in Milo Soren's son or any other sob story. I had my own to deal with.

'So' – my voice was hopeful – 'there's no offer on the table?'

'Not yet,' said Leslie. 'Milo mentioned booking a second viewing and bringing his son along too.'

That could not be allowed.

'In which case' – I tapped in my password – 'I'm officially making an offer on Starlight Cottage.' Leslie rocked back on his heels in surprise. 'I spoke to Robin last night,' I explained. 'He's agreed to buy me out. Lock, stock and barrel.'

'That's fantastic!' said Lisa, who'd been ear-wigging all along. 'I'm so pleased for you, Tilly.'

'Likewise,' said Leslie cautiously. 'But, um, sorry to remind you of the obvious. You still can't proceed.'

'Oh, but I can,' I argued. 'Especially if you give me permission to make one super-quick phone call to my solicitor. I can give her the update and get the ball rolling.'

Leslie sighed.

'By all means,' he said. 'But if Mr Soren – or anyone else for that matter – puts in an offer and is able to immediately proceed' – he shrugged – 'you know how this system works, Tilly.'

'Yes, yes,' I said, flapping a hand. I was *not* entertaining that scenario. 'May the best man win, and all that.'

'Indeed.'

'Meanwhile, please tell Mr Garroway that I'm offering the full asking price and that I'd like to buy the cottage fully furnished – if he's amenable to that. If so, ask him to give me a contents figure. You never know, he might be prepared to wait for me. Especially if other prospective buyers want to try and batter down the asking price.'

'There's an outside chance of that happening,' Leslie agreed. 'Now if you'll excuse me, *some* of us have work to do,' he added pointedly.

'Me to,' I promised, as my work phone began to ring. 'Just as soon as I've spoken to my solicitor.' I grabbed my mobile and gave Leslie an apologetic look, inwardly cringing as the landline continued to ring unanswered.

Leslie sighed and glanced at Lisa.

'Take that call, please,' he said.

Lisa immediately obliged, putting on her most seductive telephone voice. Anyone would think she was selling hot dates, not houses.

'Right,' said Leslie, as I located my solicitor's telephone number. 'I'll call Mr Garroway now. Let him know you're in the frame.'

I paused.

'Or I could do it?' I quickly suggested.

'I don't think that would be ethical, Tilly, given that you're an employee of the same estate agency Mr Garroway is using.'

'I don't know what you mean,' I said, not quite meeting Leslie's eye.

'Let's keep things businesslike and above board, eh?' said Leslie, giving me a *I know your game* look.

'Don't you trust me?' I said innocently.

'Not one little bit,' he said sternly, but he gave me a wink before returning to his office.

Wise man, my boss. A very wise man indeed.

Chapter Thirteen

Bringing my solicitor up to date took longer than anticipated. My eyes constantly flicked to my boss's office door, lest he appear again and note that, so far this morning, I'd not done a stroke of work.

'You should go after Robin's pension,' exhorted a disembodied female voice.

I could picture Annette Doyle at the other end of the line. There she was. Sitting in her smart but functional office. Face pinched. Salt-and-pepper hair cut aggressively short. A severely tailored suit. Her Clark Kent specs teamed with scarlet lipstick.

I'd only met her once and she'd terrified the pants off me. I wanted to challenge her recent interim bill but had yet to find the wherewithal to do so.

'I don't want Robin's pension,' I quavered. 'I've found a house and would like to press on with its purchase. There are other interested parties and' – my voice cracked slightly – 'they cannot be allowed to succeed.'

'Tilly,' said Annette sternly. 'I understand your desire to move forward and put your unhappy marriage behind you.'

'Good,' I said, attempting to copy her businesslike manner.

'But–'

'No buts, please, Annette,' I whimpered.

'But' – she asserted – 'the safest time to purchase a property is *after* a financial settlement. In other words, when the divorce has been finalised.'

'But I *have* a financial settlement,' I cried. 'Robin put it on the table last night.'

'His pension pot aside, there are still other matters to resolve. For example, the division of your capital assets. Your respective incomes. And other financial issues. You mentioned a savings account that you'd regularly contributed to. But we both know this is entirely in your husband's name. This isn't a five-minute job, Tilly. Clarity is paramount. Apart from anything else, it provides a more accurate picture of your financial standing which, in turn, gives a realistic insight into what kind of property you can truly afford.'

I rather suspected that this was also *legal speak* for Annette ensuring her fees were maximised. However, I didn't have the bravado to state that.

'I simply want to get a wiggle on,' I muttered.

'And rest assured that I *am* wiggling,' said Annette sharply. 'Was there anything else?'

'No,' I sighed. 'And, um, thank you,' I quickly added. Didn't want her tacking another fifty quid on the bill because I'd been surly. 'And, er, I really appreciate all your help to date.' A bit of grovelling might not hurt either.

I heaved another sigh and disconnected the call.

'Problems?' asked Lisa sympathetically.

'My solicitor says I need to be divorced before buying a house.'

'Well, that's the most sensible thing,' said my friend. 'Heavens, conveyancing is stressful enough, without having a divorce in the equation.'

'I suppose,' I said, chewing my lip. 'But this means I'm no longer in with a fighting chance against Milo Soren.'

'I hate to say this,' Lisa gently pointed out. 'But I don't think you ever were in with a fighting chance. Anyway' – she gave me a *cheer up* smile – 'if it's meant to be, it will be.'

'I hate that saying,' I grumbled.

'But it's true,' Lisa reasoned.

'I know,' I wailed.

'Don't lose all faith.' She gave a smile of encouragement. 'After all, Leslie has promised to speak to Mr Garroway about your offer.'

'I know,' I said again.

'And maybe Milo Soren's son will hate Starlight Cottage. If so, his father will be forced to look elsewhere.'

'True, but that still leaves a small army of other potential buyers all keen to view.'

My shoulders drooped at the thought of all these faceless people. Grinning smugly as they clutched their shiny mortgage offers. Delighted they were in rented accommodation and chain-free.

As I slumped over my keyboard, my phone dinged with a text. I straightened up and made a long arm. A message from Robin.

Samantha will be with you at six o'clock this evening.

'Fabulous,' I hissed.

'Good news?' asked Lisa hopefully.

'Not really,' I sighed. 'After work, I can expect a visitor. The Bald One wants to look around the house. Do an inventory. Make a list of what's staying and what's going.'

'I thought Robin was buying everything?'

'He is, but I don't think Samantha is wild about it. On the day of completion, she's organising a skip on the drive. Presumably to chuck out what isn't being kept.'

'Fair enough,' Lisa shrugged. 'If I were buying my partner's ex-wife's house, I wouldn't want it furnished. I'd prefer to start again. A fresh slate, so to speak.'

'Me too, but that means spending money – something Robin doesn't particularly like doing. Oh, Lisa,' I wailed. 'I don't know what to do.'

'About the Bald One?'

'No.' I pursed my lips. As far as I was concerned, Samantha could swivel. 'I'm talking about Starlight Cottage.'

'Sit tight,' she advised. 'All will be well. You'll see.'

'I hope you're right.'

'I know how to make things a tiny bit nicer.' She reached into her handbag. 'Ta da!'

Lisa produced a packet of chocolate cookies. As she waved them in the air, my eyes lit up.

Life is always better with biscuits.

Chapter Fourteen

Come six o'clock, the biscuits had long been polished off and life was back to being challenging.

I'd barely finished giving Cindy a hasty evening walk when Samantha turned up. She parked her immaculate Mercedes on my driveway just as I was letting myself into the house. I wondered sourly what Robin was paying his PA to enable her to swan around in such a swanky car.

The driver's door opened. A pair of long slim legs and stiletto heels were revealed. As Samantha exited the Merc, a gust of wind uplifted a waterfall of blonde hair. She turned to face me, and I tried not to feel envious about her flawless skin and immaculate makeup.

I felt distinctly at a disadvantage. My own legs were encased in scruffy joggers and muddy boots. My hair was windswept, and I had a red nose from the cold evening air.

How does she manage to drive in those three-inch heels, muttered Cindy.

'I was just thinking the same thing,' I murmured. 'Hello, Samantha,' I trilled.

Turning away, I unlocked the front door, wondering if Samantha felt awkward about this visit. I certainly did.

'Hey,' she said, catching me up. 'Good to see you, Tilly.'

Blimey, she was a cool customer. The last time we'd met, she'd been sprawled across Robin's desk, and those long legs had been wrapped around my husband's hips.

'One sec,' I said, reaching for an old towel I'd left by the front door. 'Let me just wipe my dog's paws before we go inside. She's a bit muddy.'

Stooping down, I set to work. Cindy was used to this and obliged by dutifully holding out each paw for me.

'What a well-trained dog,' said Samantha in delight. She reached out to pat Cindy's head.

'Careful,' I warned. 'She's not very good with strangers.'

Samantha immediately snatched back her hand while Cindy – was it my imagination? – gave me a look of rebuke.

'She's a rescue,' I said, as if that explained everything.

'I suppose you can't be too careful about dogs with an unknown history.'

Cindy gave me another reproachful look.

I am the kindest dog in the world. How DARE you make me out to be some sort of mutt-case.

I flashed her an apologetic look.

'Come in,' I said to Samantha. 'Let me give my dog a chew, and then I'll show you around.'

I walked into the kitchen, Cindy at my heel, and reached for her treat jar. Extracting a large beef strip, I passed it to her. For a moment our eyes locked.

I know this isn't easy for you and I understand, she seemed to say, before gently taking the chew.

'You're one in a million,' I whispered.

'What?'

I straightened up to see that Samantha had silently followed me into the kitchen. She'd positioned herself at my right elbow.

'I was talking to my dog,' I said.

An expression passed over her face. One that let me know I was a little weird.

'Do you always talk to your dog?' she frowned.

'Yes,' I said, my tone defensive. 'I think every pet owner talks to their cat or dog. It's a perfectly normal thing to do.'

'Is it?' she pulled a face. 'I once had a goldfish. I didn't talk to it.' She gave a derisive tinkle of laughter. 'Please don't tell me that *you* would have!'

I gave her a serious look.

'I think I'd have instead opted for dropping a line. Anyway' – I ignored Samantha's look of confusion – 'as you can see, this is the kitchen.'

I swept an arm wide, inviting her to look around. To admire the extension with its fashionable atrium ceiling. The showy bifolds that issued out to the patio. I walked across the room and gazed at the garden beyond.

A lot of work – and expense – had gone into this home improvement. I'd spent many a happy moment sitting in one of the strategically placed tub chairs. Kindle in one hand. Cuppa in the other. Or simply relaxing and enjoying views of the garden, while my husband took over the lounge.

Robin had usually been horizontal on the sofa watching footie. On other occasions I'd sat here alone. While my husband *worked late*. Likely horizontal again. But this time on his client sofa. Twat.

Bad word, said Cindy, trotting over to me.

Yes, I silently agreed. But sometimes it's a very satisfying word.

Samantha was looking around, a proprietary look on her face.

'This house is smaller than I remember,' she said.

I let out an involuntary gasp. Robin had assured me that he'd never brought her here! The bastard. Samantha caught my expression and smirked.

'Slip of the tongue,' she said. 'Robin once showed me some pictures.'

'Of course he did,' I said sweetly. 'Still, at least this room is bigger than your current kitchen*ette.*'

I leant forward to straighten one of the tub chair's cushions. Out of my peripheral vision, I saw Samantha's mouth purse. I'd annoyed her with the *kitchenette* comment. Good.

She moved across the room and joined me. Her eyes swept over the garden beyond. I could tell that my cherished plants and frothing tubs didn't interest her. Instead, she reached out and touched one of the heavy window drapes.

'Robin and I will be installing shutters throughout. If you want' – she gave me a gracious look – 'you can take these with you. After all, curtains are so old-fashioned.'

This time it was my turn to compress my mouth. In the point scoring stakes, we were now one all.

Samantha was keen to let me know that my taste wasn't hers. As we moved from room to room, she declared that carpets were *so last year.* Sideboards had apparently been out of vogue since the beginning of time. As for freestanding wardrobes, what century was I living in?

'Oh, a king size bed,' she said, as we walked into the master bedroom. 'That will be the first thing to go in the skip. I'll be ordering a custom made seven-footer.'

'Yes, I can see that you'll need some extra room,' I said, looking pointedly at her hugely inflated chest. Surely, they weren't real?

'Oh dear, oh dear,' she sighed, nodding at the bedside cabinets. 'Those can definitely go.' She sashayed over to the ensuite, pausing for a moment in the doorway. 'I've seen the most *fabulous* bedroom furniture in John Lewis,' she confided. 'Robin is going to love it.'

Samantha stuck her head around the bathroom door, then pulled a face.

'As I thought. A new bathroom will be top of the list.'

What a bitch!

'That ensuite was completely refurbed last year,' I said, an edge to my voice.

'Yeah, but shower cubicles went out with the ark.' She gave a pitying smile. '*Everyone* knows that wet rooms are all the rage.' She sighed theatrically. 'Never mind. I love a project. It will be my pleasure to do up this house. Naturally I'll be posting everything to Instagram.'

'Naturally,' I agreed, thinking that right now I'd love to bundle her into the shower, turn the dial to hot, take a snap, then upload with appropriate caption:

Oh dear. I seem to be having selfie-steam issues.

Chapter Fifteen

Leslie, true to his word, forwarded my offer on Starlight Cottage to Albert Garroway.

At the end of the week, my boss sought me out during the lunch hour. He approached my desk just as Lisa and I were having a heated discussion about how we'd blow a lottery win if our numbers came up.

'Sorry to interrupt, ladies,' said Leslie. There was something about his tone that instantly had me on red alert. He looked at me. 'I've heard from Mr Garroway.'

Lisa shot me a worried look.

'Oh, yes?' I said ultra casually. My stomach wasn't fooled and contracted into a tight knot. I put my half-eaten sandwich to one side. 'And?'

'Albert was thrilled to be offered the full asking price,' said Leslie carefully.

'Right.' I put my hands in my lap. Twiddled my thumbs nervously. 'Did you also mention that I was interested in buying it fully furnished?'

Leslie nodded.

'Albert said he was certainly open to a potential buyer purchasing the contents in their entirety – even his late wife's paintings. He confessed he'd never really appreciated Audrey's artwork and that, in his honest opinion, her canvasses were nothing more than a lot of blobs. Certainly, they hold no sentimental value.'

'That's surely good news for me,' I said, feeling a flicker of hope.

'Yes,' Leslie nodded. 'And, um, that's the only good news.'

'Okay,' I said, my thumb twiddling going into overdrive. 'So, what's the bad news?'

Leslie's mouth compressed.

'Albert said he was hugely sympathetic to your situation. He also said that if he hadn't fallen head over heels in love with a retirement flat in Dorset, he'd be happy to wait for however long it took for your divorce to finalise.'

'So why can't he wait?' I quavered.

'Because the retirement flat is a newbuild. Exchange of contracts must take place in twenty-eight days.'

'I'll ring my solicitor,' I said, reaching for the phone. 'I'll tell her to put a rocket up Robin's bum and–'

'Albert's accepted another offer,' Leslie interrupted.

The air whooshed out of me.

'No,' I whispered, shaking my head.

'I'm afraid so, Tilly. At the end of the day, the prospective purchaser was holding all the right cards.' Leslie held up one hand to tick off on his fingers. 'First, no requirement for a mortgage. Second, not in a chain. Third, solicitor already appointed and likely being instructed as we speak.' He let his hands fall back to his sides. 'I'm sorry.'

'Oh, Tilly,' said Lisa sympathetically.

I had a sudden need to know who had succeeded where

I'd so miserably failed.

'Who is the buyer?' I asked in a wobbly voice.

Leslie gave me look.

'Do you really need to ask? It's Milo Soren.'

'Terrific,' I said bitterly. 'I thought he first had to get his son's approval?'

'It wasn't quite like that, Tilly. Milo simply wanted to involve his lad. Apparently, he's had a bit of a tough time lately. Anyway, moving house is a massive gamechanger in people's lives. Perhaps Milo wanted his son's approval because – well, for whatever reason – *he* needed confirmation that he was making the right decision.'

'Well, isn't this hunky dory,' I said bitterly. 'I now have a sale going through on my house, but no place to go.'

'I told you, silly,' Lisa piped up. 'You can live with me until you've found something. There's no rush. You can take as long as you like.'

'Thanks, Lisa. That's very sweet of you. I don't wish to seem ungracious, but this wasn't what I'd envisioned at this stage of my life. Approaching fifty. Borrowing my bestie's sofa. Nothing to show for five decades on this planet except for a suitcase bunging up my mate's hallway.'

'Stop being so negative,' said Lisa. 'It won't be forever.'

'Lisa's right,' said Leslie. 'And just think' – he put a sympathetic hand on my shoulder – 'the next time you make an offer, you'll succeed. Vendors will be biting off your hand to have a purchaser like you.'

'Except none of them will be selling Starlight Cottage,' I said sadly.

Chapter Sixteen

Two months later, on a cold January afternoon, I moved out of the marital home.

It was most peculiar walking away from everything. Well, *almost* everything. Apart from the stripped beds, the house had otherwise appeared occupied. It certainly hadn't looked unloved or neglected, like some places did when the inhabitants left.

Robin had insisted on everything being left in its place, just as it had been before he'd suddenly found himself living in Sexy Samantha's tiny flat. Therefore, *our* cutlery remained in the kitchen drawer. Likewise, the cups, saucers, plates and glasses. They remained in the cupboards. Even the larder continued to hold its usual stock of tinned goods. Long life milk. Tubs of gravy and custard. A jar of instant coffee. Even a large box of PG Tips.

The bulk of Robin's shoes – of which there were many because there had been no room in Samantha's *supermarket freezer* – had continued to languish in the cupboard under the stairs. Robin had even insisted the vacuum cleaner and ironing board be in their usual place. And they were.

In my opinion, I thought it somewhat weird. Not, maybe, from Robin's perspective. My husband was a stickler for the familiar – apart from keeping his wife, of course. But surely it was odd from Samantha's perspective?

But then I'd dismissed the thought. I didn't care if Robin – after being catapulted into the unknown – now craved the familiar like a security blanket. Nor did I care if Samantha dumped everything in the skip that had turned up on the drive. All I *had* cared about was leaving the house in immaculate order.

I'd given in to a strong urge to deep clean the place before Samantha's arrival. Consequently, every cupboard and drawer had been emptied out, cleaned, then neatly repacked or stacked.

China and glassware had gleamed. The hot cupboard's shelves had been left with freshly laundered towels and bedlinen. The larder had been forensically taken apart and tidied.

Much had ended up in the dustbin. How was it possible to have tins of food dating back to the Covid years? And what about that box of fancy herbal tea? It had still been in its cellophane packaging. But the *Best Before 2011* date had seen it joining the detritus.

I'd also forked out and paid to have the oven and hob professionally cleaned. The fridge and freezer, too. The freezer had been quite a challenge due to not being defrosted for some four years. Yes, slobby. But at least I'd been able to call myself out, rather than have Samantha do it. Afterwards, all the appliances had positively sparkled.

Whatever hadn't been thrown out, had gone to the charity shop. I'd dramatically streamlined my wardrobe.

Several coats and shoes had been culled. Also, jeans – *how many in the cupboard?* – along with sweaters, t-shirts, skirts and dresses. Some garments hadn't been worn in years.

I'd emptied the bookcase of my old romance novels and psychological thrillers. All the photo albums had gone to the dump. Robin hadn't wanted to keep them. Not even of our wedding day.

I'd laboriously photographed everything with my phone. I didn't know if I'd ever bring myself to look again at those pics. But at least I knew the option was there for a digital trip down Memory Lane. When my heart had healed.

Perhaps, in a year from now, I'd tap into my phone's *library*. Scroll back, back, back. Look at the day I'd married Robin. Regard impartially the professional shot of us laughing as confetti whirled through the air. Maybe I'd feel completely detached as I studied the young bride looking adoringly at her new husband. The git.

After the dustmen had been, I'd gone to town on the bins and recycling boxes. They'd been left to soak in bleach, then scrubbed vigorously. I'd even mown the lawn, wiped down the mower, then stowed it neatly in the garage.

No way was I having Sexy Samantha walk into my house – well, hers now – and run a manicured finger over surfaces as she checked for dust. That couldn't happen. I was not prepared to give her the smallest chance in trashing either my housework or standards. Even though my ego had clamoured to leave the place messy and grubby, my pride hadn't let me.

Just before completion, Robin and Samantha had

requested to visit the house together. Robin had given some ridiculous excuse. Something about his young girlfriend needing to know the precise measurements of certain windows.

As they'd stepped into the hallway, I'd been aware of a tension between them. As they'd gone into the lounge, I'd offered them both a cup of tea. Leaving Samantha wielding a metal tape measure like a sword, I'd gone off to the kitchen.

Waiting for the kettle to boil, I'd overheard Samantha raising her voice to Robin. I hadn't been able to hear her every word, but my ears had captured enough to understand the gist of her agitation.

'…armchairs are hideous… don't care if they are only two years old… don't like them… not staying… black leather sofa… John Lewis… yes, expensive… it's called *class*.'

Oh dear. Good luck with that, Robin.

On the day of completion, I'd posted the keys through the letterbox in accordance with Robin's instructions. I'd then loaded Cindy's basket into the rear of Octavia, along with a suitcase and two boxes that contained all my worldly goods. Cindy had hopped into the front, and we'd set off to Lisa's tiny ground floor maisonette in Longfield.

I'd cried all the way.

Chapter Seventeen

I was indebted to Lisa. She'd thrown me a lifeline. Put a roof over my head.

Finally, I could surf the internet and look at suitable properties for Cindy and myself, confident I was in a great position. The fact that nothing currently appealed didn't matter too much. Lisa had said I could stay at hers indefinitely.

January came and went. I continued to scan properties online like they were going out of fashion. So far everything was either too expensive or required a ton of work. Apartments were aplenty, but not feasible when having a dog.

February arrived. The first weekend of the new month was a wet one. Lisa had absented herself by going to Spain for a long weekend. She was attending the wedding of an old school friend who'd traded England for sunnier climes.

I spent Saturday morning giving the maisonette a thorough vacuuming, before making the bathroom and kitchen sparkle. However, the place was tiny. The job was done in less than a couple of hours. How to spend the remainder of the day? Cindy gave me an enquiring look.

Walkies?

'You've already had a walk today.'

So let's have another one!

I considered for a moment. Earlier, we'd driven to Meopham, and I'd parked at the office carpark. We'd then walked a good couple of miles along the road. Up to the windmill, a local landmark. We'd then strolled around the Common which, because of the rain, we'd had to ourselves.

We'd eventually walked back to Octavia, hugging the narrow pavement that edged the A227. It was a busy road and not the place to let a dog like Cindy off the lead. She could so easily get distracted by a squirrel and be under the wheels of a car in a nanosecond.

Walkies, again?

My dog's eyes, like two chocolate buttons with a star at each centre, silently implored me.

Please? Pretty please?

'Okay,' I agreed. I peered through the kitchen window. 'Bonus,' I informed Cindy. 'It's stopped raining.'

This was good news because no rain meant no whiff of damp dog. A soggy doggy wasn't the greatest smell, especially in a place as small as this one.

'We'll go for that second walk,' I informed Cindy. She wagged her tail. 'But not around Longfield or Meopham.'

Oh, then where?

'Somewhere nice,' I assured.

Will there be squirrels?

'Lots of squirrels,' I promised.

A moment later, I'd swapped her every-day-collar for one fitted with tiny jingle bells. My dog might be obsessed with grey fluffies, but I didn't condone her catching them. When Cindy dashed off, collar jingling like Santa's reindeer, local wildlife were alerted. They swiftly took cover.

Minutes later, we were both inside Octavia. As we headed out of Longfield and towards Meopham, Cindy's nose was almost pressed against the window. She was eager to work out where we were going. Eventually, she gave a little yip of excitement.

Ooh, we're going to Trosley Country Park!

'Um, no,' I said, signalling right. Octavia's engine started to whine as she began the steep ascent to our destination.

Oh, Mum, no! Why are you driving to Starlight Croft?

'Because, at the top of the hill, there's beautiful woodland to explore.'

Yeah, right. But I'm not daft. You have an ulterior motive. Am I right, or am I right?

'I don't know what you're talking about,' I said innocently.

I crouched over the steering wheel. We were now at the point where the road narrowed to a singletrack country lane.

You've come for a nosy, haven't you? A sneaky peek at Starlight Cottage. And maybe to catch a glimpse of the new owner. Milo Soren.

'Possibly,' I admitted, pulling a face.

You never met him, did you?

'No,' I sighed. 'I made sure I was out of the office when he came in to see Leslie. I didn't trust myself not to fall at his feet and beg him to buy something somewhere else.' I sighed again. 'Anyway, it's done now. He lives here, and we don't.'

So much for your chat with the universe.

'Indeed,' I agreed.

I wonder what Milo Soren is like?

'Lisa said he was in his forties, goodlooking, but harassed. I think she was possibly batting her eyelashes at him but didn't get anywhere.'

There's a pub in the village. After our walk, can we go there? I fancy a sausage sandwich followed by a huge slice of chocolate cake.

'You can't eat chocolate cake,' I pointed out. 'It's toxic to dogs. Anyway, let me concentrate. This road is a bit of a challenge and' – my heart sank – 'oh, bugger. A transit van is coming towards us. Looks like a courier. Sod it. He's not giving way either.'

I don't think he can. You'll have to reverse for him.

'Just cosmic,' I muttered, changing gear.

As Octavia shot back, back, and back some more in a rather kamikaze fashion, I swore under my breath. I'd been bullied into complying with the other driver. Big vehicles always took advantage of smaller ones. A case where size definitely mattered. All I needed now was a vehicle coming up behind me and then I'd be well and truly stuck.

Bet you're glad you didn't move here after all, eh?

'Nope,' I retorted, although I wasn't sure my neck agreed. The muscles were now protesting from maintaining a one-hundred-and-eighty-degree angle.

A small layby came into view. Sighing with relief, I squashed Octavia into the hedgerow. I then screamed as a cow's head popped over the leafy foliage. She regarded us benignly before letting out a mournful moo.

'WOOF!' barked Cindy, making me jump again. I clutched my chest as Cindy let rip. 'WOOF, WOOF, WOOF, WOOF, WOOF, WOOOOOOF!'

Dog and cow stared at each other as the van driver rattled past. Its wingmirror missed Octavia by a whisker.

'You're welcome,' I huffed. 'Did you see that? He didn't bother to say thank you.'

Never mind the van driver, Cindy frowned. *Did you hear what that cow said to me?*

'No,' I said, looking at my dog.

This wasn't good. Not only was I having entire conversations with my pooch, but apparently a cow was joining in too.

She told us to moo-ve it.

'Ha!' I rolled my eyes as we set off again. 'Keep your paws crossed that we don't encounter another vehicle. Oh, and one more thing. I love our chats, Cindy, but I draw the line at including cows.'

That's a shame. I was going to tell you a cow joke – Cindy sniggered *– but you've probably herd them all.*

Chapter Eighteen

We arrived at Starlight Croft without any further traffic encounters. I silently thanked the universe, then immediately retracted the gratitude. What had the universe done for me? Diddlysquat. My polite request to live at Starlight Cottage had been totally bypassed.

We were now parked opposite the cottage. I glanced around the lane, half hoping to spot Hetty Cartwright and Shep the border collie. Hetty had fancied herself as an intuitive. She'd told me I would move to this village. What a shame she'd been wrong.

I looked at Cindy in the rearview mirror. She was sitting upright on the rear seat, ears pricked, head on a swivel. I wondered if she, too, was looking for Shep. However, Starlight Street remained quiet. There was no sign of anyone.

Can we get out, Mum?

'In a sec,' I said. 'Let me just have a moment.'

I feasted my eyes on the cottage. The place that had once been all my hopes, all my dreams. Yes, there I was. Opening the front door. Taking a parcel from the postman. Exchanging pleasantries. Hetty walking by. Spotting me. Pausing to *yoo-hoo*.

'Fancy joining Shep and me? We're going to the woods.

Be warned, it will be very muddy after last night's rain.'

'I'd love to! Let me fetch my wellies. Cindy and I adore mud and puddles.'

And then, as we set off, Hetty glancing at me. Her face almost messianic. Ice-blue eyes blazing. The bright white hair looking like a saint's aura as she nudged me in the ribs.

'I *told* you that you'd end up living here one day. You didn't believe me, did you?'

Well, no, Hetty, I didn't. And unfortunately, despite you claiming to be the village oracle, the fact remains that you aren't, and your prediction was way off beam.

Someone is home, said Cindy, interrupting my thoughts.

I sat up straighter. Peered myopically at a ground floor window. Activity was going on within.

'You're right,' I breathed.

It must be him. The new owner.

'Milo Soren,' I hissed, as if he were Severus Snape.

I narrowed my eyes to bring everything into sharper focus. A curtain had been lifted to one side. The outline of a man filled one window. I caught my breath as he paused, one arm still holding the curtain. The man's back tensed. His shoulders stiffened. It wasn't great body language.

He's spotted you, said Cindy.

'Yes,' I whispered.

I'm not getting a good vibe. I think you should drive off.

'Don't be silly. I have as much right to park here as anyone else.'

Yes, but you look a bit obvious. I mean, you're not a visitor, are you? What else could you possibly be doing, other than loitering?

The curtain dropped, and the man disappeared. I exhaled rather noisily, unaware that I'd been holding my breath.

'It's okay, he's gone,' I said.

I think you spoke too soon.

The front was opening. The man was pulling on a pair of shoes.

He's coming over, squeaked Cindy.

'It's fine,' I assured. 'He's probably popping to the corner shop to get some milk, or something.'

There isn't a corner shop.

'Well, okay, maybe the farm shop. The Strawberry Shed sells milk.'

He doesn't look like he's off to do shopping. More like emoting.

The man was now walking along the garden pathway. His eyes locked on mine. My heart did a few unexpected skippy beats. Milo Soren was extremely good looking. He also looked vaguely familiar. With those chiselled cheekbones and film star looks, he could have teleported straight in from Hollywood.

He was heading over, clearly intent on saying something. I automatically sucked in my stomach, even though he couldn't see my muffin top. At least I'd put on some lippy and mascara this morning, so wasn't looking like a complete has-been. Wow, he really was gorgeous.

I buzzed down the window and gave him a winning smile. Perhaps he was going to ask me if I was lost. I could say yes. Pretend that I'd taken a wrong turn off the A227.

And he'd pull a handy map from his back pocket. Show me where I needed to go. Our hands would unexpectedly touch. And sparks would fly.

It's amazing what the brain can imagine in two seconds, and right now mine was in overdrive. It continued to whip up something both flirtatious and romantic:

Milo: 'Good morning, fair lady.' (Yes, my brain had parachuted straight into an Edwardian soap drama.) *'Can I help you?'*

Me: 'Greetings, sire.' (Looks up shyly. Blushes prettily.) *'I appear to have incorrectly navigated these barren lands.'* (Delivers tiny swoon.) *'And, stupidly, left home without my carafe of water.'* (No plastic bottles in this scene.)

Milo: 'Why, beautiful maiden, you must be parched to pieces.' (Did Edwardian men say *parched to pieces*?) *'But do not be distressed. Let me be chivalrous. Come into my humble dwelling for refreshment. Indeed, only an hour ago, my manservant finished treading the grapes. A very robust red. It is incredibly full-bodied – much like you, if I might be so bold.'*

Me: 'Why, squire! Your words are like pretty musical notes to my delicate ears.' (Waggles head to show off sexy hearing apparatus). *'Lead me to your abode… and your boudoir… and your bed…'* (Clutches heart and faints clean away from desire.)

I gazed adoringly at Milo Soren.

He didn't gaze adoringly back. Instead, he hunkered down by Octavia's open window and jabbed a forefinger at me.

'I thought so,' he said, eyes blazing. 'I recognised the car. There aren't too many bright orange Fiats about. You're the woman who nearly flattened me in a Sevenoaks carpark.'

Chapter Nineteen

'By some appalling coincidence' – Milo scowled – 'our paths cross again.'

Not a coincidence, Cindy piped up. *My mum deliberately came here to have a nosy–*

'Hush,' I said.

Milo's eyebrows shot upwards.

'Are you telling me to be quiet?' he snapped.

'Um, I was speaking to my dog,' I blustered. Now wasn't the time to confess I had an affinity with Dr Dolittle. 'She was being noisy.'

'No, she wasn't,' said Milo.

'Woof.' Cindy gave an obligatory yap.

'Hush,' I said again. 'See?' I smiled nervously. 'Noisy.'

'What are you doing in Starlight Croft?' he demanded.

'I happened to be passing.'

'Rubbish,' he snapped. 'You've been parked outside my house and staring at my property for ages. What are you doing? Giving it the once over.'

Told you, Cindy huffed. *He thought you were casing the joint.*

'I said hush.'

'Woof.'

'Can we at least get our timing right?'

'Woof.'

'Hush.'

Milo put his head on one side, evidently bewildered. He looked from me, to Cindy, then back to me again.

'There was a burglary at the manor house last week. The police believe that the criminal isn't the usual type of villain. By the very nature of being female, *you* tick that box.'

'Are you implying that I'm a crook?' I gasped.

'I'm asking' – his tone was now ominous – 'why are you parked outside my house? And why are you studying it with such obvious interest? Were you trying to assess if there's a dog on the premises? Or a bell box on the outside wall? Or maybe a ring doorbell? Or could it be that you were looking to see if I have CCTV cameras?' His chin jutted. 'Because I can tell you now, I have *all* those things. And just in case you're in cahoots with someone else, can I suggest you revise your driving skills. It's very important, when making a getaway, that you don't mow people down in the process.'

'I didn't mow anyone down,' I retorted.

'It was a narrow escape though, wasn't it?' he said belligerently. 'And not content with almost running me over, you nearly took out an innocent couple too. In fact, I'm amazed you've not yet been banned for reckless driving.'

'I've had enough of this conversation,' I spluttered. 'How dare you criticise my driving or insinuate that I'm a thief. If you must know, I came to Starlight Croft to… to… to look up an old friend.'

'What's your friend's name?' he questioned.

Yes, what was my imaginary girlfriend called?

'Hetty,' I said defiantly. 'Hetty Cartwright.'

'Hetty lives at Fern Farm. You're going the wrong way.'

'I'm not stupid,' I said haughtily. 'Before visiting Hetty, I was going to take my dog for a walk in the woods.'

'Which are over there,' he said, jabbing a finger.

'And that's where I'm going,' I snapped. 'So, if you don't mind' – I pushed open the driver's door, forcing him to take a step backwards – 'my dog and I will now be on our way. Meanwhile, please take your ring doorbell and have a good time watching a rerun of an innocent woman being intimidated by a bully of a man. In fact, I've a good mind to report you to the police for harassment.'

'Based on your suspicious behaviour, I'm sure they'd be delighted to talk to you.' He gave me a thin smile. 'Tell them Milo Soren is happy to make a statement.'

'I might just do that.' I stuck my nose in the air. 'Good day, Mr Moron.'

'Soren,' he snapped.

Chapter Twenty

'Horrible man,' I seethed, as Cindy and I headed off on foot.

How had I ever thought Milo Soren goodlooking? He might look like Antonio Banderas, but he didn't have any of film star's charm. Together, Cindy and I ducked through a gap in a nearby hedge. We were now on a public footpath that led to the woods.

'If he were the last man on Earth, and I were the last woman, and it was up to us to repopulate this planet, then humanity would die out,' I ranted.

Sorry to tell you this, Mum, but it would die out anyway. You're too old to have babies.

'Don't remind me,' I grimaced. 'It's a sore subject.'

I know, Cindy soothed. *But I did tell you it wasn't a great idea parking outside Milo's place or staring at his house for ages. You did look a bit, you know, unhinged.*

'That house that should have been mine,' I said bitterly, as we paced along. 'I don't think I'm ever going to find anything that compares to Starlight Cottage.' My shoulders drooped. 'It's all very well living at Lisa's for the time being, but I really want a place of our own.'

What about that two-up-two-down in Gravesend?

'It's on a busy road. I don't think I'd sleep at night with

such a heavy volume of traffic.'

You'd eventually get used to it.

'Believe me, there are some things that the passage of time does not ever allow you to get used to.'

Ah, said Cindy meaningfully. *I know what you're hinting at.*

'Yeah.' I kicked a stone viciously. Watched it skim along the pathway, hit another stone, and then bounce sideways into some grass. 'Not a day goes by where – at some point – I don't think about it. What might have been. If I'd been a little older. A little wiser. If circumstances had been different.' My eyes brimmed. 'Sometimes I have a good day and realise that twelve hours have passed without me thinking about it. And I tell myself that the inner peace of those twelve hours was blissful. Such a relief. And then, equally, I'm horrified. I ask myself: what sort of person have I become to have permitted twelve hours of amnesia? It makes me feel like such a bad person.'

You're not a bad person.

'I'm not sure the Law of Karma would agree with you. After all, look how the subsequent years have played out.'

I still don't think you're a bad person. More… a sad person. In the last few months your whole life has changed. This time last year, you lived in a lovely part of Meopham. You had a house full of treasures collected with a man you expected to grow old with.

'Whereas now I live out of a suitcase, sleep on a sofa, and can fit all my worldly possessions into a cardboard box.'

And you have me, of course.

'Indeed,' I smiled. 'What would I do without you?'

Possibly be like Shirley Valentine and instead chat to the walls.

Cindy paused to scan the overhead trees. She then gave a yip of excitement and strained at the lead.

Much as this conversation has been fascinating, can you let me run free? This wood is heaving with squirrels, and I want to chase a few.

'Fair enough,' I sighed.

I stooped and unclipped the leash. My dog instantly took off like a supersonic rocket. There wasn't an inch of fat on her. Perhaps I should be more like Cindy and, well, *shift*. It was all very well walking a pooch every day, but a jog might be better. It would burn more calories. Which might diminish the muffin around my midriff. And talking of muffins, I could kill a chocolate one right now. Perhaps if I did a bit of running, I could later spoil myself with a treat.

The Strawberry Shed stocked all manner of yummy cakes. My stomach rumbled at the thought of a giant Victoria sandwich full of fresh strawberries and whipped cream. Perking up, I broke into a jog and pounded after Cindy.

After ten minutes, I wondered if I'd worked off a thousand calories. I wasn't sure which part of me ached the most – my legs after leaping puddles, or my breasts which had bounced painfully due to not wearing a sports bra. Winded, I came to a standstill and held my sides. A stitch threatened.

I was too out of breath to call my hound to heel. After two minutes, I still sounded like a heavy breather up to no good in a phone box. I leant forward, placed my hands on my knees and wondered if it were possible to pass out from hyperventilating.

Seconds later, Cindy came bombing towards me, tongue out. It looked like a pink flag fluttering in a breeze.

Did you see it? she panted.

'See what?' I puffed. I wouldn't mind letting my own tongue hang out. Currently it felt horribly hot and too big for my mouth.

The squirrel, of course! Which way did it go?

'No… and don't know,' I gasped. 'Come on.' I reached forward and clipped on her lead. 'Let's head back. I want to visit the farm shop.'

Okay, she said reluctantly.

Together, we retraced our footsteps, circumnavigating fallen branches from a recent storm.

Eventually we found ourselves back on the public footpath. Shielding my eyes and gazing straight ahead, I could see the path eventually forked. If I took a right, I'd be alongside Fern Farm's grazing land. Not that I'd venture that far. I wasn't up for crossing a stile and walking through a herd of cows. I'd read too many horror stories about dog walkers being trampled.

Instead, Cindy and I kept left. We took the path that ran alongside Starlight Street and led back to our starting point. I located the gap in the hedge that we'd taken earlier, and pushed through – straight into Milo Soren.

Chapter Twenty-One

'Watch out!' warned Milo.

'What on earth–?' I shrieked, spotting something rat-like at his ankles.

Desperate to avoid squashing the rat, I lunged forward, stumbled blindly, threw out a hand to save myself, and grabbed part of the hedge. There was an ominous snapping sound. Suddenly I was shoving a twiggy bouquet up Milo's nostrils.

'For goodness' sake,' he spluttered, clutching his nose.

A cacophony of frenzied yapping broke out. Righting my balance, I realised that the rat at Milo's feet was, in fact, a gobby chihuahua. Like its owner, it lacked any humour and had a dodgy temper. The man in question was now towering over me, dark eyes blazing.

'You again,' he glowered. 'Why don't you take more care and watch where you're going? You could have killed Rambo.'

'Rambo?' I said incredulously.

'He's very protective.'

I gave Milo a withering look.

'In other words, Rambo has Small Dog Syndrome. You gave him a name to boost his ego and, at the same time, big up yourself.'

'Big up myself?' Milo glared at me. 'I'm over six feet tall. Why would I want to *big up myself?*'

'Because, in your heart of hearts, you probably feel emasculated walking around with a dinky dog.' I adopted a mocking tone. 'Which likely explains your unnecessary aggression earlier. You feel a need – like Rambo – to bark, growl, and behave in an overzealous manner in the name of – I posted quotation marks in the air – '*protecting your property*'. Whereas the reality is you're both all mouth and no trousers. Now, if you'll excuse us. Cindy and I have better things to do than hang around in hedgerows with you and fluffball that thinks it's a Bull Mastiff.'

I made to move past Milo, but his hand shot out. Suddenly, the exit was blocked.

'One moment, lady.'

'Get out of my way,' I barked, sounding not unlike Rambo.

'Before you disappear, I'd like to set the record straight. This dog belonged to my wife. *She* named him. She also dumped him the same day that she dumped me. Fortunately, the dog fits perfectly into my cottage, whereas a Bull Mastiff wouldn't. So – no pun intended – I can thank my wife for small mercies. And before you further criticise the size of *my* dog, I'd like to point out that you drive a car the size of a cotton reel which isn't great for the size of *your* dog.'

'Are you implying that my dog is too big for my car?' I said, eyes narrowing.

'What do you think?' said Milo sarcastically.

'Cindy has plenty of room on the back seat,' I countered.

'The last time I looked, she was in the front. Not exactly ideal, especially when the driver is a maniac.'

He has a point. Remember that time when the traffic light turned red and–

'Hush,' I snapped.

'Woof,' said Cindy.

'And stop telling me to hush,' retorted Milo. 'I'm not a kid.'

'Then don't behave like one,' I said sweetly. 'And I'll have you know my dog loves being in the car with me.'

'Oh, don't tell me,' Milo scoffed. 'She's Thelma to your Louise, and the pair of you roar around, sunnies on, windows down, radio blaring, high fiving each other as you flatten lollipop ladies all over the land.'

'Do you know what I think?' My temper was starting to rise.

'No, but I have a feeling you're going to tell me.' Milo rolled his eyes.

The eyeroll was the last straw. It reminded me of Robin. It was what he used to do when putting me down; a rogue black sock turning his whiter-than-white underpants grubby grey... a steak that wasn't quite medium-rare... the flat sheet not smoothed before making the bed... that when I blew my nose I sounded like Nellie the elephant... and why did I say *you know* so many times in a conversation... and did I know how tedious and annoying this all was?

Milo Soren was not Robin. But the eyeroll had triggered me. Suddenly, all the past putdowns – and there were many –

rushed up from the past. Like a high-speed train, they roared through my head. I glared at this Antonio Banderas doppelganger standing before me.

'You're absolutely right, Mr Soren,' I hissed. 'Allow me to set the record straight. You are a hoity-toity, highfalutin, bit of posh, that talks tosh, and should take your toffee-nosed opinions and shove them up your la-di-da.'

And with that I shoved past him with a po-faced Cindy at heel.

Chapter Twenty-Two

What on earth's got into you, Mum?

'Do not say a word,' I warned as we powered along Starlight Street. 'Blasted man. He's so full of himself – and his dog too. Did you see it? Standing there, like it owned the footpath. Lips peeled back. And Milo wasn't much better. Grimacing for England. He looked like Homer Simpson suffering a bout of constipation.'

I thought you said he looked like Antonio Banderas.

'Okay,' I conceded. 'He looked like Antonio Banderas suffering a bout of constipation. Anyway, enough of him and his wretched mutt. Let's find the farm shop. I'm determined to get something sweet and sticky. Right now, I have an overwhelming desire to mainline on sugar.'

I marched down the lane, Cindy doing a brisk trot to keep up with me. The Strawberry Shed loomed into view. At the sight of it, I felt instantly soothed. The encounter with a prickly Milo and his haughty dog receded.

'What a delightful place,' I murmured to Cindy. Together, we went through a picket gate, then made our way to the farm shop's entrance. 'And such a contribution to the Starlight community,' I added.

I paused to read a sign on the door about the opening

hours. It concluded with a footnote that made my heart feel all warm and fuzzy.

Dogs welcome

'Come on,' I said to Cindy. 'You're allowed in too.'

As we stepped inside, an old-fashioned bell tinkled merrily overhead. I was instantly smitten with the interior. Rustic trestle tables doubled as display surfaces. Each were laden with jars of local produce. From pickles to marmalades. Jams to honey.

Another table was artfully draped with cotton products. Dishcloths. Embroidered tea towels. Cooks' aprons. A third table was stacked with large keepsake tins of biscuits. Their lids showed off pictures of thatched cottages, grazing cows, and woolly sheep.

I grabbed a wire basket and began slowly perusing in almost childlike delight. This place was like Santa's grotto. Everywhere was stuffed with gorgeous goodies.

A jar of honey boasted its source as direct from the Starlight hives. I placed a pot into my basket. Moving over to the display of linen, my fingers trailed across the tea towels. On a whim, I picked up a couple. I'd surprise Lisa with them. Her dishcloths were so frayed, they were more thread than fabric.

I moved over to a large dresser. It displayed packets of multi-coloured pasta. The sizes and shapes defied the average packet of penne. My hand hovered over a bag of Conchiglioni – Italian dried giant shells. How gorgeous they looked. And… *how much?* Clearly the Strawberry Shed stocked posh pasta, not supermarket spaghetti.

Skirting the pasta, I picked up some caramel biscuits. Mm. They sounded nice. The packaging was fussy and decorative, which I knew would reflect in an elevated price. However, the description sounded so good, I nearly dribbled on the spot:

A rich and buttery shortbread layered with soft toffee and a topping of melt-in-the-mouth creamy chocolate.

Two packets found their way into my basket. I'd take one to the office to share around. However, with the other, I'd pig out in front of Lisa's telly.

I walked past a chiller cabinet. It contained trays of meat. Each was labelled *high welfare local beef.* A shiver ran through me. Would the cows, blissfully grazing in Fern Farm's fields, one day reside in this refrigerator? That was the downside of loving meat. Knowing where it came from.

I blocked the thought and moved on. Oooh, what was this? Slabs of butter. Again, produced by Fern Farm. Lovely. There was also plenty of cheese, pots of cream, and even raw milk.

I wandered over to an old-fashioned counter with – how charming – a cash register straight from my childhood. A woman, around my age, put down her gossip magazine and smiled at me.

'Hello,' she said, taking my wire basket. She peered over the counter. 'Aww, what a lovely doggy,' she cooed. Cindy wagged her tail politely. ' haven't seen you around these parts before.'

'No,' I said ruefully. 'I was hoping to buy Starlight Cottage. Unfortunately, somebody beat me to it.'

'Ah,' she nodded, picking up the honey and scanning it.

Oh. I see. The cash till only *looked* like an antique. Sometimes there was no getting away from technology.

'I'm Linda,' she said, holding the pot of honey in mid-air. 'Want a bag?'

'Please,' I nodded. 'And I'm Tilly, and this is Cindy.'

'It's lovely to meet you both,' she dimpled.

As Linda popped the honey into a brown paper carrier, I had a flashback to my chat with Hetty Cartwright. She'd mentioned her son and daughter-in-law taking over the farm. A lightbulb went off in my head.

'You must be Linda Cartwright,' I said.

'I am. How did you know that?'

'I've met your mother-in-law, Hetty. What a lovely lady,' I said, remembering the vibrant Golden Oldie. 'She rather prophetically told me that this village would become my home.'

'Hetty is a bit of a character,' Linda chuckled. 'Fancies herself as having a hotline to Heaven. She claims to know certain things before they happen.'

'Yes,' I sighed. 'It's a shame she got my prediction wrong.'

'Indeed,' said Linda. 'Usually' – she paused to scan the tea towels – 'Hetty is peculiarly right. I'm sorry you were unsuccessful with the purchase,' said Linda sympathetically. 'Conveyancing can be so stressful. Starlight Cottage is a gorgeous house. Hetty was great friends with Audrey Garroway, the lady who used to live there. It was a shock when Audrey unexpectedly passed away. Her husband was devastated. Still, I think old Albert has now found happiness in Dorset. And, of course, the cottage's new owner has sent hearts a-fluttering.'

'Oh?' I said cautiously. 'You've met him, have you?'

'Yes,' Linda nodded. She stopped scanning for a moment, keen to gossip. 'Between you and me' – she gave me a sly look – 'I wouldn't say no. Don't tell my Hugo that,' she guffawed. 'Milo Soren is a total *babe*.' She brushed one hand across her forehead, as if about to faint. 'Phew!' she giggled. 'I reckon he's in his mid-forties. He's got everyone lusting after him, from Hetty down to young Polly. She's the barmaid at the Starlight Arms and half Milo's age. It's so unfair, isn't it?' Linda pulled a face. 'Men just seem to get better and better with age. Whereas us women dry out like prunes.'

I experienced a sinking sensation in the pit of my stomach. Was that why Robin had shacked up with Sexy Samantha? Because he was maturing like a fine wine, while Samantha was still *moist*? Did the new woman in my ex-husband's life have to worry about rubbing her neck with night cream? Or whether to add *Replens* to her shopping list? And did young Polly ever resort to two slices of cucumber over her eyelids? Whereas, if I stayed up beyond midnight, I needed the whole cucumber?

'Yes, it is unfair,' I agreed.

'Mind you' – Linda added – 'Milo isn't just a babe in the looks department. He's charming with it.'

'Really?' I snorted, earning a strange look from Linda. I quickly turned it into a cough.

'Talk of the devil,' she whispered as the shop's bell gave a jaunty tinkle.

I turned in time to see the *babe* in question step inside the shop.

Chapter Twenty-Three

'Hello, Milo,' said Linda, beaming away.

Her delight at seeing the man who was my nemesis was evident – from the coy twiddling of a strand of hair, to the red blush travelling up her neck. She looked like a boiler that was about to self-combust.

Quickly, I turned away, letting my hair fall across my face. I busied myself with my pockets, supposedly seeking loose change.

'Morning, Linda,' said Milo cheerfully. He came over. 'How are you today?'

'All the better for seeing you,' she simpered. The hair twiddling went into overdrive.

'Likewise,' Milo winked. 'But don't tell your Hugo that. I don't want him coming after me with his shotgun.'

Oh *per-leeze*. Any minute now, I'd have to grab one of Linda's paper bags and heave into it.

'I have some gossip for you,' said Linda to Milo.

'Ooh, I do love a bit of gossip,' he said, adopting a camp tone.

'The lovely Tilly here was hoping to buy Starlight Cottage. Apparently, you pipped her to it.'

It was at that point that Milo looked properly at the

woman who, up until then, had presented him with her back. I swung round.

'Oh, hi,' I said. The coolness in my tone was colder than Linda's chiller cabinet.

'Ah, we meet again,' said Milo.

Linda frowned.

'Do you two know each other?'

Milo made a see-saw gesture with one hand. I butted in, before he could expand.

'We've run into each other here and there,' I explained.

'*Run into* being an accurate description,' Milo added. He peered at the contents of my shopping basket. 'Oh, what have we here? Mm, caramel biscuits. Do tell. Are they of the toffee-nosed variety?'

Linda looked on in bewilderment. She glanced from Milo to me then back to Milo. She realised something was going on here but couldn't work out what.

I shot Milo a murderous look. Linda was a nice lady. The type who could so easily become a mate. I might not live in this village, but there was nothing to stop me from visiting again. And, if I did, it would be nice to make small talk with Linda as she rang up my goods. Maybe, on the next occasion, Hetty would be here too. And we'd all giggle and gossip together about everything and nothing, as women nearly always do.

I'd been enjoying my chit-chat with Linda until Milo had strolled in. Mr Fancies-Himself-Rotten had spoilt things.

That's not strictly true, Mum, said Cindy, reading my thoughts. *Linda said that it's everybody else who fancies him rotten.*

'Hush,' I said.

'Woof,' Cindy answered.

'Why do you two keep doing that?' Milo frowned.

On the wall behind Linda, a phone began to ring.

'Excuse me, Tilly,' she said. 'I must take that call. It'll be about a missed delivery I've been chasing. Won't be a sec, and then I'll finish scanning your shopping.'

The moment Linda's back was turned, Milo rounded on me. He looked like a sleek cat that had finally cornered an annoying mouse. He affected a posh voice.

'So what else has *Modom* bought?' He peered into the brown carrier next to the cash till. 'By Jove and golly gosh. It's some highfalutin honey.' He frowned theatrically. 'Is that a wise decision?'

'Why shouldn't it be?' I hissed.

'Well, it's hoity-toity enough for me, but I'm not so sure about you. Or are you thinking about converting from da-di-da to la-di-da?'

I glared at him.

'Are you stalking me?' I hissed.

Milo threw back his head and laughed. It transformed him. The dark eyes danced with amusement, and the creases at the outer corners of his eyes deepened. It was evident, despite his sniping, that this was a man who liked to laugh. I caught a flash of very white, straight teeth and a pink tongue – a sure sign of robust health.

He wiped a tear from one eye. Apparently, my question had been so hilarious he'd literally wept with laughter. He looked at me, a smile playing around his lips.

'Am I stalking you?' he hooted. 'You flatter yourself, Milly.'

'Tilly,' I said, trying not to gnash my teeth. 'You really are the most overbearing, pompous, argumentative-'

'Ah, that's what I like to see,' said Linda, returning to the cash till. 'New customers hitting it off with each other.'

'Absolutely,' said Milo. 'Eh, Jilly?'

'Tilly,' I repeated. For a moment I considered accidentally-on-purpose stepping on his toe. A quick glimpse at Milo's foot revealed Rambo glaring up at me.

'It's always nice when two people get along,' said Linda cosily.

'Oh, we've been like the proverbial house on fire,' Milo assured.

'I can see that,' Linda winked at me. 'The sparks are positively flying. Aye, aye, Milo. Don't go breaking Tilly's heart now, will you!'

Chapter Twenty-Four

It was with regret that I said goodbye to Linda, but it was a relief to get away from Milo.

'Lovely to meet you, Tilly,' Linda called after me. 'Come back and see me soon.'

'Take care, Dilly,' Milo yodelled. 'Especially in that racy little car of yours.'

Evidently, he wasn't going to forgive me any time soon for calling him Mr Moron – or nearly running him over. No doubt he was thrilled to bits that his parting comment would wind me up.

I tried and failed to come up with an icy retort just for Milo. One that went right over Linda's head but landed in Milo's nether regions – and preferably delivered frostbite to his testicles.

I had a sudden vision of Milo in bed with Linda and Polly the barmaid, and the three of them peering woefully at his damaged meat and veg. A case of two birds and one stone.

Blimey, where had that thought come from? I shook it away and headed off to Octavia. Moments later, the goods from the Strawberry Shed were in her boot.

Mum, I'm starving.

'You and me both,' I said. 'Come on. Let's go and check out the pub. I'll order bangers and mash and share the sausages with you.'

Apart from anything else, I was curious about *young Polly* – the barmaid who apparently lusted after Milo. Not that I cared. I was simply being a nosy parker. Because, well, I had nothing else to do right now. Lisa was away. My parents were in Cornwall. I had no one else with whom to spend the rest of the day – other than my beloved Cindy.

Together, we walked along the lane. The Starlight Arms eventually came into view. It was, like all the buildings around here, quaint and pretty. The pub's exterior showcased several hanging baskets filled with winter pansies and trailing ivy.

To one side of the pub was a beer garden. In summer it would be picture perfect. Right now, it featured trestle tables not dissimilar to those inside the Strawberry Shed. Several planters were scattered about, their flowering shrubs adding a splash of colour.

A rustic sign shaped like a pointed arrow was engraved with a message to visiting patrons:

A warm welcome to all our customers!

For the umpteenth time I found myself wishing that I lived in this village. For one tiny moment I allowed myself a little daydream. That I'd taken a short stroll from Starlight Cottage to the Starlight Arms, darling Cindy at side. One woman and her dog. On a sausage mission.

As we stepped over the threshold, my senses reeled. The aroma of roast beef hung in the air. It mixed perfectly with the smell of ale, furniture polish, and kindling.

The pub boasted a quarry-tiled floor, overhead beams, and recessed lighting. The bar area sported a highly polished oak counter. It ran almost the length of the entire area. Tables and chairs were dotted about inviting visitors to huddle and talk privately. Several were already occupied with hungry patrons tucking into mouthwatering dishes.

My eyes flicked over the diners' plates. Shepherd's pie… mac cheese… pork chops and apple sauce… a full English… a roast with golden puffs of Yorkshire puds. Ooh, yummy.

To the left was a feature fireplace. A vast inglenook housed a wood burner. Logs filled the space around the stove, which was currently burning brightly. The glow was both visually and physically warming. And – yippee! – there was an empty table right by the fire. I mentally marked it, then headed over to the bar.

A pretty brunette, somewhere in her twenties, gave me a welcoming smile.

'Can I help you?'

Ah, this must be Polly the dolly. Or should I say dollybird?

That's a bit bitchy, Mum.

'Sorry, I didn't mean that.'

Polly's smile wavered.

'Mean what?'

'Oops.' I gave a tinkly laugh. 'I'm on the phone.' I tapped the side of my head, apparently touching a Bluetooth earpiece which Polly couldn't see on account of my long hair.

Oh, Muuum, Cindy sighed. *I wish you wouldn't do things like this. It's so obvious you're blagging. You don't have a microphone.*

I pulled my hair forward, so it was almost covering my mouth.

'Yes… yes… that's fine… okay… bye-eeeee,' I trilled through my tresses.

I cleared my throat. Gazed at Polly. She was looking at me like I was a couple of Yorkshires short of a roast.

'I'd like bangers and mash, please. Can I order a couple of extra sausages? They're for my dog.'

The pub was starting to fill up. A flurry of people came through the main door. They were rubbing warmth into their hands and stamping their feet. I looked at them with interest. First, an old boy and his wife. Next, three men wearing woolly hats. Bits of straw hung off them. I wondered if they worked at Fern Farm. Bringing up the rear was a large group of walkers. The latter were chattering and laughing. No doubt everyone was looking to fill their bellies with hot food. I was glad I'd placed my order before them, and avoided a long wait.

'Anything to drink?' asked Polly.

'A pot of tea, please. Can I be cheeky and ask for a bowl of water for my dog?'

'Of course,' Polly smiled.

She pressed various buttons on the cash till's touchscreen. As she rang up the amount, I surreptitiously studied her. She was certainly very attractive with her bee-stung lips, swishy hair and lustrous eyelashes. Were they real? I wondered whether eyelash extensions might suit me. Did she really fancy Milo? If so, I couldn't begin to compete with the likes of her.

And why would you want to compete with her, Mum? Surely you don't, ahem, fancy Mr Fancies-Himself-Rotten, do you?

'Don't be ridiculous,' I muttered. Polly's head shot up. 'Phone,' I mouthed, tapping my ear again.

Oh dear. Wrong ear. Perhaps I could make out I was wearing two earpieces. I pressed my hand against my head, as if making an adjustment.

'Yeah... yeah... that's great. Okay, bye.' I looked at Polly. 'Sorry about that.' I made a tutting sound. 'It's gone a bit crazy today.'

'Something certainly has,' she muttered.

'Sorry?'

'Nothing.' She flashed a quick smile. 'Take a seat. I'll bring everything over shortly.'

'Thanks,' I said.

I began to make my way over to the table I'd earmarked, then stopped dead in my tracks. Sitting there, for all the world as if he owned not just the table but the entire pub too, was Milo Soren.

Chapter Twenty-Five

Milo was reading a newspaper and nursing a pint. Rambo was sitting on a chair alongside him. He looked like a scaled-down canine version of Lord Muck.

I had no idea how I'd failed to spot this man and his dog prior to placing my food order, but one thing was for sure – they could both go and sit elsewhere.

Bristling, I marched over to the table and cleared my throat.

'Excuse me.'

Milo looked up and feigned surprise.

'Are you stalking me?' he enquired, parodying my earlier comment.

'You know that's not true.'

'So is there another reason why you're standing at my table impersonating Mr Angry's wife?'

'I'm annoyed' – I enunciated – 'because you're sitting at my table.'

Milo opened his eyes wide.

'*Your* table?'

'Yes. I was going to sit here after placing my food order.'

'I see.' He put down his newspaper. 'And therein lies the answer to this dilemma. So you *meant* to reserve this table but failed to pop your bag upon its surface, or hang your coat over a chair, to indicate that it was taken.'

'Are you always so sanctimonious?'

Milo considered.

'Only when I'm right.'

'Listen, Miles—'

'It's Milo, Lilly.'

'You really are the most infuriating man.'

'I could say the same of you.'

'I'm not a man.'

'Aren't you?' Milo looked astonished. 'Well, blow me down with a feather.'

'Listen.' I dumped my handbag on the tabletop, then shrugged off my jacket. I slung it over the chair opposite Milo. 'All the other tables are now taken. I'm about to eat my lunch. Whereas you are only enjoying a drink.' I sat down. 'So why don't you take your pint and tootle over to the bar? You can sit on a tall stool and chat to Polly.'

'I can't chat to Polly.'

'Why not?'

'She's working.'

'Then chat to someone else,' I suggested.

Cindy put her head in my lap. She gave me a beseeching look.

Can you pull out a chair for me? If Sir Rambo can sit at the table, surely I can too?

Milo folded up his newspaper. He set it to one side, then regarded me gravely.

'It seems I have no choice but to chat to you.'

'That really isn't necessary. And anyway' – I spotted Polly heading over with the bangers and mash – 'my dinner is here. So... toodle-oo.'

Whereupon Polly set down the bangers and mash in front of Milo. She then placed a smaller plate of chopped sausages in front of Rambo.

'Here we are,' Polly cooed. She fluttered her eyelashes and jiggled her breasts. Oh yes, she fancied Milo all right.

'Thanks, sweetheart,' he said.

Milo gave her a blowtorch smile. I was amazed it didn't melt Polly's false eyelashes. She responded with her best *I've-just-had-an-orgasm* smoulder, before turning to me.

'I'll come again in a sec.'

I stared at her blankly.

'With your dinner,' she added.

'Right,' I croaked. 'Thanks.'

Bloody hell. The chemistry between Polly and Milo was hotter than the wood burner next to me. On impulse, I picked up my dinner mat and, using it as a fan, cooled myself. Phew. If only I could take off my sweater. However, I'd be down to my bra, so that wasn't viable. Milo gave me an enquiring look.

'You were saying?'

I glanced wildly around the pub. Every single table was now taken along with every chair. Even the tall stools at the bar were all occupied. There was nowhere else to sit. Nowhere at all. Apart from here. With this blasted man. Bugger. And now I was going to have to do some swift back peddling and grovel.

I took a deep breath and shut my eyes.

'Would you mind terribly if I ate my dinner at this table?'

Milo regarded me, thoroughly enjoying my discomfit.

'What's the magic word?'

'Please,' I hissed.

'In which case, be my guest, Philly.'

Chapter Twenty-Six

Lisa – having twisted our boss around her little finger for that long weekend in Spain – returned to work Tuesday lunchtime.

She drove straight from Gatwick Airport to the office. She didn't walk into the office, rather she fizzed. She was like an energy drink. Bubbling over. The high spirits were due to hitting it off with one of her mate's wedding guests. A man, naturally.

'I'm not kidding you, Tilly' – she paused to cram one of the Strawberry Shed's caramel biscuits into her mouth – 'Juan is gorgeous. Divine. I've only got to look at him and I swoon.' That last word caused her to spray crumbs all over her keyboard. 'In fact, I think he might be *The One*.'

I felt a frisson of anxiety, as if the inner sanctum of my world had been threatened. And then I told myself not to be ridiculous. To relax. After all, Lisa lived in Longfield. This Juan chappie lived in Barcelona. There was distance between them. Some fifteen hundred miles.

My bestie reached for another biscuit. The expression on her face was gooey, like the biscuit's caramel centre.

'I'm in love,' she sighed.

'You're in *lust*,' I countered. 'Not that there's anything

wrong with that. But think of Phil.'

'Whatever for? He bogged off.'

'Then think of your allegiance to Ronnie.'

'Who?' she frowned. 'Oh, my rabbit. Well, that's fine. Ronnie's batteries have gone flat. Which is excellent timing. I no longer need a vibrator,' she beamed. 'I have the real thing.'

'Yeah, but as Juan isn't around, you might as well recharge Ronnie. And remember' – I held up one finger – 'there are lots of perks to having a pink rabbit. No smelly socks to pick up, for starters.'

'Really, Tilly' – Lisa shot me a wounded look – 'I thought you'd be pleased for me.'

'I am, I *am*,' I assured, reaching for a biscuit too. 'It just seems' – I shrugged helplessly – 'like a whirlwind romance. I don't want you getting hurt.'

Juan had likely already moved on. Realistically, what were the chances of Lisa seeing him again? She then said something that briefly winded me.

'He said he'd try and come over this weekend.'

My head shot up. The caramel biscuit hovered mid-air.

'What?'

The word came out like a pistol shot. Lisa rolled her eyes.

'Look, I wasn't going to tell you. Well, not immediately. But now you leave me no choice. Juan has told me he loves me. Now *please* don't rain on my parade. He's going to sort out some annual leave so he can stay in England for a bit.'

Bloody hell. Couldn't he get *a bit* back home? Why did

he have to come here for *a bit* – especially with me under Lisa's roof. Two's company. Three's a crowd. Etcetera.

Lisa had a light in her eyes that I hadn't seen for a long time. It was the inner glow of a woman who believed she'd found her soulmate. A twin flame. One that happened to look like an Adonis and was no doubt a stud between the sheets.

She licked some melted chocolate from her fingertips, then smacked her lips with appreciation.

'Pass me another biscuit, Tilly.'

'They've all gone.'

'Have they?' She looked momentarily appalled. 'Never mind. Anyway' – she straightened up – 'I can't wait for you to meet Juan.'

I inwardly sighed. Let Lisa have this moment. Juan probably wouldn't show up. I mean, what would the travel costs be going backwards and forwards from Espana to Blighty? Humungous, that's what. Perhaps he'd expect Lisa to stump up the readies to see him. Or maybe he secretly had a wife and three kids. It wouldn't be the first time Lisa had got stung by a married man. No doubt he would let her down by text.

Leesa. Eeet is meee. Juan. The One. But I no more The One. Love Juan x

In which case I'd offer my bestie a shoulder. Give her wine to drown her sorrows. In fact, I could take her to the Starlight Arms. We could sit by the wood burner, and she could tell me all about the dastardly Spaniard who broken her heart. And I could tell her all about Milo and… and…

I paused. Tell Lisa what about Milo? Well, that he was a most annoying man. Although Milo was hardly in the same category as a boyfriend. He wasn't even a friend, for that matter. And anyway, Lisa wouldn't give a flying fig about my encounter with Milo. Or how he'd handfed sausages to his snooty dog. Or the way Polly had continuously found excuses to come over to our table. Bizarrely, that had irritated me more than itching powder.

My thoughts were interrupted by Lisa's phone giving a loud *dinggg.*

'Ooh,' she squealed girlishly. 'A text from my man.'

Uh-oh. Here it was. The message that would give her the brush off.

'*Eeeep*,' she squealed in excitement. 'Juan says his boss has given him the thumbs up. He's having some time off and – *yayyy* – he's now coming to England tomorrow.'

'Tomorrow?' I bleated. 'How did he manage to get a flight at such short notice?'

'Silly,' she tutted. 'He doesn't need to take a plane. Juan is an international lorry driver. He can *drive* to the UK. He says he's leaving Barcelona right now. He can spend the next fortnight with me. He's also looking at rejigging his contract so that all his driving jobs are in England.' She paused to read the rest of the message. 'Oh, how romantic,' she beamed. 'He says he can't live without me.' She hugged herself in delight, then sighed dreamily. 'My gorgeous man will soon be with me.'

I nearly choked on my caramel biscuit. Lisa's maisonette had one bedroom. And I was on the other side of a very thin wall, sleeping on her sofa. What if she brought him to the maisonette? What if Juan got up in the night for a glass of water and wandered naked through the lounge to the kitchen? This wasn't good. Not good at all.

'Tilly,' Lisa hissed urgently. My thoughts fragmented. 'Do you know that guy?'

I stared at her uncomprehendingly.

'What guy?'

'There's a bloke standing outside the shop. He's been there for ages, pretending to study the properties for sale in the window. He keeps looking this way and staring at you.'

'Really?' I frowned. 'Why would he do that?'

'How should I know? You'll catch him looking if you turn… now!'

Intrigued, I swivelled my typing stool and locked eyes with a young man. Lisa was right. He was indeed looking at me. I wondered why. Was he a client, checking to see if I was in today? Was he dithering about coming into the shop for a one-to-one meeting?

I raised my eyebrows enquiringly. The guy hastily looked away. A second later, he'd turned on his heel, leaving me staring after him. I felt strangely disturbed but couldn't think why.

Chapter Twenty-Seven

On Wednesday evening – after a quick shower and change of clothes – Lisa left the maisonette to meet Juan, who'd checked into a B&B.

'See you,' she cooed.

'Laters,' I trilled. After the front door clicked shut, I turned to Cindy with a sigh of relief. 'Phew. Thank goodness *Juan the One* isn't coming here.'

Why's that?

'Well, it's obvious, isn't it? Lisa doesn't want you and me overhearing them in the bedroom. I mean, when you're in the first flush of lust, you want to yodel a bit. You know. Make a bit of noise. Presumably Juan has booked a hotel for the two of them to stay in.'

Cindy regarded me silently.

'Ah,' I nodded. 'Agreed. This is not an appropriate conversation. It's blurring the parenting boundaries.'

Indeed. Can I have a biscuit?

'Okay.'

Later, Lisa returned home looking like a woman who'd not only died and gone to heaven, but also astral travelled around the universe.

However, there had been no romantic hotel. Instead, the

pair of them had been in Juan's lorry in a layby off the A2.

By the weekend, there was a shift in Lisa's mood. I could tell she needed to get something off her chest.

'Listen, Tilly. And please don't be offended.' I was sitting in front of her little television working my way through a plate of cookies. Despite the relaxed setting, Lisa's vibe was making me tense. 'I know I said you could stay here forever – and that still stands – but the thing is…'

'Yes?'

'My romantic trysts with Juan have been taking place in the cab of his lorry. The landlady of his B&B is from the dark ages and doesn't permit overnight visitors. His lorry is cold and uncomfortable. I'd like to bring him back here. You know' – she gave me a meaningful look – 'to entertain.'

'Of course,' I said. 'Don't mind me. I'll keep a low profile. I'll make sure the telly's volume is loud, so I don't hear the two of you at it.'

'Ah.' She made a face. 'I'd rather you go out.' She made another face. One that was horribly apologetic but, at the same time, told me she wasn't going to back down. 'Perhaps you could take Cindy for a long walk.'

'Um, okay,' I said uncertainly. Lately, the February weather had been one of cold driving rain. This had been punctuated with strong winds. 'We can make ourselves absent for an hour or two.'

'Make it three,' she said quickly.

'Right,' I quavered, telling myself that it was only for a few more days.

After all, Juan's annual leave would soon come to an end.

Even though he was changing his contract, he still had to return to Barcelona to give notice on his accommodation and pack up his belongings.

The die was then cast for the remainder of Juan's stay. However, there's only so much walking one can do in wind and rain on a dark winter's night.

Instead, I spent much of the time driving around with Cindy. Together, we checked out the locations of houses to potentially view. I would turn into various side streets, pull over, then try and get a feel for the area.

One such evening I allowed myself to feel a ripple of enthusiasm. I was discreetly parked outside a pleasant, terraced property in an attractive residential road.

'At last,' I said to Cindy. 'We might be getting somewhere.' I nodded at the little house in our view. 'What do you think?'

But Cindy's focus was elsewhere. A gang of youths had materialised, seemingly from nowhere. Despite the horrible weather, they stood on the street corner drinking beer. Every now and again they pushed and shoved each other. Presumably this was meant to be joshing. Their conversation was loud and peppered with swearing.

Eventually a man opened his front door and asked them to move. He said their noise had disturbed his baby son and upset his exhausted wife.

The youths retaliated with more expletives and lots of finger action. They eventually moved on, but not until they'd thrown their empty tins across the man's garden.

'Prats,' I muttered.

Did I want to buy a house where these lads liked to hang out? The answer was no. No doubt these yobs would one day grow up and go away, but there were always younger versions ready to pick up the mantle.

Disheartened, I checked out other areas. And then, one night, I found myself back in my old road.

Aye, aye. What are we doing here? said Cindy.

'Oh, I don't know,' I sighed.

I do. You're tormenting yourself, that's what.

I sighed again.

'You could be right. I wonder what Robin and Sexy Samantha are up to?'

I peered into the darkness. The curtains in my old home were drawn against the night. Samantha hadn't got her own way about those shutters. I wondered if she'd succeeded elsewhere. Had she persuaded Robin to dump the old marital bed in favour of something bespoke, or whatever it was that she'd wittered on about when I'd shown her around. I pondered if they were both happy and glad of the decisions they'd respectively made. She to shack up with a much older man. One who self-consciously combed his hair a certain way to cover a bald spot. And whether Robin was tolerant of his young partner applying fake tan then getting it all over the pristine white linen he'd always favoured.

I looked up. There was a glow behind the bedroom curtains. The light was on. Perhaps Robin and Samantha were doing it right now. Like Lisa and Juan.

And then I found myself thinking about Polly the barmaid. Whether she'd finally bagged Milo. And, if so, were the two of them currently shagging for England at Starlight Cottage?

Everyone seemed to be at it. Apart from me.

Chapter Twenty-Eight

'He's there again,' Lisa whispered, leaning across her desk.

'Who?' I said distractedly.

I'd just come off the phone from a potential customer who wanted a valuation. Mr and Mrs Daley were looking for a family home. They wanted a house with three bedrooms, maybe four. If they went ahead with the sale of their two-bedroomed semi in Borough Green, I might be their first viewer. Their property sounded both charming and suitable for Cindy and me.

Meanwhile, the developing relationship between Juan and Lisa meant I was even more desperate to move out of the little maisonette. Even if Juan hadn't appeared in my bestie's life, there was no getting away from the fact that her sofa wasn't doing great things for my back.

'Tilly, pay attention,' she hissed. 'This must be the sixth time I've seen that chap hanging around outside. He's definitely checking you out.'

I turned and, once again, caught the young man staring at me. He immediately looked away, then pretended to be studying the window display.

I frowned. Lisa had a point. The man did seem to be checking me out. I wondered why. After all, he was much younger than me. He gave off the vibe of… wanting to talk… but not having the courage to do so. Which made no sense. After all, what was such a big deal about coming in and chatting about a property?

Perhaps the guy felt anxious about speaking to our mortgage broker. Or embarrassed at not having a big enough deposit. Or, for that matter, a big enough salary. Perhaps he thought I was Home and Hearth's mortgage broker. Should I go out and tackle him? Say, "We don't bite, you know. Come on in. Let's talk."

This time I met the man's gaze and stared back at him. He was a tall chap, and his face seemed strangely familiar. I felt something stir in the pit of my stomach. A memory. No… no. It couldn't be. He couldn't possibly be… surely, he was too young. Wasn't he? Even so, I suddenly felt on edge. Rattled.

The man casually took a step to his left. His face was now obscured by the many display photographs.

'Why are you frowning?' asked Lisa. 'Do you know him?'

I shook my head.

'No, I don't know him. But…'

'What?'

'He reminds me of someone.'

'Maybe that's because you've seen him around. You know, locally. And you've just not properly registered his face before now. Sometimes people come in here and chat to us and then, days later, I realise I've seen them before at the Post Office. Or the local Spar.'

'No,' I said. I've never seen him locally. Or anywhere else for that matter.'

'So who does he remind you of?' Lisa asked nosily.

'Someone from the past.'

'Recent or dim and distant?' she prodded.

'Definitely dim and distant,' I said, turning back to my work.

Lisa waited for me to enlarge, but I didn't. My body language said it all. Subject closed.

Chapter Twenty-Nine

The night before Juan returned to Spain was a gamechanger for me.

'He's staying the night,' Lisa announced, during our lunch hour. 'Juan is leaving England tomorrow. I'm distraught. So, I've made that decision. I want to wake up with my boyfriend beside me,' she said dramatically. Her chin wobbled like a jelly in an earthquake. 'And anyway, it's about time you met him.'

'Right-oh,' I warbled. 'So, um, I take it you don't mind if I stay in tonight too?

'Oh,' she said. Her brow furrowed as she worked out the logistics of her housemate's presence while having hot sex. 'Well, I suggest you meet Juan first, then go for a walk. Give us a few hours, as previously. Just be aware that, this time, he'll still be there when you get back. But we should have, you know' – she flashed a meaningful look – 'be finished by then, so hopefully won't disturb you.'

'Excellent,' I quavered.

That evening, Juan arrived bearing two bouquets. One for his girlfriend. The other for the gooseberry occupying his girlfriend's sofa.

'For you, Teely,' he said gallantly, before thrusting the

flowers up my nose.

'Thank you,' I said. 'That's very kind.'

But I might as well have been talking to myself. His attention was already divested in Lisa.

I took a moment to surreptitiously study him. Juan was only a little taller than my bestie, but broad in stature. He was attractive in a dark-haired spaniel-eyed way. He was now giving Lisa all the smoulders.

'For you, *cariño*,' he said huskily, presenting her with a dozen red roses.

Lisa instantly melted like ice-cream in a heatwave. She endlessly simpered and giggled. At one point she sounded like a hyena that had sucked on a helium balloon. Juan didn't seem to notice. It was obvious that the pair of them were besotted with each other.

Lisa rustled up a risotto for the three of us. I gamely made conversation throughout the meal, but they hardly touched their food. Mostly they appeared to be mentally undressing each other over the bowl of parmesan.

Now and again Juan managed to take his eyes off Lisa long enough to answer my nervous chatter. Yes, he liked being a lorry driver. No, long distances didn't bother him. Yes, the risotto was gorgeous. Just like the cook. Although neither the cook nor he had made any further headway with their meal. They continued gazing into each other's eyes, lost in love. Or lust. Or maybe a bit of both.

Leaving them to marvel at each other, I forked up my dinner faster than Cindy eating a rare steak. Two things were of vital importance. First, eat. Second, leave the maisonette.

As swiftly as possible.

'Mm, that was *delicious*,' I said loudly.

Neither of them replied. I was talking to myself. Juan and Lisa were emotionally elsewhere. The zingers scorching back and forth between them were enough to induce a giant peri-menopausal hot flush.

'Phew,' I said, picking up my serviette. I ineffectually flapped it about. 'Lovely meal. Very… warming. I think I'll cool off by taking Cindy for a walk.'

I looked from Juan to Lisa. Zero response. They were totally lost in each other.

'Right, I'll be off then. See you later. Um, you know, *much* later,' I added.

After all, I didn't want either of them thinking that I'd be back in ten minutes. The last thing I wanted was to find them stripped down to their undies… Lisa sprawled across the table... wine glasses knocked over… liquid dripping to the floor… squashed risotto all over the place.

'Er, laters,' I trilled.

I watched, momentarily transfixed, as the pair of them began, almost in slow motion, to lean towards each other. A lip lock was imminent. Juan's left hand was already gravitating towards Lisa's breast. *Eeep*! Get me out of here.

I stood up and, in my haste to get away, promptly knocked over my chair. Whistling for Cindy, I nearly tripped over her, failing to see her already at my heels.

Mum! What are those two DOING?

If it was possible for a dog to boggle, then I swear the one at my side was doing just that.

'Never you mind what they're doing,' I said under my breath.

Seconds later, the pair of us had crashed out of the maisonette.

Outside, it was *way* too cold to walk. I opened Octavia's passenger door. Cindy hopped in. Seconds later, the little car's engine roared into life. I spun the wheel, and we shot backwards – thankfully there was nobody behind us – then I hit the accelerator.

Without a second thought, I set off in the direction of Starlight Croft. No, I wasn't going to stalk Milo Soren. Or make pithy banter with him. Nor was I going to exchange eyerolls with his snooty dog.

Right now, I just wanted to retreat. Have a quiet drink. Sit by a lit wood burner. Stare aimlessly at the dancing flames within. And try and work out where the hell I was going in my life. Because one thing was for sure. Juan might be going to Spain in the morning, but he would return. It was only a matter of when.

As I drove up the steep hill that eventually would become Starlight Street, Octavia's headlights swept over the numerous hedgerows. The twin beams picked out squat bushes and the sweeping curves of the singletrack lane.

It was on a particularly narrow bend that I made the decision to abandon the idea of looking for a house to buy. The whole thing would take far too long. I needed an alternative solution. It was more sensible to find something instantly available. Like a room to rent. There must be someone, somewhere, looking to rent out their spare bedroom. Perhaps an empty nester, glad to have some company. Or maybe a pensioner, looking for extra cash to help with the winter bills.

Decision made, I instantly felt happier. Lighter. Parking outside the Starlight Arms, I switched off Octavia's engine, then walked towards the entrance with Cindy.

The door creaked back on its hinges as I swiftly glanced around. Oh, lovely! The wood burner was loaded with kindling and logs. It crackled and popped, soothing me like a comfort blanket. I decided to order a hot chocolate and cadge some biscuits for my pooch.

As I headed towards the bar, my heart skipped a beat. For there, chatting with Polly the barmaid, was Milo Soren.

Chapter Thirty

As I walked towards the bar, Milo looked my way. He raised one eyebrow. Polly broke off her conversation and came over.

'Hello, again.' She flashed a professional smile. 'I recognise you.' Her expression said it all:

This is the woman who thinks she's wearing not one, but two telephone headpieces, and has imaginary conversations with precisely no one.

'Hi,' I beamed. I arranged my features into an expression that acknowledged her thoughts but also added a caveat:

Just humour me. I'm not bonkers – at least, not all the time.

'What can I get you?' she asked.

'A hot chocolate with all the trimmings, please.'

'Certainly.'

As she turned away to make the drink, Milo moved closer. I inwardly groaned. It appeared that Lord Rambo wasn't with his master this evening. Perhaps the snooty chihuahua was at home, reading the newspaper and smoking his pipe.

'Hello, again,' said Milo. His eyes flickered with amusement. I braced myself, wondering what word play he was about to engage in. I didn't have long to wait. 'Is this the moment where I ask if you're stalking me, or have we both exhausted that line of conversation?'

'Good evening,' I said formally. 'And yes. I think we're both done with that dialogue.'

His mouth twitched.

'Does this mean that we'll be making other… *dialogue*?'

I shrugged.

'No need. After all, I wouldn't want to spoil your tête-à-tête with young Polly.'

'Ooh, I detect an edge to your voice. Now why is that, Billie?'

I narrowed my eyes.

'You know perfectly well that my name is Tilly.'

I'd neatly avoided his question regarding the edge to my voice. But he was right. I hadn't meant to be irritated by his chit-chat with Polly, but some inner emotion had betrayed me.

I'd sounded jealous. Like a woman vying for a man's attention while knowing the competition was too stiff. That she didn't stand a chance. Now why should I feel like that? After all, I did *not* fancy Milo Soren.

I think you might have a tiny crush on him, Mum.

'Hush,' I muttered.

'Woof,' said Cindy.

'Oh, not that again,' said Milo in exasperation. 'What is it with you two?' He glanced down at Cindy. 'Hush,' he said.

She cocked her head to one side and gave him an

enquiring look. Milo muttered something under his breath.

'What was that?' I said sharply. 'Did you just call my dog a weirdo.'

'No.'

'Yes, you did.'

'No, I didn't.'

'Yes, you did.'

'Oh no I didn't.' His eyes were doing that glittery thing again. 'Have we suddenly dropped into a panto? Don't tell me,' he guffawed. 'Any moment now a pantomime horse will shuffle in. Polly will ask if it wants a pint, and the horse will reply, *I wouldn't mind two halves.*'

'You're so funny,' I said sarcastically.

'Thank you,' said Milo, as if I'd paid him a great compliment. 'And I did not call your dog a weirdo. Confession time. It was *you* I called a weirdo. You must admit, it is odd telling your dog to be quiet when she hadn't made a sound.'

'But she *did* make a sound,' I countered. 'It's just that… that… *I'm* the only one who heard her.'

'I see,' said Milo dryly. 'So, amongst your many talents, you also have bionic hearing.'

'Yes,' I said defiantly.

Wretched man. Why couldn't he go and talk to someone else? Like one of those old boys over there – the one that looked like he might expire before finishing his pint.

Polly reappeared with the hot chocolate. As she set the cup down on the counter, she picked up on my icy vibe. She gave Milo a knowing look.

'Are you winding up the customers, Milo?' she teased. 'Don't let Cilla find out or she'll have your guts for garters.' Polly gave me a conspiratorial look. 'Cilla is the pub landlady and a force to be reckoned with.'

'Right,' I said. 'Good to know.'

'Cash or card?' asked Polly.

'Oh, um, card, please,' I said, reaching for my handbag.

My heart sank. Oh no. Such had been my haste to get out of Lisa's maisonette, I'd come out without my purse.

I began delving into various pockets, feeling for loose change. There was none. My face flamed as Polly stood there, patiently waiting, Milo all the while looking on.

As I started to shed layers of clothing in my frantic search for some readies, his eyes widened at the woman giving herself a strip search on fast forward.

He put up a hand to stop me, before I got down to my smalls. His touch nearly rocketed me out of my undies.

'How much is the drink, Poll?' he asked.

'Four pounds,' she said.

'Here.' He handed her a fiver. 'Keep the change.'

'Thanks, darling.'

Darling.

Bloody woman. Bloody man. Bloody hot chocolate.

This was Lisa's fault. Her and Juan and their scorching lust. I should never have accepted the invitation to sleep on her sofa. And I might as well lob some blame at my ex-husband too. After all, I wouldn't be in this predicament if Robin had kept his dick in his trousers.

'Are you okay?' asked Polly looking concerned.

'Never better,' I grimaced.

'Are you sure? Only… you seem to be hyperventilating.'

'She's fine,' said Milo.

He picked up my hot chocolate. With his free hand, he steered me – as one might an old lady – to a couple of armchairs by the wood burner. Cindy quietly followed.

Are you okay, Mum?

I couldn't answer. Milo's touch had fired a line of zingers up my arm and into my brain. They were now exploding in a blast of stars and colour. I momentarily closed my eyes, desperately trying to ignore the effect he was having on me.

I'll take that as a no, said Cindy.

I let out a low moan. This could not be happening to me.

'Right, Tilly,' said Milo, pushing me down. I collapsed into one of the chairs. He set my drink on a side table, before sitting opposite me. 'How about you tell me what really brings you back to this village, especially at this time of night?'

Chapter Thirty-One

'Honestly, I'm not stalking you,' I said, my tone defensive.

'I thought we were done with that *dialogue*,' said Milo. 'Although I do find it strange that wherever I go, you pop up.'

'Look,' I sighed, reaching for my hot chocolate. 'You heard it for yourself via Linda when we were both at the Strawberry Shed. I wanted to buy Starlight Cottage. I fell in love with the house – and this village. However, it wasn't meant to be. But there's something about this place that resonates with me. Consequently, I find it hard to stay away.'

I shrugged helplessly and removed a marshmallow from hot chocolate's whipped topping. I popped it into my mouth. Yuck. I quickly swallowed it down. How disappointing. It was odd how some things looked so attractive on the outside but weren't so nice on the inside. A bit like my ex-husband.

'Anyway' – I turned my attention back to Milo – 'for some ridiculous reason, I find it comforting to revisit Starlight Croft. Apart from anything else, it's a lovely place to walk Cindy.' I nodded at my dog. She was now stretched out by the wood burner, warming her belly. 'I appreciate my words might sound somewhat pathetic, but hey, so what.'

Frankly I didn't care what Milo Soren, young Polly,

Linda Cartwright, Hetty, or even Uncle Tom Cobbly thought about me.

'I see,' said Milo. 'So, that bit of chat you gave me about practically being besties with Hetty Cartwright, was a load of baloney.'

I flushed at the memory of Milo catching me loitering outside his house – and me claiming that I was looking up an old friend.

'I've only met Hetty once,' I confessed. Milo looked astonished. 'But we got on so well' – I added defensively – 'that I hoped to bump into her again. You see, she'd claimed to be, well, a sort of psychic, and got my hopes up about the future.'

'Everyone in this village knows that Hetty is eccentric,' said Milo. 'So, are you saying she gave you some s ort of prediction?'

'Yes,' I sighed. I took a sip of my drink, getting whipped cream on my nose in the process. Terrific. I foraged up my sleeve for a tissue. There wasn't one.

'Here,' said Milo, reaching into his pocket. He passed me an immaculate folded cotton handkerchief. 'Keep it. I have a dozen more in my drawer at home.'

'Thank you,' I said, taken aback.

I wasn't sure if I was surprised at his gesture, or the fact that a man liked Milo owned proper hankies. It seemed so old-fashioned. In which case, this was his second act of kindness. The first being the purchase of the hot chocolate.

As I wiped away the cream, my senses immediately reeled. The scent of Milo's aftershave had impregnated the cotton. I caught notes of cedarwood, sandalwood, ginger and a hint of lemon. I wondered what man-fragrance he wore. Bizarrely, I had an urge to buy a bottle and douse myself in it.

'So what did Hetty tell you?' Milo prompted.

'I can't remember her exact words,' I said miserably. 'But it was something along the lines of… her seeing me around the village – and living at Starlight Cottage.'

'Certainly half of that prophecy has come true.' Milo gave a lopsided grin. 'I for one have seen quite a bit of you around here.'

'Ha!' I gave a bark of mirthless laughter. 'Indeed. Even so, I'd set my sights on Starlight Cottage. I'd even daydreamed about living there, despite knowing you were a strong contender in the bidding.'

Milo looked puzzled.

'How did you know that?'

I gave him a sheepish look.

'I work at Home and Hearth Estate Agents in Meopham. Mr Garroway, the vendor, marketed the property with my employer. I viewed the cottage before its details were uploaded online. Quite simply, Milo, I fell in love with the place.'

He sighed.

'Look, I'm sorry you were disappointed.'

'The best man won,' I said, attempting a carefree shrug.

I took another sip of hot chocolate. The whipped cream had now collapsed into itself, sinking within the cup's depths. Milo's handkerchief was spared another mop up. Instead, it was my eyes that were now threatening to put the hankie to use. There was some unwanted activity going on in the tear ducts. I blinked rapidly. No, I was not going to cry. This was *not* the moment to be a wuss.

My brain began to give my heart an urgent pep talk; I was a strong independent woman who'd simply encountered a blip along the road of life. At some point I *would* find a new home for Cindy and me.

'So what actually brings you to the village tonight?' Milo pressed.

'Honestly? I'm currently sofa surfing at my bestie's place. However, things have recently changed. Put simply, this evening I needed to escape.'

'Why don't you tell me all about it?' he invited.

And whether it was because Cindy was now quietly snoring, or because the stove's flames were crackling and popping in such a hypnotic manner, or simply because all background noise had receded so that Milo and I seemed to be in our own private bubble... all I knew was that he'd asked a question. One that had triggered a release response. And suddenly I was unburdening. Pouring out my heart to a man I'd met only a handful of times. A virtual stranger who, confusingly, I also felt as if I'd known forever.

Chapter Thirty-Two

'That's quite some story,' said Milo, as I burbled myself to a standstill.

'Sorry to bore you,' I said. I stared into the depths of my cup, as if it might reveal some answers to life's problems. 'I didn't mean to ramble.'

'You didn't,' he assured. I was surprised at his sincerity. 'Sometimes it's good to offload.'

'I don't even know you,' I said, giving a strangled laugh. 'Whatever must you think?'

He gave me a measured look.

'I think it's best to offload to strangers. It's cathartic. You could tell me your deepest, darkest secret, knowing that – after tonight – you might never see me again and therefore your secret would remain safe.'

'I've only ever confided my deepest, darkest secret to Cindy,' I said honestly.

'You can share it with me too, if you wish.' He made a criss-cross over his heart. 'I won't tell a soul.'

'I don't think so,' I said, but this time I smiled. 'There's a chance we might have mutual acquaintances, so I'd rather not divulge anything further. Apart from anything else, you don't exactly live a million miles away,' I pointed out. 'We could bump into each other again at some point. Maybe in the Strawberry Shed. And then I'd be ducking behind Linda's chiller cabinet thinking, "Oh, crikey. There's that guy who knows my deepest darkest secret." It would be mortifying. But hopefully, after tonight, our paths won't cross again for a long time.'

'Unless we're stalking each other,' he said gravely.

I smiled again, liking his dry humour.

'We are not stalking each other,' I assured.

For a moment, neither of us spoke. I stared into the embers of the wood burner, watching the outer edge of a log light up. It glowed redly. Eventually, the spark dimmed, turned to ash, and dropped out of sight.

'I once stalked my ex-wife's new partner,' said Milo abruptly.

For a moment, I was too surprised to say anything.

'Are you being serious?' I said eventually.

'Straight up.' His gaze was still on the burning logs. He continued to stare at them. 'Stalking is when two people go for a walk, but only one of them knows about it.'

'Funny,' I countered.

'Actually, Tilly' – he tore his eyes away from the fire – 'I'm being serious. Oh, don't look at me like that. Don't tell me you didn't ever-so-slightly lose the plot when you walked in on Robin and Sexy Samantha.' He saw me flinch. 'Bingo. The only difference between you and me is that you probably did your stalking via social media.'

I flushed.

'Yes, okay,' I admitted, shamefaced. 'I did look her up.

Quite a few times. I wanted to see what she was posting.'

'No you didn't.' Milo shook his head. He gave me a knowing look. 'You wanted to see how you *compared*.'

I caught my breath. Ten out of ten to Milo. He'd hit the nail on the head.

'Bingo again,' he said softly. 'You had an all-consuming curiosity about what she looked like. Was she fatter than you? Thinner? Taller? Shorter? Prettier? Does she have long hair? Or is it short? And then – even worse – you wondered whether to model yourself on her. Whether to dye your hair the same colour as hers. Maybe put on a few pounds and have more curves. Or go to the gym and become a Skinny Minnie. You see, the ego clamours to be heard. It loves to tell us that we're not enough. That we need to be like the person our loved one is with. That we need to be blonder. Or darker. Or wear more lipstick. I'd bet my last lotto pound that you even considered getting your lips plumped up. Maybe you got as far as making an appointment with a beauty salon. One of those places that gives eyelash extensions so long you could sweep the road if you looked down.'

Milo was now hitting so many nerves, it was like being assaulted by hot needles. Yes, my ego had urged me to check Sexy Samantha's newsfeed. Almost daily. And yes, I had flagged the differences between us.

'If I didn't know better' – I raised one eyebrow – 'I'd say you were in cahoots with Hetty Cartwright. Do you fancy yourself as some sort of clairvoyant? If not, you're an accomplished mind reader.'

'It's not rocket science,' he shrugged. 'It's what us humans are like. Simply being human. Reacting to our humanness.'

I gulped down the last of my hot chocolate then carefully set the cup down on the table.

'You're absolutely right,' I admitted. 'I did look up Samantha. Frequently. And maybe for a while I was a bit… obsessed. But I learnt something from it.'

'Tell me.'

'I realised that it didn't matter how many diets I put myself on… how many highlights I added to my hair… how much filler I injected into my lips… how long the eyelash extensions were… or whether I wore skirts with hemlines around my backside… because nothing – absolutely *nothing* – could ever give me the one thing Samantha has.' I paused. Took a deep breath. 'Youth,' I said simply. 'She's twenty years younger than me. It's impossible for me to be twenty-nine-years old again. Even if I booked a plastic surgeon and asked him to pin my jawline around my ears, I'd only ever knock off a few years. Samantha has what I no longer have – and that's not just my husband,' I said wryly.

For a few moments, Milo said nothing. Instead, he stared at me. Whatever he was about to say, he looked like he was choosing his words carefully. Then he shrugged, as if not bothered about how his words came out.

'First,' he said. 'You don't need a facelift. You're fine as you are. In fact, you're beautiful.'

I was so flabbergasted at the unexpected compliment, I was momentarily silenced.

'Second,' he continued. 'You have something that Samantha doesn't have. And it's something she won't gain for two more decades.'

I looked at Milo in bemusement, still reeling from his earlier words.

'What's that?' I croaked.

'Isn't it obvious?' he said gently. 'You've been on this planet longer than her. You've experienced an additional twenty summers of life. Think of all the lessons that's brought. What you have over her' – his eyes softened – 'is wisdom.'

Chapter Thirty-Three

'I like that,' I said to Milo. I sat back in my chair. Grinned. 'Wisdom,' I repeated. 'Wow! That makes me feel *so* much better.'

My spirits were rising faster than a hot air balloon. Not only did Milo think I was beautiful, but he also thought I was wise. Well, okay, maybe not as wise as a tawny owl. After all, I'd once nearly run him over. But, thanks to my age, I was *wiser* than Sexy Samantha. And that cheered me up no end.

There was something else in the mix. A shift. I was starting to feel an affinity with Milo. He too had experienced the breakdown of a marriage. He'd also questioned whether – as a spouse – he fell short in some way. He'd understood the need to check out the opposition. To make comparisons. He too had keenly felt not just the loss of his partner, but also the loss of his confidence. His self-esteem.

I privately wondered why his wife had walked away. Frankly it beggared belief. The guy was gorgeous. Sex on legs. And, okay, I'd initially thought him a horrible man, but now… well… he was rapidly showing me another side. One of compassion. Sympathy. Understanding. He knew exactly how I felt because he'd been there too.

'Did you really stalk your wife's new partner?' I asked.

Milo looked embarrassed.

'I did,' he admitted. 'I didn't know the person. Rather, I knew *of* them. I'd heard their name bandied about. Quite a bit, actually. Good old *mentionitis*. It was someone Martha worked with. There was an unexpected situation where the two of us happened to be in almost the same place at the same time. I hadn't been spotted, so I followed them. God knows why. And whilst I didn't impersonate Inspector Clouseau scuttling between lampposts, I did nonetheless spend several minutes spying on them. And tormenting myself.' He spread his hands wide. 'As you do.'

'I'd have done the same thing,' I confessed.

I had a sudden overwhelming curiosity about Milo's ex-wife. What had *she* been like? Had she gone off with a younger man? Perhaps, not content with her Antonio Banderas lookalike, she'd swapped Milo for a toyboy.

'And, er, there's no chance of a reconciliation?' I asked nosily.

'None whatsoever.'

I looked at Milo expectantly, waiting for him to enlarge. Instead, he dropped his gaze. Looked at his fingernails. Apparently, his thumbs were a sudden source of fascination.

Okay, he wasn't going to expand. How annoying. But surely if I dug carefully, I might unearth some juicy reveals in another minute or two? I just needed to tread delicately through his emotions. It was like picking at a loose bit of yarn. If I badgered him enough, his whole story might unravel.

'So, I take it your wife fell out of love with you,' I

prompted.

Milo took a deep breath, then exhaled gustily.

'I guess so,' he shrugged. 'That said, Martha and I still keep in touch. And she's not far away. West Kingsdown, to be precise. It's about five miles from here. Every now and again we have a coffee together. Sometimes with her other half,' he added.

'No!' I said, staggered.

Would me and Sexy Samantha ever be like that?

Hey, Samantha! Fancy meeting up in Costa later? You can tell me how it's going with Robin. Does he still forage up his nose for bogies when he thinks nobody is looking? x

And perhaps Samantha would reply accordingly:

Hiya, Tilly! It would be SO good to swap notes. I have LOADS of moans about Robin! Who better to understand than someone who spent years picking up his festering socks and underpants?! Can't wait to meet up xxx

Milo was talking again.

'Martha says she still loves me. Just that she's no longer *in* love with me.'

'Hm,' I said, my tone sceptical. 'Sometimes that's a case of leaving the door open – in case they have a change of heart and want to come back.'

Milo gave me a smile that said otherwise.

'There will be no change of heart on Martha's part. Trust me on that one.'

I still had the feeling there was more to this story. What was he withholding? He wasn't being very fair. After all, I'd practically regurgitated my entire married life to him. From yearning to start a family with Robin, to how Mother Nature had decided otherwise, right up to discovering Robin and Sexy Samantha *at it*. Milo knew all about my fleeing to the Stag Theatre. How I'd been so distressed to the point of nearly flattening him and others. I'd moaned about Sexy Samantha dissing my curtains. The carpets. The furniture. How she'd snidely revealed that she'd been in my house previously. Likely rolled around in the marital bed while I'd been away in Cornwall. And how I'd moved in with my bestie, only to be repeatedly asked to absent myself so she and her new man could make out.

I'd told Milo everything. Well, almost everything. But now I was feeling shortchanged. I wanted to know all the details of his marriage breakdown. From how he'd discovered Martha was cheating on him, to how *he* compared himself to the new man in her life.

Come on Milo, I silently urged. *Spill the beans.*

Chapter Thirty-Four

'Did you ever have children together?' I pressed.

'Nope.' Milo shook his head. 'Martha made it clear from the start that she wasn't the motherly type.'

'Oh,' I said, flummoxed.

I could have sworn that my boss had said the buyer of Starlight Cottage had a son. Perhaps Leslie had muddled Milo with someone else.

Ah, well. Just because Martha hadn't wanted kids, it didn't mean she was strange. Some women simply weren't maternal.

Years ago, I'd worked with such a female. Lorraine had made no secret of the fact that she didn't like kids. She'd referred to them as *brats*. On one occasion, after returning from a foreign holiday, she'd moaned on and on about the flight home being unbearable due to a crying baby.

Women like Lorraine were the ones who shot pained looks to harassed mothers at supermarket checkouts.

I'd once helped a young mum in such a situation. Her baby – used to being fed on demand – had protested loudly at not being put to the breast while at the checkout. The woman had tried – and failed – to pack a week's worth of shopping in five minutes flat. Eventually, she'd broken down and howled at both the checkout lady and the chuntering queue.

'I can't cope! Gah-huh-huh-HUH!'

At this point it had been debatable who'd been making the most racket – the mother or the baby.

Unable to stand another moment, I'd dropped my wire basket and pushed my way to her side. I'd told the woman to go and feed her baby while I packed her shopping. Everything had been bagged up and set to one side. However, a lady – with a most unfortunate dental arrangement – had chuntered loudly to anyone who'd cared to listen.

'I don't know why women bring their kids to supermarkets. I mean, what's the point? All they do is cause bedlam at the checkout.'

When I'd later regaled the story about the toothy woman's opinions, Lorraine had looked down her long nose at me.

'I'd have agreed with that woman,' she'd sniffed. 'That young mum should have left her screaming child with a babysitter. Good thing I'd not been in that queue, or I'd have put her straight.'

Mother Nature had never tapped Lorraine on her shoulder pads and sent her gooey eyed over kids. In fact, she'd have likely fainted at the thought of exchanging her power suits for elasticated waistbands and nipple shields.

'Did you mind not having children?' I now asked Milo.

'What a lot of questions you ask,' he said. But I could see he wasn't offended. More... amused. 'No, I didn't mind Martha not having my baby. And I'll tell you why.' Finally, I felt like Milo was about to reveal something of significance. 'You see, I actually ended up adopting.'

'Oh,' I gasped aloud.

A penny began rattling around in my head. It clanked this way and that. Finally, like that game of *Kerplunk*, it fell down a chute and gave me a lightbulb moment.

Of course! Martha hadn't had babies because... she was infertile! She'd been unable to give her husband kids. Just like *me* not being able to give Robin any babies. Good heavens, what a coincidence.

'I can see your brain racing ahead,' Milo smiled. 'Joining up all the dots. But I suspect you're way off beam. You see, Martha and I didn't actively seek to adopt a child.'

I frowned.

'I don't understand. How can you adopt a child if you didn't mean to adopt a child?'

'Let's back-peddle for a moment.' He made a rewinding motion with one hand. 'I had a much older brother, Jerad.'

'Had?' I said, picking up on the past tense.

Milo nodded, his face suddenly sad.

'Jerad and his lovely wife, Sue, were killed in a car crash.'

'Omigod,' I breathed. 'I'm so sorry.'

'It's fine,' he said with the air of someone who'd told this story many times. 'It was several years ago. Time doesn't heal – contrary to what people say – but it does bring acceptance. I've finally got my head around it.' Nonetheless, his eyes were bright for a moment. 'Sue and Jerad had a son – my nephew, JJ. They were a lovely family, until tragedy struck. The three of them went to Broadstairs for a long weekend.

They stayed at a typical seaside guesthouse, enjoyed the beach, paddled in the waves, and ate fish and chips out of newspaper. Except, on the way home, they had a tyre blowout.' He paused to collect himself. 'The car accident that followed proved to be a fatal one.'

'They all died?' I said in horror.

Milo shook his head.

'My nephew was spared. Thank God for small mercies.' He shifted in his seat. A regrouping gesture. 'There was never any question about JJ's future. He came to live with Martha and me. We officially adopted him. Suddenly Martha was *Ma* – fitting given the new role thrust upon her. And although I was still Uncle Milo, and could never replace *Dad*, JJ started calling me *Pops*.' Milo grinned with delight. 'And I love being called that.'

'So you ended up with a son after all,' I said.

'Indeed.'

'And what of Martha? Does she keep in touch with your boy?'

'Absolutely,' Milo confirmed. 'Despite not having any maternal instincts, Martha has been a good mum. JJ is only back home with me because he's come out of a serious relationship.' Milo pulled a face. 'I don't know the full ins and outs. Apparently, the girl let him go. Her loss. Since then, he's met young Polly. And it seems to be going well, albeit with caution. So, watch this space.'

'Polly?' I frowned. 'But I thought…'

'What did you think?' said Milo, looking amused.

'Nothing,' I said quickly.

So, Polly wasn't lusting after Milo. She was lusting after Mr Soren Junior. Linda at the Strawberry Shed had got that bit of gossip wrong.

'Well,' I said, blowing out my cheeks. 'That's quite a story.'

'It is,' he nodded. 'All's well that ends well.'

'Not quite,' I disagreed. 'Regarding Martha's new partner. You said you followed the person. Tormented yourself because of making comparisons. Are you now happy in your own skin?'

Milo laughed out loud.

'I've always been happy in my own skin, Tilly.'

'But… but…' I looked at him in confusion. 'You said…' – what were the words he'd used earlier? – 'something about *not being enough.*'

'I did,' he acknowledged. 'But there's one thing I've omitted from this tale.' He steepled his fingers together, as if in prayer, then regarded me pensively. 'Martha left me for another woman.'

'*Whaaat?*' I squawked.

'Don't look so incredulous. These things happen. Martha got to forty and announced – just like the proverbial worm – that she'd *turned.* That there was no going back. She was totally transparent. Said she'd met a woman at work and fallen in love. I did briefly – we're talking a nano second – consider transitioning to win her back, but then dismissed the idea.' He gave me a deadpan look. 'I've managed to rise to several challenges in life, but I'd never get away with my size elevens in kitten heels.'

Chapter Thirty-Five

'So... so... wow,' I spluttered, my brain reeling.

First, Milo's wife hadn't swapped him for a toyboy. Martha had exchanged him for another woman. She wasn't interested in men with dangly bits between their legs. She was interested in women with...

No, don't go there, Tilly.

I hastily shook away an image of a Clare Balding lookalike wearing a sturdy white bra, plain underpants and sensible shoes – with coordinated overgarments, obviously. It was unlikely that Martha's partner paraded around in just her underwear teamed with a pair of lace-ups. Meanwhile, there was no chance of Martha wanting a reconciliation with her gorgeous husband. This, in my humble opinion, was simply marvelous.

Second, Milo wasn't interested in young Polly, or vice versa. Instead, the pretty barmaid was fluttering her eyelashes at JJ. Excellent news indeed. May the two of them fall madly in love, have ten children and live happily ever after.

I suddenly felt inexplicably happy.

Why's that? came a voice from ground level.

I snuck a quick look at Cindy. She was flat out.

I might appear to be asleep, but I'm just pretending.

What a very interesting conversation the two of you have had. Why is it 'marvelous' that Martha has hooked up with a woman, and why is it 'excellent' that young Polly isn't romantically interested in Milo?

'H–'

Do not say 'hush' because I'm not going to oblige with a woof.

'Sorry?' said Milo.

'H-How nice to know your story,' I said instead. 'It's… well, I guess what I'm trying to say is… helpful to know I'm not the only one who has experienced heartache.'

Milo shrugged.

'I think everyone on this planet experiences that at some point. Some of us several times over. It's rather the way of life. At school we make friends. Then we cry our eyes out when Jane takes her skipping rope and goes off with Vanessa. Or John scoops up his football and says, "You're not good enough to be part of Meopham United." It's devastating. We get knocked sideways by the tragedy of it all. We droop home. Have a good bawl, and believe we'll never recover. Little do we realise that it's all groundwork. That we're laying the foundations for what will come when we're older.'

'Yes,' I agreed. I was silent for a moment, wondering how to find out one more thing. Sieve through the sands, so to speak. Ask the question that was now burning through my brain.

Just come out with it. Ask him straight, urged Cindy.

No, I silently retorted. I can't do that. It would look too obvious.

I cleared my throat.

'Thank goodness you and me are so resilient.' I gave a tinkling laugh, as if making light of such a heavy conversation. 'We've come out of our respective marriages battered but not broken.' I heaved a theatrical sigh.

Oh God, Cindy snorted at my feet. *You'll be holding up a placard next. One that says, 'Call me!'*

'And, er... I expect... um...' I gave Milo my best meaningful look – 'well, I'm sure we will both be ready to date again one of these fine days in the not-too-distant future.'

I'll bet anything you're now giving him a winning smile.

I didn't deign to answer, but it was true that the outer edges of my mouth were curving upwards.

Milo's eyes locked with mine. I held his gaze. Quite brazenly, I thought. Neither of us spoke. Neither of us glanced away. The look went on and on. Something was happening here. Something seriously wonderful – aside from a stirring in my loins and a warmth in some erogenous zones.

Do NOT give him any come-hither looks, warned Cindy.

And still we continued to gaze at each other. Ignoring Cindy, I gave Milo my best smoulder. He shifted in his seat. Leant forward slightly. I mirrored his body language. He opened his mouth to speak, and I found myself holding my breath. This was it. He was going to suggest we have a date together. Omigod! This was amazing. After all the crap with Robin. After feeling rubbish at being replaced by a younger woman. After Lisa chucking me out so she could get it on with Juan. After feeling like the only woman in the world who wasn't wanted by someone, things were about to change.

'I am,' he said quietly.

'Fantastic,' I murmured, leaning forward a bit more. Any second now, I'd be in his lap.

'In fact' – he suddenly leant backwards, and his next words took the wind right out of my billowing sails – 'I've been dating for a while.'

Chapter Thirty-Six

'W-What?' I stuttered.

It was as if one of Polly's cold pints of lager had been flung in my face. I collapsed backwards in my chair, desperately trying to compose myself.

'That's w-wonderful,' I said, thinking it was anything but.

Bloody hell. I mean *bloody hell.* What had that bit of *look-into-my-eyes* been all about then? How had I read it so wrong?

Because you're out of practice, said Cindy.

Too flipping right, I huffed.

And I'd just like to point something out. You seem to have changed your tune over Milo Soren.

I tried to compose my features into a blasé couldn't-careless arrangement. I had a nasty feeling I looked more like someone who'd been slapped around the face with a wet flip-flop. To say I was stunned was an understatement. Milo was speaking again.

'Wonderful?' he questioned. He gave a snort of derision. 'I'm not sure I'd describe my foray back into the world of dating quite like that. To be perfectly honest, I was so shattered by Martha's betrayal, I felt a need to prove myself.

In other words, I've behaved like a total tart. I downloaded one of those dating apps and nearly got repetitive strain injury from swiping right. I said yes to any woman who was interested. I didn't care what they looked like. Young or old.'

I had a sudden mental picture of Milo in bed with a pensioner. There she was. Blue bubble-perm pressed against his pillowcases.

'Not *that* old,' he added, as if reading my thoughts. 'And not that young either,' he added hastily. 'Somewhere between thirty-five and fifty,' he clarified.

'Good to know,' I gasped, plucking a drinks coaster from the side table. I vigorously fanned myself. I was hot, bothered, and out of sorts.

'As long as they gave me the thumbs up on the app, then I was thrilled to bits.'

'Awesome,' I muttered, abandoning the coaster.

'You see, it meant that – despite my wife no longer wanting me – I was still desirable to other women. And that was all I needed to know. My ego had taken a battering. My confidence had sunk not just to the floor, but down to the depths of the foundations. Obviously, I stopped behaving like that after a few weeks. Ended the one-night stands.'

'Jolly good,' I croaked.

I wondered what dating app he was on. Whether I could download it.

'You see' – he shrugged – 'there comes a point when one-night stands don't do it for you.'

'Well, quite,' I said, as if I engaged in them every other day of the week.

I'd never had a one-night stand. It struck me how naïve I was. Before Robin, I hadn't even had many boyfriends. In fact, I could count on one hand how many men I'd slept with. What would Milo make of that? Well... he'd probably think I was a bit wet behind the ears, that's what.

And why had I got to nearly half a century in age but never left behind me a trail of devastated lovers? I mentally dove back through the pages of memory. Had I ever dumped anyone? I had a nasty feeling it had always been the boy who'd let me go, even though it wasn't cool to admit that. Far better to say *it was a mutual decision.*

Memories came flooding back. Bittersweet ones. Yes, I'd said those words a lot in my earlier years. Even to Mum, when she'd asked why that *nice boy Timothy* had stopped coming round.

'Tim?' I'd feigned surprise. 'Oh, we decided we didn't have anything in common. It was a mutual decision.' The bloody two-timing little turd.

'In fact, I recently dated a woman for a whole six weeks,' said Milo. 'My track record is improving,' he laughed.

'Good to know.'

It really wasn't.

'She didn't take too kindly to the way I ended it,' he said thoughtfully.

'Oh?'

'I was a coward. Did it by phone. Texted her. It turned a little nasty. She got up from the sofa and slapped me.'

'I see.'

Milo gave me a strange look.

'I'm joking, Tilly. Anyway, to recap. I've seen a few women but there's currently no one on the scene.'

Until the next time he swipes right, sniffed Cindy.

Milo regarded me for a moment.

'What's up? You've gone very quiet.'

'Nothing,' I said breezily, pasting a smile on my face.

'So, what about you?' he asked softly. 'Are you being truthful about not yet dipping a toe in the dating waters?'

I pulled a face. I could hardly say that men were beating a path to my door. Not after the earlier confession about my social life being more arid than the Sahara Desert.

'No,' I said shortly, desperate to change the subject.

I didn't want to know about Milo's harem of women. Or his numerous one-night stands. Or how he'd managed to have a *relationship* for a whole six whole weeks. I felt sorry for the women, to be honest. What must it be like to be wined and dined by a guy who was hotter than chilli sauce – but then spat out like gum that had lost its flavour?

I looked at my wristwatch. The time was getting on. Hopefully Lisa and Juan were now sated, and it was safe to return home. *Home.* That was something Lisa's maisonette had never been.

'Why the glum face?' asked Milo.

'Oh, you know. I need to head back. I'm just reminded of the fact that I have no proper roots right now. It's very unsettling. Anyway, as I said earlier, I'll be rectifying that soon. My current mission is to find a room to rent. A stop gap. Then I'll push on looking for my own place.'

'Hang on a minute.' Milo put out a hand to stop me

getting up. His touch nearly sent me through the pub's ceiling. 'I might be able to help you out.'

I gave him a puzzled look.

'How?'

'When I moved into Starlight Cottage, the only thing that needed attention was the shed in the garden.'

'I remember it,' I nodded.

'I had it demolished and then replaced with one of those fancy home-office-cum-summerhouse buildings. It's completely in keeping with the cottage's overall look. I've even planted some climbing roses around the door.'

'Sounds nice. So, do you work from home?'

'Not at all. I have family in Italy. My parents are there. And one or two other relatives that I'm very fond of, and who like to combine seeing me with a bit of a jolly. In my last place, space was never a problem. However, Starlight Cottage only has two bedrooms. Currently, JJ is occupying one of them. So, when family visit, I need somewhere for them to stay. My cousins won't mind sleeping on the sofas in the cottage, but I can't expect Zio Luigi or Zia Vittoria to do likewise. Nor my parents. They're all in their late seventies. Hence my idea to replace the shed with something small but functional. The new studio has a double pull-out bed, a kitchenette area, plus a shower and loo. Everything is fully connected. Electrics. Running water. There's even a unit on the wall to provide air conditioning in the summer and heating in the winter. It's very chic and cosy if I do say so myself.'

'Sounds terrific,' I said.

'It is,' he smiled. 'So how about it?'

'How about what?'

'How about you use it until you're sorted out? You can pay me a peppercorn and keep it aired. To be honest, you'd be doing me a favour.'

My mouth fell open.

'I-I couldn't possibly impose,' I stuttered.

'You wouldn't be,' he assured. 'Tell you what. Why don't you give your bestie and Loverboy a little bit longer. Come back with me to Starlight Cottage. I know it's dark, but I've had lights put around the back garden, so you'll be able to see the accommodation.' He gave me a disarming grin and something inside me melted. 'After all, you have nothing to lose,' he added.

Only my heart, I thought silently.

Chapter Thirty-Seven

The *fancy home-office-cum-summerhouse* – to use Milo's description – was perfect as a stop gap.

'I don't know what to say,' I said.

We were standing slap bang in the middle of a twenty by ten building. It was possibly bigger than Lisa's lounge. Certainly, it was less cluttered.

A neat kitchenette was at one end. A door led to a shower room and loo. At the other end was a sofa which became a double bed. There was even a small television set upon the wall.

Underneath the TV was a large sideboard that provided storage space. On its surface was an Echo Spot. Oh good. I'd be able to have conversations not just with Cindy, but also Alexa.

Elsewhere, an occasional table had a lift-up lid. This provided further storage. Midway, between the kitchenette and sofa area, was a generous floor-to-ceiling cupboard. I opened the door and discovered a vacuum cleaner, ironing board and steam iron, also a hanging rail.

'You've thought of everything,' I said in amazement.

'Even the kitchen sink,' Milo joked. 'However, there isn't a washing machine.'

'That's fine,' I said, wondering if there was a launderette in the area. Not that it mattered if there wasn't. 'I can handwash stuff. Anything bulky can go to the drycleaners.'

'Don't be daft,' said Milo. 'I'll give you a key to the cottage. Use my washing machine.'

'I really couldn't impose.' I shook my head.

'Up to you,' he said with a shrug.

I had a sudden vision of stepping through his backdoor. Laundry basket held aloft. Milo in the open-plan area. One of his *swipe right* ladies draped across the sofa. That would never do.

'It's fine,' I said firmly. 'I can wash clothes in the shower. And there's a drycleaner two doors down from my work.'

'Okay, but the offer is there if you change your mind. Meanwhile, perhaps we should let Rambo and Cindy get reacquainted? After all, they'll be sharing the garden. We don't want any territory issues.'

'Righto,' I agreed, following Milo out of the summerhouse.

We walked along the pretty meandering path to the cottage's backdoor. Even though it was dark, I couldn't help noticing how beautiful the garden looked. Milo's electricians had created some serious mood magic around the flowerbeds and fencing. Numerous nightlights bathed everything in a soft glow. It was – dare I say it – the perfect setting for romance.

Milo let Rambo out. Seconds later the pint-sized dog had strutted over to Cindy. The chihuahua greeted her with a bit of a rumble and lots of posturing. Seconds later, he'd headed over to the apple tree to cock his leg.

'Let Cindy off her lead,' said Milo. 'She might as well romp around the garden with Rambo.'

'Will he be okay with her?' I asked nervously. 'After all, he's already marking his territory.'

'He'll be fine,' said Milo. 'He's not a German Shepherd.'

'Why is it good he's not a German Shepherd?'

Milo regarded me gravely.

'Because they mark their territory with a beach towel.'

'Oh, for goodness' sake,' I snorted. 'That's a terrible joke.'

'But it made you laugh,' he countered. 'Gotcha.' He pointed a finger at me. 'You've looked so sad ever since we left the pub. I wanted to see you if I could make you smile.'

'Well, you did,' I said. 'And I'm not sad. Not really. Things are on the up. Thanks to you,' I added shyly.

Only hours ago, I'd thought this man beyond annoying. Instead, he'd become something of a life saver.

We stood there for a minute or two. Not saying anything. Just watching Rambo and Cindy sniff each other's backsides, wag their tails, and then check out a rosebush together. Milo was the first to speak.

'Move your stuff in tomorrow.' He handed me the key to the accommodation.

'Thank you,' I said, curling my fingers around it. 'Be sure to tell your son about me. That soon a stranger will be living at the bottom of the garden. Otherwise he might wonder who I am.'

'I'll introduce you when he's next around,' said Milo.

'Currently he's with some mates. There was talk of a stag weekend in Prague. I don't like to ask questions otherwise I'm accused of being a nosy parker – which, of course, I am,' he grinned. 'A parent always worries about their child, no matter how old they are. JJ didn't tell me his return date. Which rather suggests a stag *week.* I've had too much going on in my own life lately to keep track of my son's diary too, what with setting up a new clinic and everything.'

'I see,' I said, wondering what Milo did for a living.

'I'm a dentist,' he explained, as if reading my thoughts. 'I've set up a new practice in Meopham.'

'Oh!' I exclaimed. 'That's where I work. Perhaps we'll bump into each other.'

'Maybe,' Milo smiled, before whistling Rambo to heel. 'Good boy,' he said, scooping up the little dog. 'The two of us will now walk you and Cindy back to your car.'

'You don't need to do that,' I protested.

'Nonsense,' he said gruffly. 'It's highly unlikely you'll get mugged around here. Not unless Hugo Cartwright's cows have made a break for it. A couple of days ago a few of them did just that. Hugo is tighter than my jeans after a roast dinner. He wasn't pleased to stump up the readies for new fencing. Cows aside, there's no street lighting around here. Anyway, no woman should walk anywhere late at night.'

'Well, if it's no trouble,' I said, secretly relieved.

'It isn't,' he assured. 'Oh, good. You're smiling again.'

I didn't like to tell Milo that the smile was completely involuntary. That I couldn't have stopped beaming if my life had depended upon it. Inside, my heart was singing. Even though Milo Soren was on a dating app, even though he'd likely given himself tendonitis from all the swiping right, even though he dated women faster than cars visiting a McDonald's drive-thru, none of that mattered. Because, right now, he was with me.

'And I'd just like to say' – he added, his face suddenly serious – 'you truly have a beautiful smile.'

I was so flabbergasted, I didn't know how to respond. Instead, I stood there, feeling gormless, but still giving him my *beautiful smile.*

'Won't be a mo,' he said.

He disappeared into the cottage; Rambo tucked under one arm. I clipped Cindy's lead onto her collar. A moment later, Milo was back, this time with Rambo attached to a long leash.

'Shall we?' he said, offering me an elbow.

And it seemed like the most natural thing in the world to link my arm with his and let him lead me through the garden gate.

Hmm, said Cindy. *So long as you don't get led up the garden path.*

Chapter Thirty-Eight

A few minutes later, Milo and I arrived at Starlight Arms' carpark. The place was almost deserted. Together, we walked over to Octavia.

I opened the passenger door for Cindy. Before hopping inside, she briefly touched noses with Rambo. I wondered, somewhat fancifully, if she and the little dog had just given each other a kiss goodnight. As I shut the door behind her, I wondered if Milo might kiss *me* goodnight.

'Thanks again,' I said, lingering by the passenger door. 'You've been a knight in shining armour.'

'It was my pleasure to rescue a damsel in distress,' he said gallantly. 'As I mentioned before, you're doing me a favour keeping the accommodation aired.'

I hovered by Octavia's passenger door. Cindy was sitting ramrod straight on the front seat. She peered through the window at Milo and me.

Are we going or what?

'I'm hoping for–'

I instantly clammed up. Dear Lord. That had been a close call.

'Hoping for what?' said Milo, puzzled.

'Hoping for Lisa and Juan to be asleep when I get back,'

I improvised. Holy moly. I'd nearly said *hoping for a kiss*. I really should stop having imaginary conversations with my dog. One of these days it was going to land me in trouble.

'Right,' I said brightly. There was nothing more to say. 'I'll be off.'

'Bye,' said Milo.

Okay, he wasn't narrowing the space between us. There was no movement on his part to take a step forward. He wasn't even doing any of that previous eye-meet thing. Just standing there benignly. With Rambo. One man and his dog. Bugger. Right, move, Tilly.

I walked to the driver's door. Opened it. Gave a fluttery wave. A final cheery smile. Apparently, he thought it beautiful, so from now on I'd be beaming at him like a floodlight at a football stadium.

'See you tomorrow,' I chirped, giving him one last chance to do something. Anything.

'You will indeed,' he answered.

And still he stood there. No quick dart round to the driver's side. No last-minute plaintive cry:

Wait! Don't go, Tilly. My life is meaningless without you.

Cindy shot me a look.

Can I just point out, Mum, that as from tomorrow you will be living at the bottom of this guy's garden. Therefore, you will feature in his life on a daily basis.

'Yes, thank you for pointing that out,' I muttered testily.

Octavia's engine turned over. Milo took a step backwards. Mental note to self. *Do not run him over.* I reversed slowly, then pushed the gearstick into first. As Octavia changed direction and her wheels crunched over the carpark's shingle, Milo suddenly appeared on my right. He then surprised me by knocking on the driver's window.

Omigod! Was this it? Was this the moment he would beg me not to leave until he'd kissed my luscious lips?

I hastily buzzed down the window.

'Yes?' I said breathlessly.

He stooped down so that he was on eye – and lip – level with me.

'I just wanted to say…'

'Yes?'

'Before you go…'

'Yes?'

I stared at him, slightly wild about the eyes. What did he want to say before I went?

Your eyes shine like a thousand stars in the sky…

Your skin glows like early morning dew on grass…

Your hair is silkier than Rambo's fur…

No, that wasn't very romantic. What about…

Your smile lights up my life…

No, that was boring. Maybe…

You're so hot, you're the reason for global warming…

Yes, better.

You're like a camera. I want to take you to a dark room and see what develops…

Now we're talking.

You're like a light switch – you turn me on…

Omigod, yes, yes, yes!

But wait. Something else was happening.

Milo raised one hand. Reached through Octavia's window. Tucked a strand of hair behind my ear. As his fingers brushed against my cheek, it was as if hot pokers were touching my skin. I had a horrible urge to grab his fingers, stick them in my mouth and suck the living daylights out of them. I was now gripping Octavia's steering wheel so hard, my knuckles had turned white.

'Just to say…'

For God's sake man, drawled Cindy. *Spit it out.*

'I'm very glad we're now friends.'

And with that, Milo straightened up. Turned around. And, without a backward glance, sauntered out of the carpark, Rambo at his heels.

It took a full sixty seconds for the zingers to subside and several more minutes before I was in any fit state to head down Starlight Street.

Chapter Thirty-Nine

I got back to Lisa's to find the lights off and no sign of life. I assumed she and Juan were both in bed and asleep. I paused, cocked an ear. There were no faint sounds of murmured pillow talk.

I crept about in the dark, carefully negotiating furniture, then let Cindy out for a final wee. A sudden noise behind had me spinning around. The torch from Lisa's phone eerily lit up her face.

'Blimey,' I whispered. 'You look like something out of a Halloween Fright Night.'

'Cheers,' she muttered indignantly. The light went off. 'Where on earth have you been?'

'Out,' I said simply.

'I know that.' I sensed her eyeroll in the darkness. 'But you've been gone for hours.'

I shrugged.

'Well, you wanted the place to yourself. I obliged.'

'Even so,' she said, blowing out her cheeks. 'I started to worry. Where have you been?'

'I went to the pub.'

'You can't have done,' she said. 'Juan and I ended up getting dressed and went to The Cricketers for a nightcap.

We didn't see you there.'

'That's because I didn't go to The Cricketers.'

I let Cindy back inside. She crept across the room and collapsed into her basket with a groan of contentment.

'So where did you go?' Lisa prompted.

'The Starlight Arms,' I replied.

'The Star–'

She broke off and this time gave a huff of annoyance.

My eyes had now adjusted to the shadows. I could make out her features thanks to moonlight spilling through the lounge windows. The curtains hadn't been drawn against the night.

'Why do you keep going to that village?' she grumbled. 'It's ridiculous, Tilly. You're behaving like someone obsessed. Tormenting yourself. Look' – she touched my arm – 'don't take this the wrong way, but have you thought about counselling? I think, after everything that's happened in the last few months, you might benefit from talking to someone impartial.'

'Oh, for goodness' sake,' I sighed. I flopped down on the sofa that I had yet to make up as a bed. It suddenly dawned on me that this would be the last night I'd spend here. Hurrah! 'I don't need to speak to a counsellor. Or see a psychiatrist. Or do online therapy. Or – for that matter – take up yoga or reinvent myself.'

'Now you're being silly,' she said, sitting down beside me. 'I'm only looking out for you.'

'Well, thank you, but there's no need. And actually, I have some news.'

I shifted on the sofa so that I was facing her. Lisa was still peering at me in consternation.

'You have good news since I last saw you?' she frowned.

'That's right,' I nodded, unable to resist smiling. 'I'm moving out tomorrow.'

'What?' she squawked. Her neck tucked into her shoulders, as if dodging a bullet. 'What are you talking about, Tilly?' she hissed.

'I went to the Starlight Arms and bumped into Milo Soren. Remember him?'

'How could I ever forget?' she said disdainfully. 'Of course I remember him. He's the new owner of Starlight Cottage. A man you cannot stand. So, what did you do? Empty your drink over his head? Cause a rumpus? Get barred?'

'On the contrary,' I said, as happiness bubbled up inside me. 'We got chatting. He's actually really nice. And then we went back to his place.'

'Hold it right there, lady.' Lisa stuck one hand up like a lollipop lady about to stop the traffic. 'What the blazes are you saying? Did you go back to Starlight Cottage and get your leg over?'

'Don't be daft,' I snorted.

'I don't believe you,' she harrumphed. 'I can see your eyes shining. They're like two twin headlamps.' She peered at me in the gloom. 'You've definitely shagged him.'

'I definitely have not,' I countered.

'Bet you wanted to.' She waggled a finger at me.

'That is classified information,' I retorted.

'Omigod!' she crowed. 'Don't tell me that you've got the hots for Milo Soren.'

'That is also classified information,' I giggled.

'I'm going to put the kettle on.' She stood up. 'And I'm telling you now, madam, you are going to spill the beans.'

I flopped back against the sofa, making several squeaking noises to myself. I then wrapped my arms around my torso so that I was hugging myself. For a moment, I tried to pretend it was Milo hugging me. Unfortunately, there were no zingers, so my body wasn't fooled. Neither was Lisa. She was staring at me from where she was standing, slowly shaking her head.

'My oh my,' she said wryly. 'You have got him bad.'

Chapter Forty

By the time I'd brought Lisa up to date and told her all about Milo's offer of moving into his guest accommodation, she was agog.

We were briefly interrupted by Juan. He wandered out to see what was going on. Lisa sent him back to bed and said she wouldn't be long. Juan blew her a kiss, then bid me goodnight, before retreating to the bedroom.

'Goodnight, Teely,' he said, in his heavy accent. 'It wazza nice to meeta yooo.'

'You too,' I said.

Lisa and I then had a hushed conversation with Lisa immediately breaking her promise that she would shortly return to Juan's side. However, the snores coming from next door told me he wasn't missing her.

Lisa then prattled on about Juan, Juan, Juan, and peculiarly I burbled on about Milo, Milo, Milo.

'But Tilly,' she said eventually. 'You can't move into this guy's *garden*, for heaven's sake. You're not thinking straight.'

'Of course I'm thinking straight,' I countered. 'It's perfect for me.'

'It's a glorified garden shed,' she snapped.

'It really isn't,' I said. 'It's more like a studio apartment and rather amazing. Yes, there *was* a garden shed. But Milo replaced it. It's all pukka. Honest. The place is even connected to mains drainage.'

'So's my garden hose,' she said wryly. 'Look, you've had terrible mentionitis, and I don't need to be Einstein to realise that you have a thumping great crush on the guy-'

'I absolutely do not,' I protested as my neck did a giveaway flush. I was glad of the gloomy light.

'And I've seen Milo Soren with my own eyes' – she swept on, ignoring my denial – 'so I totally get where you're coming from.'

'Lisa, you–'

'Even so,' she interrupted. 'You're acting impulsively. There is no need to rush out of my place. Okay, I know it's not an ideal situation. However, Juan has things to do in Spain before he returns. Therefore, you have plenty of time to get registered with an online rental company and find, oh, I don't know, student digs, or something.'

'Student digs?' I scoffed. 'Can you really see me sharing a house with a bunch of uni kids? I can visualise it now – a kitchen sink bunged up with pots and pans. An overflowing dustbin – complete with split liner. Damp laundry festooned over every radiator. My food being 'borrowed' – possibly my clothes too. Not forgetting the whiff of funny fags twenty-four-seven.'

'No self-respecting student will want to borrow your clothes,' Lisa countered.

I noticed that she hadn't contradicted the rest of my verbal thumbnail sketch about life in a student house.

'Thanks, but no thanks,' I said. My tone was final.

'Then at least stay here until Juan returns,' she begged. 'I can't bear to think of my bestie living in a garden shed.'

'I've already told you, it's not like that.'

'You know what I mean,' she huffed.

'Apparently, Milo is Italian. He had the outbuilding overhauled especially for when his family visit.'

'Fine, fine.' She threw up her hands. 'It's your life. Just don't blame me when you have chilblains, and your clothes smell of damp, and you constantly have the sniffles due to living in a garden.'

'I won't,' I said. There was no convincing her, so I gave up. Instead, I put out a hand. Touched her on the arm. 'Thank you for being concerned. For caring. I know you mean well.'

'If things don't work out, you can always come back here for a while.'

'Things *will* work out,' I insisted. 'Anyway, it's only a stop gap.'

'Stop gaps can last a while,' she said. 'I mean, how long is a piece of string?'

'In this case, the string is short,' I assured. 'Especially as I feel like I'm finally getting somewhere with the house hunting.'

'Have you found something you like?' she asked in surprise.

'No,' I said carefully. 'But I've done a lot of research. Driven around. Checked out areas.'

'Good,' she said, standing up. 'Give me your cup.' She

held out one hand and I passed her my empty mug. 'I'll dump these in the sink and wash them up in the morning.'

'I think it already is the morning,' I said regretfully. 'We've been talking for ages. Heavens, it's half past one. We're going to feel like death warmed up tomorrow.'

'Er, about tomorrow – or, rather, today,' said Lisa, suddenly bashful. 'I'm going to stay with Juan until the very last moment. I'll be in about lunchtime. Can you make up an excuse to tell Leslie?'

'Oh, Lis-*aaa*,' I wailed. 'I hate telling porky pies. Leslie always gives *the look*. You know what I mean. Where he says nothing, but his eyes morph into a lie detector machine. And you know I'm rubbish at lying.'

'Tell him I had an upset tummy.'

'Can't you phone in and tell him yourself?'

'No, silly, because he'll know I'm lying from my voice.'

'I'll tell him a half-lie,' I conceded. 'I'll say that you forgot to set your alarm and that when I last saw you, you were racing around like a lunatic, putting your tights on back to front. He knows the roads will be heaving with parents doing the school run, so that gives you until about 10 o'clock – at an absolute push.'

One thing about the stretch between Longfield and Meopham was the number of schools. There were three junior schools plus a vast secondary, all within a mile of each other. At certain times of the morning, it was carnage on the A227, what with school buses and rush hour traffic in the mix. It was even worse if some of the mums – and there were many – wrestled pushchairs from their boots. This was a sure sign that Mothers' Meetings were imminent on various pavements all over Meopham.

'Okay,' said Lisa reluctantly. 'Getting in at ten rather than midday is better than nothing. So, I guess tonight is your last night in my humble abode?'

'It is,' I beamed, then hastily killed the smile. Lisa's sofa – and new love life – might not have been great for me, but she'd been a true friend. Supportive, kind and caring. 'I shall miss you.' I stepped forward and gave her a big hug.

'Silly,' she said, squeezing me back. 'I'll see you at work every day.'

'That you will,' I assured. 'But I want to say thank you. For everything. You're a diamond.'

'Stop it,' she said, as I let her go. We were now both sniffing a bit. 'When will you pack up your stuff?' she asked gruffly.

I swiped a hand quickly over my cheek.

'I'll pop back in my lunch hour tomorrow. Load up Octavia. Then, after work, I'll head over to Starlight Croft.'

'Okay,' she said. 'And maybe – when you've unpacked and sorted yourself out – I'll pop over with a bottle of wine. We'll share it while you give me a guided tour of your garden shed.'

I burst out laughing.

'You're on.'

Chapter Forty-One

When the alarm went off on Friday morning, I felt beyond bleary-eyed. And then I remembered what day it was.

Today was the day I was moving in with Milo Soren. Well, not moving *in* with him, but you know what I mean. Soon I would be ensconced at the end of his garden. Perhaps he would knock on the door around seven o'clock. See how I was. Suggest a takeaway together? Or wait, he might have his son there. Perhaps the three of us could have a curry all together. And later – after I'd gone *home* – JJ would turn to Milo and give him some frank man-to-man straight talking.

'Pops! Stop swiping right. Instead, focus on the gorgeous single woman living mere feet from you.'

Yes, something like that anyway. And Milo would look at his son in amazement. His eyes would widen.

'Omigod, JJ. You're right. Up until now, I simply thought of Tilly as a rather annoying female. But the scales have fallen from my eyes.'

'Good. In which case, are you going to ask her out?'

'I'd like to, son. But I don't want to frighten her off. She's not long out of a disastrous marriage. I'll have to tread carefully. Woo her gently.'

I sprang off Lisa's sofa with an alacrity that wasn't the

norm. My back gave a twang of protest. It wasn't used to skippy behaviour. I instantly reined in the manic joy. The last thing I wanted was a sudden slipped disc. Although…

I paused for a moment. Allowed myself a small daydream. Me with a dodgy back. Prostrate on Milo's bed – after having collapsed prettily upon it.

Or, hang on. Why would I be in Milo's bedroom? No, that didn't work. We'd need to be in the garden accommodation. Yes, perhaps, after dinner with Milo and JJ, I'd had a spot of bother converting the sofa into a pullout bed. The mechanism had jammed. I'd had to return to the cottage and ask Milo to help me. JJ had miraculously disappeared. Gone to see Polly. An urgent request to help change a beer barrel. Or similar. So, together, Milo and I had walked to the summerhouse.

'See,' I would say, pointing to the offending lever/button/knob. 'It's stuck.' I'd give it a wiggle by way of demonstration. And then; 'Ouch, my back!'

'What's wrong with your back?'

'I think I've slipped a disc.'

Actually, no, not a disc. That was rather dire. I knew someone who'd done the same and been in agony. Had to have two operations. I didn't want to be out of action for weeks on end. Or in agony. Rewind.

'Ouch, my back!'

'What's wrong with your back?'

'I think I've pulled a muscle. Ooh, ouch, ouch.'

Cue soft music. Rose light fills the room as…

Milo manfully instructs Tilly what to do: 'Lean on me.'

Tilly obeys and receives a belting zinger: 'Like this?'

Milo receives a belting zinger in the trouser region: 'Lean harder!'

Tilly vibrates from a second zinger: 'Ooh…'

Milo suffers uncontrollable trouser steepling: 'Ahhh…'

Tilly looks up wantonly: 'Milo…'

Milo gasps: 'My darling. I want to make passionate love to you.'

Tilly puckers up: 'Yes, yes, yes!'

'Are you okay, Tilly?' said a bemused voice.

My eyes snapped open. I turned to see Lisa standing there. She had her hands on her hips and was regarding me curiously.

'Fine,' I squeaked.

'You looked like you were kissing the air,' she said, eyebrows raised.

'*Nooo*. I was simply lost in thought. Thinking about everything to do today. Closing my eyes helps me concentrate.'

'Does it indeed,' she muttered, moving to the kitchen area.

'I thought you were having a lay-in,' I said, keen to change the subject.

I headed over to the backdoor and let Cindy out for a wee.

'I am,' said Lisa, reaching for the kettle. She stuck it under the tap and blasted water into it. 'I'm making Juan and me a cup of tea. Then going back to bed for an hour.'

'Budge over,' I said, coming up alongside her. I removed

one of Cindy's upturned food bowls from the drainer. Locating a tin of dog food, I forked some meaty chunks into the bowl.

'Poo, that stuff pongs,' said Lisa, wrinkling her nose. 'Want a cuppa?'

'Please,' I said gratefully. I set the bowl down on the floor, then let Cindy in. 'But if you don't mind, I'll quickly use the bathroom first. I promise to have the fastest shower in history while you're waiting for that kettle to boil.'

'Fine,' Lisa nodded. 'Something's certainly coming to the boil,' she added under her breath. I pretended not to hear and scampered off to the smallest room in the house. Seconds later her voice floated after me. 'And don't get in a lip lock with the shower nozzle.'

Chapter Forty-Two

'You're late,' said Leslie, as I crashed into the office. 'And where's Lisa?'

Since moving in with my bestie, she and I had taken it in turns to share the drive from Longfield to Meopham. However, thanks to Juan, that wasn't the case today.

The brief commute to work had been even more appalling due to a motorist getting in a row with a cyclist. The screaming match that had subsequently taken place had blocked vehicles and caused a cacophony of blaring horns. Consequently, several motorists had joined in the argument. One had been an old boy. He'd intimidated a female driver by aiming his walking stick like a hitman at target practice.

By this point I'd had my window down, eavesdropping on the fracas. Eventually an irate lorry driver had telephoned the boys in blue. I'd overheard him ranting on the phone.

'Stop hiding in the bushes at Kings Hill with your speed cameras and get over here. There are several people calling each other *Jesus Christ*, plus a pensioner impersonating Basil Fawlty. He's insisting everyone's cars are going to have *a damn good thrashing*.

'The traffic was mental this morning,' I said breathlessly.

I hastened over to my desk, shrugging off my coat

enroute. I was aware of Leslie's eyes following me. His inbuilt lie detector was boring into my back. I slung my jacket over the chair and chucked my handbag under the desk. Leaning over the keyboard, I flipped the switch on my monitor.

'Also' – I quavered – 'Lisa overslept. But she'll be here shortly.'

Leslie made a harrumphing sound.

'How is it that some of my employees live miles away but manage to get here before the two members of staff that only live in the next village?'

'They obviously managed to dodge the mayhem,' I gulped, flopping down on my seat. 'Lisa and I aren't often late.' I entered my login code. 'Can I make you a nice cup of coffee, Leslie?'

Personally, I was gasping and – thanks to last night's sleep being on the sparse side – caffeine was necessary. And if my boss had a couple of handy matchsticks to prop up my eyelids, that would be even better.

'I've already had a drink,' said Leslie. 'Anyway, I'm going out. I'll be back after lunch. Appointments,' he added by way of explanation. 'Hopefully Lisa will be here before my return.'

He flashed me a meaningful look. One that conveyed he wasn't stupid and, traffic issues aside, I'd failed the lie detector test.

As soon as he'd left, I sent Lisa a text relaying the same, and asked her to let Cindy out again before she left the maisonette.

She turned up just after eleven, looking sexually sated but also puffy-eyed from crying.

'How am I going to get through the next few days without Juan,' she groaned, collapsing over her keyboard. Her head shot up when Leslie unexpectedly came through the door.

'You're back early,' I twittered, wondering if he'd copped Lisa's arrival seconds earlier.

'Forgot some papers,' he explained curtly. Leslie glared at Lisa. She was now pounding her keyboard. 'Good *afternoon*,' he said pointedly.

'Now, now, Leslie.' Lisa paused from her typing. Gave him a winning smile. 'I wasn't *that* late this morning.'

'You're still half asleep though,' he grunted. 'You might want to check your typing. After all, you haven't switched on your monitor. I suggest you work your lunch hour to make up the lost time.'

'Fuckity-fuck,' Lisa hissed as Leslie stalked off.

'Nice try,' I giggled, just as the phone rang. 'Home and Hearth Estate Agents. How can I help you?'

'Er, is that Tilly Thomas?' said a male voice.

'Speaking,' I confirmed.

And then the line went dead.

'Strange,' I said, hanging up.

My thoughts fragmented as the phone rang again, this time with a different caller. Lisa and I kept our heads down. The office was unusually busy today and the phone rang nonstop.

By lunchtime, Lisa and I were still flat out. I abandoned

the original plan of spending the lunch hour loading up Octavia with my belongings. I'd now have to do that after work instead. I knew Cindy wouldn't be cross-legged thanks to Lisa letting her out.

I glanced over at my bestie. She caught my eye. I mimed if she wanted me to get her a sandwich to eat at her desk. She nodded.

I stood up, shimmied into my jacket and reached for my handbag. As I walked towards the main door, a pair of familiar legs were visible behind the window display. I yanked the door open, and the rest of the person came into view. It was the young man Lisa had previously caught staring at me. This time he was supposedly studying properties for let. As I stepped onto the pavement, he looked my way.

'Hello,' I said automatically.

'Hi,' he replied warily.

I felt a frisson of anxiety. After all, this was a man who frequently swung past my workplace, stared at me working within, made out to be looking at the window display, but never ventured inside. Was he like one of those yobs I'd seen on that street corner?

However, this guy wasn't a teenager. So maybe unlikely. Even so, he made me feel uneasy. Had he seen me driving Octavia about? My bright orange Fiat did rather stand out. Had he *targeted* me?

Ah ha! There goes that woman from Home and Hearth Estate Agents. I now know that she's single and likely vulnerable. All I need do is bide my time. Plan the right moment. Then grab her handbag and run.

What did the police advise when it came to dealing with a wannabe mugger? Challenge the person? Let them know that you were on to them? Or run like the clappers in the opposite direction? I didn't have a clue. Nonetheless I felt compelled to call this guy out. To let him know I was on to him. Knew his game.

I gripped my bag tightly and looked him in the eye.

'Not yet found a house?' I challenged. My voice sounded harsh, and my gaze was unwavering.

'Er, no. Actually… I'm not looking for a property,' he confessed.

'Indeed,' I jeered. Blimey, he wasn't even going to bluff about his loitering. My eyes narrowed. Two slits of icy flint. 'So, what *are* you doing outside my place of work?' I demanded.

'Well…' he began, then trailed off.

It came to me that his voice sounded familiar, although I couldn't initially place it. And then I twigged. I'd heard him speak earlier. That dropped phone call.

'Is that Tilly Thomas?'

And then the line had gone dead.

Omigod. This man was a stalker in the true sense of the word. Not content to mooching around outside my place of work, now he was ringing me up too. The question was… why?'

When I next spoke, my voice was like a pistol shot.

'What do you *really* want?' I scowled.

'To talk to you,' he said simply.

My nostrils flared. Dear God. This guy wasn't even going to deny he'd been trailing me.

'You called me this morning,' I accused. 'And then you hung up.'

'I did,' he said softly.

My free hand began to pat-pat behind my back. Where was the shop's door handle? It was suddenly of vital importance to be back inside the office. Surrounded by other people. Preferably with a few handy monitors to lob at this man who, even now, was advancing towards me.

Chapter Forty-Three

'Don't be frightened,' the guy implored.

Was he for real?

'I'm not scared,' I whispered. I was terrified.

Frigging jelly babies. Where was my gung-ho when I needed it – the fight or flight response? I seemed to have neither wings on my heels to run, nor strength to stand and fight. If I could just lift one of my legs. Knee him in the nuts. Or command my foot to give a well-aimed kick to the shins.

But despite my brain's frantic commands, my body wasn't responding. I felt as weak as a rag doll – and petrified with it. My stomach lurched, as did my bowels. For one horrible moment I thought I might disgrace myself.

The man was almost upon me. Clenching my buttocks and gritting my teeth, I took a step backwards, still blindly groping for the damned handle on the office door. Where the bloody hell had it gone? I needed to scream. To alert Lisa… the others… *any*one… that I was being mugged in broad daylight. Right before their eyes – if any of them could deign to look this way.

But what if this man wasn't going to mug me? What if he planned to murder me instead? Perhaps he was one of those people who'd become addicted to violent video games.

And reprogrammed his brain. And was now hellbent on *taking out* all forty-nine-year-old blonde women.

Your mission, if you choose it, is to go totally nuts.

I risked a quick look at his hands. He wasn't carrying a knife. Or a gun, for that matter. But maybe he was hiding his chosen weapon within his jacket. After all, it wasn't zipped up.

A sudden breeze lifted his open jacket. I caught sight of an inner pocket. There was a telltale shape within the lining. A mobile phone – not a weapon of mass destruction.

'Stay away from me,' I hissed. 'Or I'll scream.'

'Please don't do that,' he begged, as the distance between us closed.

He put out a hand. Touched my handbag. I wanted to shove it into his face, but my arms refused to work. I opened my mouth to waggle my tonsils, but all that came out was a hoarse squeak. He was now towering over me. My eyes widened in horror. This was it. I was going to die. Either that or faint.

I leant back against the office door, just as Lisa opened it. I fell backwards, cannoning into her. Righting my balance, I scuttled behind her.

'What the bloody hell is going on out here?' she demanded, glaring at the man.

'I meant no harm,' he said. Intimidated by Lisa, he stuck his hands in the air, like a terrorist surrendering to the SAS.

'Help,' I croaked.

My legs were starting to feel most peculiar. In the absence of my brain failing to instruct my pins whether to run like a frightened deer or stay and fight like Kung Fu Panda, they seemed to be in a state of confusion. They were juddering violently, as if wanting to flee, but my feet weren't obliging. Instead, I seemed to be sinking down to the floor while my legs impersonated Michael Flatley doing an Irish dance.

'Help,' I bleated again.

I was now sprawled across the large doormat, complete with company logo and greeting message. *Welcome to Home and Hearth.* Except all that was visible was …*come…to…earth.*

'Dying,' I panted, still clutching my handbag to my chest. 'Seriously.'

'Don't be so melodramatic, Tilly,' said Lisa bossily. 'Get up. If Leslie comes back right now and sees this bit of drama, our jobs might be on the line. On the other hand, if I've saved you from being mugged, I might be up for promotion.'

'I was *not* mugging anyone!' said the guy, aghast at such an accusation.

Everyone inside the office was now staring at the man framed in the doorway. This unwanted spotlight of attention had turned him scarlet with embarrassment. He gave Lisa an earnest look.

'I've been trying to pluck up the courage to talk to this lady for ages,' he explained.

He was now so red, even his ears were glowing.

'Got a thing about her, have you?' Lisa demanded.

Her forefinger shot out, like a 007 gun. She waggled it about in a threatening manner.

'Into older women, are you, sonny?'

'No!' he protested. I'm a regular guy.'

'There's nothing *regular* about your behaviour,' Lisa insisted. She stepped forward and prodded the guy with her 007 finger. 'I've a good mind to call the police.'

'Whatever for?' said the man in horror.

'Because you've behaved like a total creep. So, what do you say' – prod, prod, prod – 'about that, eh?'

The guy lowered his hands and batted Lisa's finger away. Despite still being puce from embarrassment, he was now also annoyed.

'I'm *not* a creep and I promise I meant no harm.'

Panting slightly, I stuck out my own 007 forefinger. It wobbled from side to side like an EasyJet flight in the grip of turbulence.

'Who the bloody hell are you?' I gasped.

The guy glanced from me to his slack jawed audience. He gave an imperceptible shake of his head, then turned his attention back to me.

'I was hoping to be discreet. To talk to you in private,' he explained. 'But it's backfired big time.'

'Cut the crap,' said Lisa. 'Tilly has asked a question. Have the decency to give her an answer.'

'Very well,' said the man.

As his eyes locked on mine, something deep in my soul violently shifted. I gasped aloud as emotions – buried from long *long* ago – broke free from their moorings. They rushed up. Through the layers of the past. Through the sands of time. Then smashed their way through a thick wall of ice. It was as if a giant pneumatic drill had shattered a North Pole glacier.

Recognition.

In that moment, I felt two things. Utter joy and deep despair. You see, I knew this man.

He was now watching me carefully. Observing the further emotions streaming through my body. Rippling over my face. Disbelief. Incredulity. And absolute heartbreak.

He nodded, and his face said it all.

Confirmation.

It verified what my heart knew, but what my brain was desperately trying to process. And then he spoke the words aloud.

'I am your son.'

Chapter Forty-Four

'What are you talking about?' Lisa spluttered. 'Tilly doesn't have kids.'

'I'm her son,' the man repeated.

'You really are a sicko.' Lisa rounded on him furiously. 'My friend has never had children. She was unable to. Dooo... yooo... understand?' she enunciated. 'Ah, yes! I see I now have your full attention.' She gave the man a satisfied smirk. 'It is impossible for you to be related to Tilly, because she is infertile. Always has been.'

'Actually,' I croaked. 'That's not completely true.'

'W-Wha–?' Now it was Lisa's turn to look gobsmacked. 'Don't be absurd,' she hissed. 'All those years of trying for a child with Robin. Or did you make that up?'

'No,' I shook my head. 'That much is true. I couldn't seem to fall pregnant. But there was another time...'

I trailed off. Gulped hard. Tears were now spurting out of my eyes, like an ill-fitting hosepipe attached to a leaking outdoor tap.

Candice, another member of staff, stepped forward.

'Excuse me,' she interrupted. 'There's obviously some deeply personal and highly emotive stuff going on here. Tilly, why don't you and this gentleman go into Leslie's office?

He's not due back for a while. You can both chat in private.'

'Well excuse *me*,' said Lisa officiously. 'Nobody is talking to Tilly without me being present.' She rounded on the hapless man again. 'We only have *your* word about this and I, for one, am not convinced. So, if you don't mind' – she stepped aside to let the man pass – 'get yourself in there.' She jerked her head in the direction of Leslie's office. 'Yes, that's the one. Go in. I will be personally interrogating you.' Lisa was now in full Detective Inspector mode. 'Come on, Tilly.' She took me by the arm and frogmarched me into Leslie's office. She paused to address Candice and the rest of the staff. 'That's it, folks. Floorshow over.' She shut the door in their astonished faces, then propelled me over to Leslie's chair. 'Sit.'

I didn't so much sit as crumple. Omigod. *Omigod*. My heart was banging like an Olympic sprinter. I was starting to feel horribly sick and out of sorts. Lisa and the guy sat down on two client chairs placed on the other side of Leslie's desk.

'Look,' said the man. He leant forward in his chair. Put his elbows on Leslie's desk. Steepled his fingers together. 'I'm so sorry if this has come as a shock.'

'Just a bit,' I croaked. My vocal chords had shrivelled up.

'Shall we start at the beginning?' he suggested.

I nodded weakly.

'Please can you tell me your story first?' I whispered.

He gave the ghost of a smile.

'That's probably a good idea, although I will want to hear your story too.'

'Of course,' I said meekly.

'You're not the only one,' Lisa muttered, shooting me a look. One that said *I can't believe what's going on here – and why did you never confide in me?* 'But first' – she stood up – 'I think we all need a stiff drink.'

Lisa went to Leslie's drinks cabinet. It was reserved for special clients and bigwigs higher up the management chain. She was momentarily distracted by a piece of paper wedged between some bottles. A note of some sort. She read it, then pushed it back into place before pouring us all a pick-me-up. Seconds later, the three of us were nursing a brandy apiece.

'Right,' she said, flopping down in her seat. 'Do tell. Tilly and I are all ears.'

It struck me that my bestie – along with all my work colleagues – had discovered my deepest, darkest secret. It was something I'd never shared with anyone. Not even my ex-husband.

A part of me wondered whether I wanted Lisa in this room, as the past caught up with me. But then I realised the past already *had* caught up with me, and in the most public way. Indeed, the past was sitting opposite my trembling body, looking at me across Leslie's leather-topped desk. It made no difference whether Lisa stayed or not. She knew. Everyone knew. My secret was out. This man was my son.

I stared at him. His face was drawing me like a magnet. I was incapable of dragging my eyes from him. My God he was beautiful. He really was. And I didn't even know his name. As if reading my mind, he told me.

'I'm Jake.'

'Jake,' I repeated. I said it with awe. Reverence. As if

he'd just said *I'm Jesus.*

'Did you give me that name?' he asked.

I shook my head. Tears were once again streaming down my face, although I wasn't crying. It more like… my body releasing. I knew there were going to be many more tears. Possibly enough to fill a paddling pool.

'It's a great name,' I whispered. 'Please, Jake. Carry on.'

'I always knew I was adopted,' he said quietly. 'It was never a secret. My mum' – he shot me a look of apology, one that said I wasn't yet privy to that label – 'well, she told me from the start. She and my dad were waiting to receive me before I was even born.'

I swallowed hard as Lisa shot me another questioning look. One that said *people were waiting to take your baby before you'd given birth?* I ignored her. No one would understand. No one, unless they were me. My focus remained on this man. Jake. My son. And I was sucking up every single word coming out of his mouth, like a parched marathon runner necking water.

'I never had any issue about my mum and dad not being my biological parents,' he continued. 'They told me I was their son. And that was that. I even looked a bit like my dad.' Jake gave a half laugh. 'People said I also had his mannerisms.' He shrugged. 'Learned behaviour, I guess. Even so, I grew up completely untroubled by the word *adopted*. It just didn't register on my radar.'

A part of me was relieved to hear him say this. Another part of me felt destroyed.

'My parents were wonderful,' he carried on. 'Strict when

they needed to be, but also very loving. They were the best,' he said simply.

My heart squeezed at those words. What *I* would have given to be told I was the best.

'I never wanted for anything,' said Jake. 'Mum and Dad both worked hard, and we all enjoyed the benefits of their earnings. We had terrific holidays. Cornwall was a firm favourite. Sometimes we went abroad too. Growing up, I was like any other lad. Riding a bike. Playing football. Doing my best at school. Life was good. Years passed. And then two things happened, but not at the same time.'

'O-Oh?' I said, feeling a sense of foreboding. Please tell me this darling boy hadn't fallen in with the wrong crowd. Experimented with drugs. Drink. Ended up on the wrong side of the law. I was way off beam.

'My parents died,' he explained.

'I'm sorry,' I murmured.

'Other family members gathered around. I was supported,' he shrugged. 'Nonetheless, a part of me felt…' – he struggled to find the right words – 'like a boat that had lost its mooring. I was still in the harbour, bobbing about, but I wasn't… *connected*. For the first time I felt… out on a limb.'

'Is that when you decided to search for your biological parents?' asked Lisa.

Jake shook his head.

'No. I parked those feelings to one side. I told myself that this inner sense of disconnection was due to bereavement – and eventually things did settle down. But then a second thing happened. By this point, a few years had passed. I was in a serious relationship.'

I felt my heart momentarily lift at the thought of this young man – my son no less –being independent. Meeting the girl of his dreams. I swiped one hand across my sodden cheeks.

'Things between me and Hannah were good. We were in love. We'd bought a house together. As far as I was concerned, she was my future, and I hers.' He swallowed. Paused. Took a breath. It was obvious that he was struggling to maintain his composure. When he next spoke, his voice was calm but loaded with pain. 'And then Hannah suggested we start a family. That was when I fell apart.'

Chapter Forty-Five

'Fell apart?' I whispered. 'What… as in… had a nervous breakdown?' My heart squeezed.

Jake shook his head.

'No, not like that,' he sighed. 'It was more… asking myself how I could bring a new life into this world, when I'd never bothered to find out who I truly was. If that makes any sense,' he added. He shifted in his seat. A regrouping gesture. 'Hannah wanted the two of us to create a brand-new human being. For me, this was a massive trigger. I suddenly had this overwhelming urge to find out who I really was. Who had I been when I first came into this world?'

'My beautiful baby boy,' I sobbed.

For a moment Jake glared at me, then the fierce expression softened.

'I needed to find the man and woman who'd made my flesh and bones.' He rubbed his forehead. A stress response. 'It became an all-consuming desire to find the two people who'd created my *essence*. Can you understand?'

I stared at him mutely, while Lisa slowly nodded.

'Yes,' she said.

'Unfortunately, it didn't make sense to Hannah,' he said sadly. 'At first, she was patient with me. She said it was probably common to want to know more about one's origins. What one's birth parents did, and so on. She understood my curiosity. The need to know what was *inside* me. My parents had brought me up as their own, but they'd died. They couldn't answer the questions suddenly whirring in my head. Unfortunately – despite them never making a secret of my adoption – when I looked for the paperwork, there was none. At least, nothing that gave me a lead on where to start. Time went by, and Hannah began to get impatient with me. She wanted to crack on. Start a family. Instead, her partner seemed to have morphed into someone with a messed-up head. Suddenly her calm, level-headed boyfriend was a mess of wildly swinging emotions. From anger and hurt. To abandonment. Despair. I didn't know if it was an early mid-life crisis or a ridiculously belated adoption trauma. All I *did* know was that I felt confused and lost, and I refused to bring a new life into this world when I had unanswered questions about my own life.'

'Can I interrupt for a moment?' asked Lisa.

'Of course,' said Jake.

'How old are you?' she asked.

I was instantly reminded of Jake's bright red face only half an hour earlier when he'd stood in the main office with everyone watching the drama unfold. Now it was my turn to have a flaming face.

'He's thirty-four,' I muttered.

Lisa's mouth fell open.

'Thirty-*four*?' she squawked. 'That means' – her brow furrowed as she struggled with the maths – 'you couldn't have been more than…'

'Fifteen,' I nodded, my face burning with shame. 'I was fifteen when I gave birth.'

'Holy moly,' she breathed.

'I did wonder if you were no more than a kid when you carried me,' said Jake. 'In a way, it makes it easier for me to come to terms with. Even so, I still have questions to ask.'

'Of course,' I whispered.

'I mean' – Jake shrugged – 'I'm not expecting some instant parent-child bond to come about just because you're my biological mother.'

My tear ducts involuntarily squirted more water. How could I even begin to explain that – despite holding my newborn for a few precious seconds – the invisible umbilical cord had always been there. Well, for me anyway. I could remember pouring my heart out to Cindy in one of our imagined conversations.

Not a day goes by where – at some point – I don't think about what happened. What might have been. If I'd been a little older. A little wiser. If circumstances had been different. Sometimes I have a good day and realise that twelve hours have passed without fretting about it. I tell myself that the inner peace of those twelve hours was blissful. Such a relief. And then, equally, I'm horrified. Ask myself what sort of person I've become to have permitted twelve hours of amnesia. It makes me feel like such a bad person.

Cindy had reassured me that I wasn't. At least, I like to think she had.

I now understood why Jake had seemed so familiar when I'd first caught sight of him outside my place of work.

A part of my mind detached. Whooshed backwards. Lisa telling me to *turn now*. Of locking eyes with a nameless stranger. Feeling disturbed, but not knowing why.

Well, now I knew. Jake had reminded me of Nicholas. Nicholas from long ago. So long ago, that I'd still been at school. As had Nicholas.

'So' – Jake ventured tentatively – 'did you not have a family with your husband?'

I shook my head.

'No, although I wanted to,' I confessed.

'Did you tell your husband about me?' asked Jake.

I shook my head.

'No. My parents knew. Obviously. And people in authority. It became a taboo subject. My folks and I… we haven't discussed it in decades. Coping mechanisms on all sides, I suppose. But there were no more babies. I told myself it was karma paying me back. I'd received the gift of a child once, then given the gift away. So why should I be blessed again?' I took a shuddering breath as my eyes continued to leak. 'There was even a part of me that wondered if I'd somehow programmed my body not to have a baby as a form of self-punishment.'

'Oh, Tilly,' said Lisa. 'Don't be daft.'

'Really?' My chin jutted defiantly. 'It was no more than I deserved.'

Jake shook his head.

'You were fifteen,' he pointed out. 'And now, if you don't mind, I'd like to hear your story. The details of how I came to be.'

Chapter Forty-Six

Where to begin? When I was thirteen? With a small pair of budding breasts and starting to notice the opposite sex?

Or perhaps fourteen? Yes, fourteen is the better starting point.

By this point I was taller than my girlfriends. I had hips and curves whereas my friends were late to the puberty party, their figures still boyish.

I was never confused about my gender. The only *experimenting* I did was with the cheap makeup bought with pocket money. I was blessed to never experience teenage spots or puppy fat. I had long blonde hair and legs like Bambi. Whenever out of school uniform, lorry drivers would honk their horns. Jack-the-lad brickies, high on scaffolding and testosterone, would wolf whistle.

I can remember my mother laughing on such occasions. She'd flick back her hair, believing the attention was for her. My father wasn't fooled. He would stick his fingers up at the lorry drivers and swear at the lads leering from the scaffolding. He'd cry, "It's a good thing you're up there and not down here, or you'd need more than a hard hat to protect yourselves."

London nightclubs were for celebrities. Locally, discos were for ordinary people. Such folks could be found in any pub pretending it was a trendy establishment. Obviously, you had to be eighteen to get in, but with a face full of makeup, a short dress and heels bought with my paper round money, entry wasn't a problem.

I used to meet up with Marie, the only other girl in my class who – like me – could pass for eighteen.

We'd both tell our respective parents that we were going round to each other's houses to study and have a sleepover. So, while Mum and Dad thought I was at Marie's place labouring over algebra and, later, watching trash telly, instead we'd hole up at the local shopping precinct's public loo. In front of a well-lit mirror, we'd transform ourselves. We might have been schoolgirls who loved to race their bicycles downhill, legs stuck out at an angle, but we'd also wanted to play grownups. And as any adult will attest, part of being a grownup is understanding the responsibility that goes with it.

I met Nicholas one Saturday evening. Marie and I had taken a bus into Brighton – my then hometown. Loud music had been pouring out of the pubs. One had stood out. It had drawn us like moths to a megawatt lightbulb.

An obligatory bouncer had given us the onceover. We'd felt empowered. Unlimited. Fourteen going on twenty-four. In other words, overconfident and horribly naïve.

We'd walked in with no issue. And there, at the bar, had been a couple of lads. They'd looked our way. Nudged each other.

It transpired that Nicholas and Callum were mirror-images of Marie and me. They were fifteen to our fourteen. However, thanks to some Italian and Greek heritage, they'd both sported some hair on their chests. They'd displayed this fluff by undoing several buttons on their shirts. Their clothes – leather jackets and jeans – gave them a look that shouted *sexy young men* rather than *teenage boys*.

With a pint apiece already inside them, they were giving off a vibe. Self-assurance. Marie and I were totally fooled when Nicholas and Callum told us they were nineteen.

'And how old are you?' said Nicholas, catching hold of my hand.

'Nearly twenty,' I giggled, delighted at hoodwinking him.

'What's your tipple?' he asked, as the barman approached.

'Pernod and black,' I said without hesitation.

I'd never tasted the drink, but had once overheard Marie's older sister, Caitlin, saying that Pernod and black was *the height of sophistication*. As Caitlin was every teenage girl's idol, I'd mentally filed away the info. I'd accepted the drink and instantly felt like an *It Girl*. Putting the glass to my lips, I'd nearly heaved.

'To us,' said Nicholas.

He'd clinked his glass against mine. I'd downed the disgusting drink like someone swallowing cough medicine.

But teenagers can't hold their drink. Nor do they have a bottomless purse due to being schoolkids. They also have a lower boredom threshold than adults. So, still kidding each other that we were older than our years, we left the bright lights and headed to that other place where teen relationships progress. McDonald's.

Chapter Forty-Seven

I looked at Jake.

'So that's how it started,' I said. A thought suddenly occurred to me. 'Have you traced Nicholas?'

'I... know where he is,' he said cautiously.

I gulped. I hadn't allowed myself to think of Nicholas in decades. Not properly. Obviously, my thoughts had occasionally strayed that way. I'd wondered where he was living. If he'd met someone. Married. Had a family. Ever given our own child a thought. But as fast as such thoughts had entered my head, another part had quickly shut them down. And as for looking Nicholas up on social media – that was a no. Mentally, for me, it was too iffy a path.

But now a can of worms was being opened. Jake knew where Nicholas was. And my curiosity was piqued. How could I not find out more about Nicholas given that our son was here at my place of work?

'So, you haven't spoken to him?' I whispered.

'No.' Jake shook his head.

'How did you find him?'

'The same way I found you.' Jake's eyes were unblinking. 'So many people do those DNA things. You know, *find out your heritage*. People buy them as gifts for their loved ones. After all, they make unique presents. A simple swab of the mouth. Then wait to find out if you're distantly related to Prince William.' He gave a derisive snort. 'It makes interesting reading. It makes comparisons to others who have posted off their samples. Consequently, you know exactly *who* you're related to. Once I knew you were likely my birth mother, it was simply a case of tracing your whereabouts. In today's world, that isn't hard.'

'Does Nicholas still live in Brighton?'

Jake shook his head.

'No, and for now, I'd like to hear more of your story. You've told me how my biological mother met my biological father, but nothing else.'

'What bit do you want next?' I asked, as fresh tears slid down my cheeks.

'All of it,' he said simply.

And, head bowed, inwardly dying of shame, I continued my story.

How, after an evening of consuming cheap burgers in a bun, Marie and Callum had splintered off leaving me and Nicholas alone. We'd gone back to his place. Except, of course, it hadn't been *his* place. It had been his *parents'* place. They'd been away overnight. Visiting relatives. They'd entrusted Nicholas with the keys to the house. To feed the cat. Take the dog for a walk. Not to throw a wild party.

Once back at his place, he'd showed off. Poured gin and tonics from his parents' cabinet. We'd got drunk. He'd pushed me down on the sofa. Asked how many *men* I'd slept with. I'd quaked upon hearing that word. Even in my gin-sodden befuddled state, it had registered that I was in dodgy territory. There was a world of difference between a teenage boy and a *man*. I'd told him the truth. That I was a virgin. And not nineteen. Instead, I'd told him I was seventeen. He'd done the same. Said he was a seventeen-year-old virgin.

We'd giggled, as if we'd shared the naughtiest secret ever. He'd then taken my face between his hands and gently kissed me. And then he'd suggested we *fool around*. See what happened... if anything... no pressure. And so, we had.

But, fuelled by gin and teenage hormones, we'd ended up doing an awful lot more than *fooling around*.

I'd stayed the night. Very little sleep had been had. We'd discovered sex. And we'd stayed up all night long indulging in it.

The following morning, exhausted, we'd given each other lingering kisses good-bye. We'd exchanged phone numbers. Secreted the bits of paper away in back pockets. And we *did* see each other again. Although we both quickly rumbled each other's true ages.

After that, there was little chance to be together intimately. His parents didn't go away again, and mine never went away without taking me with them.

It was only when I didn't have a period for about three months, that I felt a frisson of alarm. But I didn't tell a soul. Not even Marie. In my head, confiding in someone would have made the problem real. Whereas ignoring it meant the problem might go away. Such was a frightened fourteen-year-old's logic.

I wore baggy sweatshirts over my school uniform. My

fifteenth birthday came – and still no period. At weekends I took to wearing my dad's unwanted denim shirt. It was so enormous, two of me could have fitted within its frayed seams. Until, of course, there was undeniably two of me in the tummy area.

I can still remember my mother one day looking at me. Making a comment about my weight gain. Suggesting that I stop snacking. She'd playfully poked me in the stomach. But her finger hadn't disappeared into a soft roll of puppy fat. Instead, she'd prodded a round, firm abdomen.

Mum had stopped dead in her tracks. She'd glared at me. Demanded I undo my father's shirt. I'd refused.

'Do it!' she'd roared. 'NOW!'

'I will not,' I'd retorted, defiant. 'How *dare* you insinuate I'm fat. And how *dare* you demand me to strip. I've a good mind to ring Childline.'

She'd gone ballistic. Lunged at me.

For a moment I'd thought she might hit me. I'd instinctively thrown up my hands to cover my face. Instead, she'd grabbed the opening of the shirt. Yanked it apart. Buttons had pinged off in all directions and bounced across the floor. And my very established baby bump had been revealed in all its glory.

She'd inhaled sharply. Taken a shocked step backwards. I'd slowly lowered my hands and seen the colour drain from her face. She'd moved her head from side to side, unable to believe what she was seeing.

'Oh my God, Tilly,' she'd quavered. 'What have you done? You stupid, *stupid,* child.'

The brief remainder of my pregnancy had passed in a blur. Nicholas's parents had been informed. We were banned from seeing each other. Shortly afterwards, his parents had moved away, taking Nicholas with them. My parents eventually did the same. But not before I'd given birth at Brighton General Hospital.

My school had been informed. Well, the headmistress. I'd ended up being home schooled. Marie and my classmates were told that, due to unforeseen circumstances, I would not be returning to school. Phone calls from friends were intercepted. I remember Marie once coming to the house and my mother turning her away.

A social worker had been assigned to me – supposedly to provide support and counselling. Ultimately, she'd facilitated the adoption process. For make no mistake, my parents had told me I could not keep the baby. Mum was insistent.

'You're still a child yourself, and we're not raising it. It's not right, Tilly. You must put this behind you. Dad and I will help you to do that. To move on. To get your life back on track. Thank God there are people out there who can't have kids. Who are desperate for a baby to love and raise as their own.'

Ever since my missed period, I'd been in denial that a tiny human being had been growing inside me. Even when I'd felt the baby moving, I'd told myself it was wind.

I won't lie. I will admit that it was a relief to have the situation taken out of my hands. To comply. To do as I was told. To think of it as a blip. A child-woman who, afterwards, would have a clean slate. A shiny new future.

Labour had passed in a haze. I remember the pain. Of gulping gas and air. Afterwards, a sweet midwife had placed my newborn in my arms.

'Congratulations, Tilly. You have a beautiful little boy.'

I'd looked down at the darling little face. My son's eyes had opened. Tried to focus on mine. I'd marvelled at his shock of dark hair. The perfect nose. The rosebud mouth. The soft curve of his cheeks. The tiny arms and legs. The perfect fingers and toes. The miniature shell-like nails. The social worker – furious with the midwife – had snatched my baby away.

'No bonding!' she'd exhorted. 'I'm thinking of *you*, Tilly.'

I'd left the hospital emotionally numb.

Dad had been at the wheel of the car. Mum in the passenger seat. I'd sat in the back, slumped over – body language like any other teen.

What the outside world hadn't known was that *this* teen had a *linea nigra* on her stomach and wore padded knickers to absorb *lochia*.

My parents had chatted throughout the journey to our new home in Kent. The conversation had been a little forced but determined. Nothing chaotic or scandalous had ever happened. They were starting over in a new area. Nobody knew the history of Malcolm and Sylvia Thomas or their daughter Tilly. We were a respectable family. Hurrah!

As far as Mum and Dad were concerned, my pregnancy was a subject never to be discussed again. And it wasn't.

The years passed. I grew into a young woman. Privately

I always felt as if there were two of me in one body. The old Tilly – the girl who'd had a baby while still a child herself – and the adult Tilly. The latter went on to marry Robin Jameson. Tilly Jameson longed to settle down and start a family. But her longing was never fulfilled.

Periodically, my mind would whoosh back. Back to a sunny day in July where, terrified, lonely, and in pain, I'd delivered a tiny human being. When I'd briefly held my baby boy, I'd been flattened by an overwhelming sense of love. And when that social worker had whisked him away, it was as if I'd been bereaved.

Chapter Forty-Eight

'And that is how that chapter of my life ended,' I whispered.

I looked at Jake through sore eyes. My cheeks feel tight from all the tears.

'Oh my God,' said Lisa. She looked appalled. 'You poor thing.'

'I'm sorry you had to go through that,' said Jake quietly. He sounded sincere.

I regarded him blearily.

'I'm sorry you had to go through it too,' I said flatly. 'I want to apologise for being such a stupid, irresponsible, idiotic, pathetically immature teenager who behaved so foolishly and...'

'Hey,' Jake interrupted. One hand shot out and enclosed mine. 'It's okay.' The gesture had been spontaneous, but nonetheless surprised us both. A physical connection. After all this time. So many years. 'Everything turned out okay for me,' he assured. He patted my hand. 'It really did. I'm not bitter. Do you understand? I am... was... curious. Just needed to discover some missing pieces in this jigsaw of life. And now, one piece is in place. When the second – and final – piece is in place, then I'll be whole again. Ready to carry on with my life, and one day bring a little one into this world. I'm sorry if I caused distress. It really wasn't my intention.'

'It's fine,' I said hoarsely. A fresh flow of tears leaked down my face. They dripped off my chin and puddled on Leslie's desk.

I felt wrung out but also, perversely, so much lighter. It was as if a heavy invisible cloak had been wrapped around my shoulders for so long it had barely registered. But now, it had fallen, in a heap, to the floor. I flexed my neck. Yes, everything felt so much freer.

'Do you think you'll get back with Hannah' – I asked – 'when you've found the next missing piece of your jigsaw.' I assumed he meant Nicholas.

Jake shook his head.

'No,' he said. 'That ship has sailed, and maybe for the better. Hannah has moved on, and I'm pleased for her.'

'Jake,' I said tentatively. It seemed strange saying his name. It wasn't one I'd have chosen, but I loved it nonetheless. He was still holding my hand. I curled my fingers upwards, shifting the connection. Instead of him holding my hand, now it was *my* hand holding *his*. 'I don't expect you to say yes, but…' I broke off, suddenly anxious to put my unspoken emotions into words.

'Go on,' he said quietly.

'I… would you… what I'm trying to say is… can we keep in touch? Please?' The last word came out as a pathetic whimper. 'I don't want to put you under pressure, but now that you've reappeared in my life' – another wave of fresh tears spurted from my eyes – 'I can't bear the thought of you disappearing again.' The words died on my lips as my voice petered out. 'So sorry,' I gabbled. 'I know you have your own heartache to work through. I shouldn't have put that upon you. Please forgive-'

'I'd like that,' he interrupted.

I stared at him, not quite trusting I'd heard correctly.

'How about' – he said tentatively – 'that we don't go into this relationship with any expectations?'

I nodded my head up and down so violently it was a wonder I didn't give myself whiplash. Omigod. Jake was prepared to stay in touch!

'We mustn't put each other on a pedestal,' he continued. 'We both need to stay as grounded in reality as possible.'

'Yes,' I whispered. 'And Jake, one more thing...'

I was still clinging to his hand. Careful, Tilly. Don't scare him off. But I couldn't help it. When he walked out of this office, he needed to know some words from my heart. I hadn't been able to raise him. To be a mother to him. But by God I had so much love for him. Somehow, I needed to convey that. 'I think you're an amazing person and I'm so glad you found me. So very, *very* glad. Those words are totally inadequate for how I'm feeling right now.'

He squeezed my fingers and grinned.

'Me too. And now' – he gently extricated his hand from mine – 'I have a plane to catch.' He caught the stricken look on my face. 'But I'll be back,' he assured, pulling out his mobile. 'Give me your number.'

I watched him tap the digits into his phone. I was desperate to put his details into mine, but an inner voice cautioned me not to ask. To trust that he'd get in touch again when the time was right. When he was back from wherever he was now going. I caught a flash of his mobile screen. My heart skipped a beat. Jake had listed me in his contacts not as *Tilly*. Rather, *Mum*.

The three of us stood up and made to the door. Lisa first. She opened it but paused. She turned back to me and Jake.

'I'll leave you both to say goodbye,' she said diplomatically. 'It was nice to meet you, Jake, even if it was a mega shock.'

He gave a ghost of a smile.

'And you,' he nodded.

I hovered, wanting to throw my arms around this young man – this child of mine in adult skin. But I was terrified of being rejected. Jake looked at me awkwardly.

'Would it be okay to hug you?' he asked tentatively.

'It would be very okay,' I said hoarsely.

And as I felt myself engulfed in a bear hug, my heart soared like a kite. It whooshed up to the office ceiling, and then burst through the building's very roof, rocketing into the stratosphere. And in that moment, I dared to trust Jake would be in touch again. That one word on his mobile – *Mum* – said it all.

Chapter Forty-Nine

Jake left the office just as my boss returned.

'What?' Leslie questioned. He stared at my tearstained face and puffy eyes. 'What have I missed?'

Lisa glanced at Candice and the others. Her expression dared anyone to comment.

'You haven't missed anything,' Candice assured.

'Although I think Tilly might be coming down with something,' Lisa piped up. 'I reckon she should go home.'

'It's fine,' I protested. '*I'm* fine.'

'You don't look it.' Leslie peered at me. 'You look awful.'

'Tilly started feeling unwell soon after you left,' said Lisa. 'And, as her bestie, I think you should let me take her home and look after her.'

'Do you?' said Leslie wryly. He tutted. 'Oh, go on then.' He rolled his eyes. 'But come Monday morning, I expect the pair of you back in the office bright and early.'

'Of course.' Lisa flashed our boss a grateful grin.

'There's really no need,' I objected. 'I'm not ill, just a bit-'

Leslie's hand shot up.

'If you're about to tell me it's *women's problems* then

that's too much information.'

'It *is* women's problems,' Lisa agreed. 'But I'll look after her. It's Tilly's age you see. When a woman is heading towards fifty, her ovaries-'

'I do not want to know.' Leslie edged away from my desk. 'Just go, Tilly. And look after her, Lisa. Have a good weekend and I'll see you both on Monday.'

'You will,' said Lisa cheerfully, before turning to me. 'Right, come on, madam. Let's get you home. Have those legs up on the sofa.' She gave me a meaningful look, as Leslie disappeared inside his office. 'In other words, I want the full story of you and Nicholas rehashed with absolutely nothing missed out.'

'You've heard it all,' I muttered, as I logged off the system. 'There's nothing left to tell.' I picked up my handbag and jacket. 'And anyway, I'm meant to be packing up my stuff and moving into Milo's studio.'

Lisa rolled her eyes.

'So despite this afternoon's drama, you're still intent on living in a garden shed?'

'Yes,' I said obstinately. 'But if you're offering to help me pack my stuff, load up Octavia, and then have a recovery drink at the Starlight Arms, then you're on.'

'Damn right,' said Lisa, picking up her own handbag. 'Let's go.' She turned to Candice and the other girls. 'Bye, everyone. See you Monday.'

Lisa fairly skipped out of the office, but I was slow to follow. I felt exhausted. Shattered. All I really wanted to do, was crawl under a soft duvet and sleep for a million years.

Needless to say, I perked up a bit once back at Lisa's. After all, a new chapter was about to unfold in my life. *Another* new chapter. And this time it was going to be a serene precursor to buying my own place. One without Lisa's shenanigans interrupting my equilibrium.

Together we boxed up my worldly goods – which wasn't much – and shoved everything into Octavia. Cindy hopped onto the Fiat's front seat, leaving no room for anyone else.

'No worries,' said Lisa. 'I'll follow you. After all, I'll need to get myself home again later.' She leant into the passenger side and patted Cindy's head. 'I hope you settle into the garden shed quickly. Make sure you're a good girl for your mummy.'

I'm always a good girl.

'Do you know, Tilly, sometimes I swear your dog knows what I'm saying.'

I do.

'Aww,' said Lisa, looking at Cindy fondly. 'Coochie-coo, coochie-coo, my little poochie-poo,' she baby-talked, all the while ruffling Cindy's ears. She then lifted them outwards before wrapping them under her chin, as if they were ribbons on a bonnet. 'You're such a sweetie.'

I know.

'Aunty Lisa is going to miss you.'

Likewise.

'But not your parps,' she added.

Likewise.

Chapter Fifty

It didn't take long to unpack everything.

As I shut the cupboard door on my clothes, I realised it was a capsule wardrobe in every sense of the word. When I found my next home, there was going to be plenty of cupboard space and some serious retail therapy. It would be a priority.

'This place smells musty,' Lisa criticised, sniffing the air.

'It does not,' I retorted. 'However, it is a bit nippy.'

I cast around for the gadget that operated the wall unit. Ah, there it was. Languishing on the kitchen worktop. Scooping it up, I pointed the remote at a contraption that doubled as both air conditioning and heating. Right now, the latter was required.

'There,' I said, setting the remote down. 'We'll soon be toastie. After all, it's only a small space to heat.'

'Indeed,' said Lisa dryly. 'Garden sheds are never ginormous.'

'Oh, give over,' I tutted. I flopped down on the sofa where Cindy was currently sitting. She was bolt upright. As a result, she looked rather temporary.

Are we sharing this bed later?

'Yes,' I said.

'Yes what?' Lisa frowned.

'Er, sorry. Thought you said something.'

'No, I didn't. But don't get comfortable. I thought you said we were going to the local pub.' She glanced at her wristwatch. 'I'm feeling quite peckish. Shall we have an early dinner?'

'Sounds like a plan,' I agreed.

'And a bottle of wine. Or two,' she added.

'Sure. But don't forget you're driving later.'

'Oh, sod it,' she shrugged. 'I can always crash out here with you. Didn't you say this sofa converts into a double bed?'

'Yes,' I said reluctantly. I wasn't sure I wanted Lisa staying over. I still felt tearful. Drinking lots of wine and then, later, having a good howl – alone – was high on my list of priorities. 'Won't Juan be expecting you to Facetime him tonight?'

'Yes, probably,' she sighed. 'You're right. I'll pace myself with the vino, and then drive home.'

'Good idea,' I agreed, letting her believe the thought had been hers all along. 'Come on then.' I stood up, reached for the zapper again, and turned the heating down to low. 'We'll take Cindy with us. I don't want her left alone until she's settled in.'

I shrugged on my coat and reached for Cindy's lead. Lisa followed me. Outside, the light was fading fast. She glanced over at Milo's place.

'Before we take ourselves off, shall we say hello to your sexy landlord?'

I followed her gaze. Starlight Cottage was in darkness.

'I don't think he's in.'

'Shame,' she sighed.

'Hang on,' I teased. 'I thought you were totally mesmerised by Juan.'

'I am,' she assured. 'But there's nothing wrong with a bit of window shopping,' she added carelessly. 'And having met Milo Soren previously, I can attest that he is very easy on the eye. Don't you agree?'

I gave an indifferent shrug.

'If you like that sort of thing,' I said vaguely.

Thankfully the grey light hid my giveaway blushes. I let my hair fall across my face as I locked up the studio. The last thing I wanted was Lisa seeing my flaming cheeks, or I'd never hear the end of it.

'Still, you must agree' – she persisted – 'it must be thrilling having a gorgeous guy on your doorstep.'

'Not especially,' I said, as Lisa opened the garden gate. We stepped out onto Starlight Lane and headed off, Cindy trotting obediently to heel. 'As you said, he's my landlord. Nothing more, nothing less.'

'A bloody sexy landlord though, eh!' said Lisa throatily. 'Just imagine. There you are. Sitting on your sofa-cum-bed. Watching telly. Minding your own business. And then' – she glanced at me with huge eyes – 'a humungous spider parachutes down from the ceiling. It sends you into such a tizzy, you shriek loudly. And then Milo dashes along the garden path and bursts in, demanding to know what's wrong. You're now standing on the sideboard with your skirts hitched up. You say' – she adopted a silly voice – '*Oh, Milo. Thank goodness you're here. There's a huge spider. On my bed.* And Milo will give you a smouldering look before declaring, *Fear not, Tilly. I am at your service.* And then he'd dispose of the spider... and service you.'

She guffawed loudly at this imagined situation, blissfully unaware that I'd already had several scenarios play out in my head ever since Milo had handed over the key.

'Yes, well, that isn't going to happen,' I tutted, suppressing a shudder at the idea of an eight-legged visitor descending from the rafters. 'And even if it did, I have Cindy to protect me. She's ace at catching spiders.'

There's something very satisfying about flattening them with one's paw.

'Well don't let on to Milo,' said Lisa. 'Sometimes it's good to show your vulnerable side. I think men like that. It makes them feel macho and protective. Also, you could do a lot worse than him.'

'Oh, *please*,' I said, rolling my eyes. 'Don't go all Mills and Boon on me.'

'But you have to admit' – she was thoughtful now – 'it is rather opportunist.'

'I'm not listening to this,' I declared.

'Think about it, Tilly,' she said, suddenly excited. 'You're single. He's single.'

'*La la la*,' I sang, sticking my fingers in my ears.

'Oh, have it your way,' she huffed, as the pub came into view.

'I know you mean well,' I said, patting her forearm. 'But

realistically I'm not ready for romance. Not sure I ever will be.'

'Don't be so negative,' Lisa chided, as we approached the pub's main door. She went on through. 'Ooh, this is nice.' She gave the cosy interior the once over. 'And there's a table right by the wood burner. Lovely!'

She made her way over to it and pulled out a chair. It was the same place I'd sat with Milo when he'd offered me his studio. With a pang of wistfulness, I followed her and sat down.

Chapter Fifty-One

The pub was relatively quiet. There was no sign of young Polly.

Instead, a middle-aged woman – a dead ringer for Bette Lynch – was emptying a commercial undercounter dishwasher. She had one heavily made-up eye on the freshly washed glassware, and the other on Lisa and me as we took off our jackets.

'I'll go and get the menus,' I said, before heading over to the blonde.

This must be Cilla. I remembered Polly mentioning the pub landlady. Someone who could be quite opinionated. A force to be reckoned with.

'Hello.' I smiled nervously. 'Me and my friend would like to eat here, if that's okay.'

'Of course it is, love,' she said. The stern features suddenly relaxed into a smile.

'Tilly,' Lisa fog horned. 'Don't forget to order a bottle of house wine.'

'Tilly,' Cilla repeated. She looked thoughtful. 'That's quite an unusual name. Would you be the lady that's moved in with Milo?'

I immediately blushed.

'Er, as such,' I said, my colour deepening. 'I'm renting his studio for a bit. Until I find my own place.'

'I see,' said Cilla. 'Well good luck with the house hunting.'

'Thank you,' I said, willing my complexion to return to its usual *pale and interesting.* Or *washed out,* as Robin used to say.

'Red or white?' Cilla asked. She indicated the display of wines.

'White, please.'

'Here are the options.' She held out a couple of laminated menus. 'On the board over there' – she jerked her head at a wall – 'are today's specials. I can vouch for the lamb.' She gave a satisfied nod. 'Local meat. Grass fed. High welfare.'

'Good to know,' I whispered.

Oh dear. Presumably the *tender rack of ribs in a rich wine jus* had, until recently, enjoyed grazing in one of Starlight Croft's fields. I squinted at the chalkboard. Perhaps, instead, I'd go for the seabass.

'Sit down, love,' said Cilla. 'I'll bring the wine over in a sec.'

'Thanks,' I said, taking the menus from her.

I weaved my way through the tables, then flopped down opposite Lisa.

'I can see why you've been charmed by this village,' she said, leaning back in her chair. She gave a sigh of contentment. 'If this pub is anything to go by, this this village is very' – she screwed up her face, seeking the right word –

'calming.'

'It is,' I nodded.

'And after today, you want all the calm you can get.'

I sighed gustily.

'Too right.' I shook my head sadly. 'What the heck has happened to my life? I don't recognise it anymore.'

'New beginnings,' she said sagely. 'They come to us all at some point. But flipping heck, girl.' She put one elbow on the table, then rested her chin in the palm of her hand. 'That's quite secret you hid away. To think you spent *decades* hiding it.' She blew out her cheeks, and her elbow briefly wobbled. 'How come you never mentioned it to me?'

I shook my head again.

'I couldn't. There's a part of me that looks back on that time in disbelief. Like it happened to someone else. And there's another part' – I gulped – 'where it seems like it happened yesterday.' My eyes suddenly threatened to spurt more tears.

'Don't break down,' said Lisa in alarm. 'Not here. Sorry, Tilly. I didn't mean to upset you all over again.'

'Oh, my tear ducts haven't come close to emptying.' I gave her a watery smile, then blinked rapidly. 'Panic ye not,' I joked weakly. 'I'll save them for later. When I'm on my own.'

'You need to heal,' she murmured. 'Heads up. The wine is on its way.'

We both stopped talking as Cilla delivered two glasses and the house white.

'Ladies,' she said, setting the bottle and flutes down.

'Ready to order?'

'Oh, erm…' I trailed off, hastily looking at the menu.

'The lamb for me,' said Lisa.

That sounds delicious, said a voice from under the table. *And just to remind you, I haven't yet eaten, and it's not fair that I should have to watch you.*

'Make that two.' I'd give the lion's share of the meat to Cindy.

'And plenty of mint sauce,' Lisa added.

'Coming right up,' Cilla smiled, before heading back to the bar.

Lisa reached for the bottle and set about pouring. She gave me a sly look.

'I must say, Tilly, I thought I was daring popping my cherry at sixteen.' She pushed the glass towards me, then filled the second. 'But you were light years ahead of me.' She put down the bottle, took a sip from her own glass, then regarded me thoughtfully. 'If you don't mind me saying, Tilly, you don't look the type.'

'Thanks.' I pulled a face, before taking a glug of wine. Not bad. I took another sip. 'And do, please, enlighten me on what *type* loses their virginity before sixteen?'

'Well, you know' – she shrugged apologetically – 'bad girls. Not girls like you who were nicely brought up.'

'Don't be so stereotypical,' I chided. 'You don't have to be a bad girl to do what I did. Just an idiotic girl.' I rubbed my eyes with the heel of one hand. 'A foolish girl,' I added. 'As I said to Jake. God' – I groaned – 'what must he think of me?'

'I think he's simply grateful to know some personal history,' said Lisa gently. 'He didn't look particularly shocked to discover that his biological mother had been little more than a child herself.'

'I wish things had been different,' I said sadly. 'In today's world, it *would* have been different.'

'You think?' Lisa mused. 'Do you honestly believe your mum would have said, "Oh, Tilly, darling. I'll look after Baby while you go to school." I'm not so sure. Didn't she have her own job to hold down?'

'Yes,' I nodded. 'And two wages were required. My parents were never poor, but they weren't wealthy either. Finances were always a juggling act. I was an only child because they couldn't afford to have another one, much less a grandkid.'

'So, there you go. Being a teenage mum would never have worked.'

I closed my eyes. Blocked out the pub. Mentally returned to a delivery ward from long ago. Saw myself holding a newborn in my arms. And once again I remembered a flood of maternal feelings that, even now, were impossible to put into words. I opened my eyes again. Looked at Lisa.

'I just wish the timing had been different. That it had happened with Robin, instead. I'd have given anything to be a mum.'

Lisa reached across the table and patted my hand.

'But Tilly' – she said gently – 'you *are* a mum. You always have been.'

I stared at her blankly. Her words rattled around my brain, then landed with a clatter in my heart. By God, Lisa was right. My expression changed to one of astonishment and delight.

There were many ways of being a mother. I might not have had the joy of raising Jake, but he'd started his life in *my* belly. For nine precious months it had been *my* body that had hugged him. Nurtured him. *My* body that had been a vessel for his. It had nourished him. Protected him. And finally, when he'd been delivered into the world, I'd given this precious gift to someone who hadn't been able to do what my body had done. The fact that this unknown woman had then been able to give everything that the teenage Tilly hadn't, was irrelevant.

It had been *me* who'd given Jake the gift of life. And despite being told to forget… to deny… now the glorious truth was out! Lisa had hit the proverbial nail on the head. I was indeed a mum. And nobody could take that away from me.

I raised my glass to my bestie. Gave her a tremulous smile.

'Cheers.'

Chapter Fifty-Two

Lisa, Cindy and I returned to Milo's studio a couple of hours later.

Having now eaten at the Starlight Arms and engaged in a bit of chit-chat with Cilla, I left the pub feeling like I'd made another new friend. It was such a shame there were no properties currently for sale in the village.

'I'm not going to linger,' said my bestie, when we reached the garden gate. 'You look worn out, so I'll take myself off. I suggest you have an early night.'

I looked at Lisa blearily.

'Honestly? I can't wait to get into bed.'

'Good girl.' She flung her arms around me and gave me a big hug. 'You've had an emotionally exhausting day.'

'That's an understatement. Look, Lisa…' I hesitated.

'What?'

'Can I beg a favour?'

'Sure. Spit it out.'

'This revelation today… Jake… a long ago secret…'

'Yes?'

'Well, I know the cat is out of the bag at work, but I'd rather leave it there, if you don't mind.' I nodded my head meaningfully at Starlight Cottage. 'I don't want my new landlord knowing. Milo and I didn't get off to the greatest of starts. It's only recently that a thaw took place between us. He might wonder what sort of hussy is inhabiting his studio if he knew the truth.'

'I'm sure he wouldn't judge you, Tilly.'

'Maybe not, but I'd prefer the subject to remain private. I'm still coming to terms with it myself. As it is, the thought of facing everyone at work on Monday makes me feel queasy. I mean, what will Leslie say when the office gossip reaches his ears?'

'Today's news is tomorrow's fish and chip paper,' said Lisa firmly. 'And anyway, if anyone is indiscreet, I'll spread some other gossip.' She tapped the side of her nose. 'You're not the only one who has been keeping secrets.'

'Eh?' My brows knitted. 'What do you know that I don't?

She tapped the side of her nose for a second time.

'A ticking time bomb, that's what,' she declared. 'Something that would take the spotlight of attention right off you.'

'I don't believe you,' I tutted. 'Listen, you can't make things up about people. Spreading rumours and telling porky pies is wrong.'

'It wouldn't be porky pies,' she assured. 'Do you remember when I walked in on Leslie picking his nose?'

'Lisa, our boss picking his nose is hardly headline gossip.'

'It is,' she said indignantly. 'Especially when I said to him, "Leslie, is that a bogey on your finger?" and he said, "No it'*snot*. Snot, geddit?' she guffawed. 'Ha! Made you laugh! But seriously, I do know a *real* secret.' She looked about furtively, as if the entire staff of Home and Hearth might be lurking. 'Ready for this one?' She lowered her voice to a dramatic whisper. 'Candace and Leslie are having a ding-dong.'

'Stop it,' I said, clicking my tongue.

'It's true!' she exclaimed.

I looked my bestie's face. Earnest expression. Eyes wide. Blimey, she *was* telling the truth. Flipping heck. Candace and Leslie were both married – and not to each other.

'How long have you been hugging that bit of information?' I gasped.

'Since we were in his office this afternoon.'

'You've lost me,' I said, confused.

'Remember when I went to the drinks cabinet to get us all a brandy? Well, there was a love letter posted between two of the bottles. One corner of the note was poking out. I could see some of the words, and recognised Candace's loopy writing. So, I was nosy and read it.'

'What did it say?' I breathed.

'Naughty things,' Lisa winked. 'Darling Leslie, you melt me into a puddle in my panties…'

'Don't,' I snorted, clutching my mouth.

'… enjoy your meeting this afternoon and grab my boob when you're ready…'

'You're winding me up,' I said, snorting again.

'… lots of love from Randy Candy, your personal supplier of sugar tits.'

I burst out laughing.

'You cannot be serious,' I said. 'I mean, not really.'

'You'd better believe it,' said Lisa. She made a criss-cross over her heart. 'Who would have thought, eh? Sweet Candace with her tweed skirts and cardigans buttoned up to her windpipe. Nor Leslie, with his horn-rimmed glasses, and picking his nose when he thinks nobody is looking.'

'Blimmin heck,' I said, blowing out my cheeks. 'I'm gobsmacked.'

'Indeedy. And let's hope their respective spouses don't find out. Otherwise Home and Hearth will be seeing a completely different drama – which will make Jake's appearance positively tame.'

'Having been on the cuckolded end of an office romance myself, my heart goes out to their spouses. How are we going to look Leslie and Candace in the eye again?'

'Quite easily,' said Lisa firmly. 'Especially when it comes to Leslie and our annual salary reviews. Let's put it this way' – she smiled wickedly – 'if he trots out guff about poor targets being the reason for no pay rise, I might ask if he likes his tits with one sugar or two.'

'You wouldn't,' I gasped.

'Tilly, you are my best friend and I love you loads, but you are sometimes incredibly naïve.'

'Don't remind me,' I said sagely. 'I have thirty-four-year-old son to prove it.'

Chapter Fifty-Three

After Lisa had gone, I had a long leisurely shower. The water rained over my head, washing away the day's unexpected shocks and surprises.

When I emerged from the bathroom in pyjamas and a towel turban, it was to find Cindy sprawled out on the sofa-cum-bed.

'You'll have to make room for me later,' I warned. 'That space is not exclusively yours.'

Cindy opened one eye.

I'll budge up when you're ready to get under the duvet. Anyway, you can't go to bed with wet hair. You'll soak the pillow.

'I'll have a soaked pillow anyway,' I sighed. 'I want the luxury of an undisturbed fit of crying.'

About Jake?

'Of course about Jake,' I sighed again. I went to the sideboard. Rummaged within. Extracted the hairdryer. Found a handy electrical socket. 'I'm appalled that everyone at work now knows my secret.' I stood in front of the mirror and switched on the hairdryer. 'Apart from my boss,' I shouted over the noise. 'But it won't take long for him to find out. Talk about dying of embarrassment.'

Never mind that. How did you feel?

'What do you mean?'

How did you feel when this stranger told you he was your son?

I considered the question while the dryer whooshed my hair about.

'I couldn't take it in,' I answered. 'Not at first. And yet, perversely, I knew immediately who he was. I felt it here.' I touched my heart with my free hand. 'It was weird. Devastating. Shattering. But, embarrassment aside, I'm also feeling so happy, Cindy.'

I'm pleased for you. You've been burdened for too long. Your mum and dad wanted to forget it ever happened and encouraged you to do the same. But you know what?

'I know what you're going to say.' I looked at my dog, enjoying this imaginary – but therapeutic – conversation.

The truth will always out.

'Indeed,' I agreed. 'And you know what else?'

What?

'I'm glad. It's a relief. And Cindy, you should see Jake. He is so handsome. I know I'm probably biased, but he really is. All those times I saw him outside the shop window, I thought he looked familiar. And now I know why. He is so like Nicholas. But I can see me in him too. The shape of his face. His eyebrows.'

And where is Nicholas?

I bit my lip.

'I don't know.' I paused to brush some tangled hair. 'Now that I've got over the initial shock of being reunited with my son, Nicholas has been on my mind. Ever since Jake revealed who he was, so many questions have been tumbling over and over in my head.

Such as?

'Like… where is Nicholas? Will I see him again? How do I feel about that possibility? Is he married? Has he had kids?'

And what if he's not married? Cindy mused. *And what if you both met up and fell in love all over again?*

'That thought did fleetingly occur to me,' I confessed. 'But, that said, I'm not convinced we were ever *in love* in the first place. We were *kids*, for goodness' sake. What do teenagers know of love?'

Some people would say "plenty". After all, you hear stories of childhood sweethearts growing old together.

'You do,' I said, with a pang of sadness.

It was all very well revisiting the past and wondering what might have been. Whether – pregnancy aside – Nicholas and I might have been childhood sweethearts who went on to grow old together. But I also knew that the odds were likely on us fizzling out. That we'd have moved on. As youngsters so often do.

I fell silent, concentrating on finishing my blow-dry. Eventually, when my hair fell in a smooth sheet past my shoulders, I pulled the plug from the socket.

'I have other questions too,' I said to Cindy as I wound the flex around the dryer.

Tell me.

'About Jake's adoptive parents. Like… who were they?

I'd have particularly loved to meet the woman who raised him. Would I have liked her? Would she have been a kindred spirit? What did she look like? What – for that matter – did they *both* look like?'

Perhaps, if you ask Jake, he can show you some photographs.

'Yes,' I said thoughtfully. 'Yes, I'm sure you're right.'

At that moment there was a knock on the door. Cindy leapt off the sofa-cum-bed and gave a warning woof.

'Only me,' said a familiar voice.

Milo.

And despite feeling peaky and worn out, a frisson of excitement rippled down my spine. Cindy was still waiting by the door, now slowly wagging her tail.

'C-Coming,' I stuttered, reaching for my ancient dressing gown. I needed to cover my awful pyjamas. 'Two ticks,' I dithered. Was it possible to shimmy into a little black dress and add full makeup in a matter of seconds?

Don't be ridiculous, Mum. Hurry up and let Milo in.

'Yes,' I muttered, hastening to the door. 'I don't need to impress him anyway. Not that I could, even if I wanted to. After all, this is a man who is king when it comes to swiping right.'

I opened the door.

'Hey!' I pasted a welcoming smile on my face. What I lacked in glamour, could be made up for in warmth.

'God,' was Milo's opening gambit. 'You look how I feel.'

I dropped the smile.

'Thanks,' I said, taken aback.

'No offence meant,' said Milo. He gave my scruffy robe the once over. 'I popped by to apologise for not being here when you arrived. It's been a bit of a day.' He pulled a face. 'Work,' he explained. 'And kids,' he added. 'Well, just the one, but' – he grimaced – 'it doesn't matter how old they are, they're always a worry.'

I gave him a look of sympathy.

'I've had a bit of a day too.'

'Sorry to hear that. I was going to ask you if you fancied a drink at the pub, but I can see you're ready for bed. Bit early, isn't it?'

'Oh, that's kind of you. But yes, I am ready for bed. And anyway, I've already been to the pub. With my buddy, Lisa,' I added. 'For various reasons, our boss let us leave the office sooner rather than later. Lisa helped me move my stuff in, and then we had something to eat at the Starlight Arms. I met Cilla, the landlady.'

'And survived!' Milo smiled. 'Cilla is terrifying.'

'A little bit,' I admitted.

'Do you fancy a nightcap at the cottage?' Milo asked. Was it my imagination, or was there hope in his eyes. 'I haven't eaten yet and as JJ has naffed off I wouldn't mind some company while rustling up beans on toast.'

I hesitated. The thought of spending one-to-one time with Milo was making my heart do more dives than a Red Arrows plane. However, I felt hideously gauche in my nightwear.

'That would be nice,' I said. 'Give me a moment to get

changed.'

'Don't be daft,' said Milo. 'Come as you are. Who is there to impress?'

You.

'No one,' I agreed.

Chapter Fifty-Four

'Bring Cindy with you,' said Milo. 'She can keep Rambo company.'

Try stopping me, smirked Cindy. *I detect chemistry between you and your landlord, and I want to be there to witness it firsthand.*

'Don't be ridiculous,' I said aloud.

Milo looked startled.

'Why, is it a problem?'

'S-Sorry, I was talking to Cindy,' I stuttered. 'I thought she…'

'Said something?' said Milo curiously.

'I thought she woofed,' I said lamely.

'Woof,' Cindy obliged.

'L-Like that. Anyway, I'm probably hearing things. Had the hairdryer on earlier.' I slapped the side of my head with one hand. 'Blimmin thing. It always upsets my hearing. Tinnitus,' I explained, giving my head another slap. 'Ah, that's better. Gone.'

'I thought sufferers heard ringing, not barking,' said Milo, looking baffled.

'Oh, they hear all sorts,' I nodded emphatically. 'Growling. Buzzing. But, yes, you're right, it's mostly ringing.'

'How unpleasant.'

'Um, yes, it can be.'

'Have you seen a doctor about it?'

'Er, no. I once called the Tinnitus Association. It rang unanswered,' I joked feebly. Dear God, could we just get off the subject of my hearing. 'Anyway' – I stepped out into the garden and followed Milo – 'let's have that nightcap. You can tell me all about your awful day.'

'I'd rather hear about yours,' said Milo, as Cindy bounded ahead. 'It must have been ten times worse than mine for you to look so haggard.'

'Gee, you know how to make a girl feel good, don't you!'

Terrific. Nothing like being reminded how awful you looked. Oh, so what, Tilly? Just enjoy his company and going inside this fabulous cottage again.

'Sorry,' Milo apologised. 'Martha was always saying I lacked a sensitivity chip. Let me rephrase that. You look a little wan' – he unlocked the cottage's backdoor – 'but your natural beauty is undiminished.'

'Thanks,' I mumbled, embarrassed by the beauty comment, but also a tiny bit thrilled.

As we stepped inside, Rambo greeted us. The little dog looked bug eyed. He'd obviously been fast asleep.

'Out you go, boy,' said Milo. 'Go and do a wee and then I'll feed you.'

'Has he been on his own all day?' I asked, astonished at the strength of Rambo's bladder.

'No,' Milo shook his head. 'Hetty Cartwright has a key to the cottage. She kindly walks Rambo around lunchtime. I give her a tenner. She's happy to top up her pension for some cash in hand. She has Shep, of course. However, he's also a working dog, so gets plenty of exercise. Hetty likes taking Rambo up to the duck pond and back, before retiring to the pub for a gossip with Cilla and her cronies. On other days, she visits the Strawberry Shed for a coffee and pastry with Linda, and Rambo gets to hoover up all the crumbs. He loves all the attention from customers. Then Hetty brings him home again leaving him to sleep off his snacks and dream about doing it all over again the following day. I swear my dog is disappointed at weekends when he only has me for company. Anyway' – Milo waved a hand at a tall stool in the kitchen area – 'take a pew.'

I perched while Milo went to the sink, washed his hands, then located a tin of baked beans from the larder. One of the dogs scratched at the door.

'I'll let them in,' I said, hopping down from the stool.

'Thanks,' said Milo. He was now peering into the depths of the refrigerator. 'Damn,' he groaned. 'I could have sworn I had some bread in here.'

'I'd offer to give you some of mine' – I said as the dogs scampered in from the garden – 'but I've yet to do a shop. That was another reason for me eating out earlier. The cupboard was bare.' I shut the backdoor then joined Milo by the fridge. 'Oh, look,' I pointed. 'You have plenty of eggs. And cheese. What about whisking up an omelette?'

Milo looked appalled.

'But that would mean cooking.'

I raised an eyebrow.

'You call making an omelette *cooking*?'

'Yes. Don't you?'

'No,' I snorted. 'Good heavens. How on earth do two men living together survive?'

'With a microwave for frozen ready meals,' he explained. 'However' – he pulled open the freezer door revealing empty shelves – 'like you, I need to do a shop.'

'Move out the way,' I tutted. 'I'll make you a cheese omelette.' I gave him a gentle prod, ignoring the zinger that shot through my finger. 'Three eggs okay?'

'Perfect,' said Milo. 'I'll sort out our drinks.'

Well, really, Mum, said Cindy, hovering at my heels. *Nothing like taking over his kitchen and bossing him around. You'll be telling him to peel some vegetables next.*

I would if he had any, I retorted silently.

Don't forget to give me some cheese, said Cindy, as I extracted a packet from the fridge.

And me, said Rambo.

Oh, terrific, Tilly. Not only do you witter away to your mongrel, but you're also now having a conversation with a chihuahua.

Milo set a glass down on the worktop. Hello again, brandy! He perched on the same tall stool I'd vacated. I took a quick sip of my drink, then opened the tin of beans and set about whisking the eggs.

'Ah, that's good,' said Milo, taking a glug of his brandy.

'Thanks,' I said, nodding at my own glass. 'That's the

second one today' – I confessed before jokily adding – 'I try not to make a habit of it.' I tipped the beaten eggs into a frying pan. The mixture met hot oil. For a moment there was only the sound of sizzling. I reached for my brandy again, then pointed to the dogs. 'Is it okay with you if Rambo has a small piece of cheddar?'

'Be my guest,' Milo shrugged. 'Rambo isn't lactose intolerant; in case you were wondering.'

'Good.' I broke off two pieces of cheese and gave it to the dribbling dogs. 'I should have called Cindy *Gromit*,' I laughed. 'After Wallace's Gromit, who also adored cheese.' I turned back to the pan.

'Wallace and Gromit!' Milo exclaimed. His face was suddenly wreathed in smiles. 'Those two characters take me back a bit. I loved their films.

'Me too,' I confessed, crumbling cheddar into the pan.

'In fact, I have all the DVDs.'

'You still have DVDs?' I said in amazement.

'Yup,' Milo grinned. 'And don't tell anyone' – he made a show of looking about furtively – 'but I also have a DVD player *and* it's in full working order.'

'Is that so?' I teased. 'In which case, what are we waiting for?'

Milo let out a whoop and jumped off the stool.

'*The Wrong Trousers* okay?' he asked, opening a drawer by the television.

'Perfect,' I said happily.

I flipped the omelette, folded it in half, then slid it onto a plate along with the baked beans. Dumping the pans in the sink, I blasted them with hot water to soak. 'Here,' I said, turning to Milo. I handed him the plate of food, along with a knife and fork.

'Want to share?' he asked, taking the meal from me.

'No, I'm not hungry.' I picked up my brandy. Seconds later, I'd flopped down on the sofa next to Milo.

Careful, Tilly. Don't be overfamiliar. He's not your partner.

I shifted my backside a few inches away from him, then ran my fingers over the sofa fabric.

'I can't help noticing that you bought the cottage fully furnished.'

'Would have been madness not to,' said Milo. He forked up food with one hand and, with the other, made a long arm for the remote control. 'The vendor's wife had excellent taste.'

'She did,' I agreed. 'Do you know, I had dreams about sitting on this sofa in front of the wood burner on a cold evening.'

'The wood burner!' Milo cried, startling me. He chucked down the remote and put his plate to one side. 'Don't let the dogs scoff my dinner.'

'What are you doing?' I frowned.

'Your wish is my command,' he said, hunkering down in front of the burner. It had been pre-laid with scrunched-up newspaper and kindling. Picking up a box of matches from the hearth, he set fire to yesterday's headlines. As everything turned into a leaping orange ball, he plucked a log from the recess and added it to the flames. 'Ta da!' he exclaimed, before returning to the sofa and picking up his plate again. 'Ready?' Once more, he pointed the remote at the telly.

'Ready,' I confirmed, as the theme tune burst into life.

Suddenly, the room was filled with the sound of wind instruments parp-parping a catchy melody that perfectly depicted the two charming characters.

I sighed happily, sat back, and relaxed.

Chapter Fifty-Five

So much for thinking I was going to spend the night bawling into my pillow over a long-ago secret. That original plan had changed dramatically.

Instead, I was comfortably ensconced on a sofa. Next to me, was a goodlooking man. Together we were watching a classic animated film. The dogs were now stretched out in front of the burner's flickering flames. They heaved contented sighs and closed their eyes.

Milo, sitting alongside me, shifted his weight. He set down his empty dinner plate on the floor. As he moved back, was it my imagination or was he sitting a tad closer? Certainly, his leg was now brushing against mine.

With a trembling hand, I sipped my brandy and tried to ignore the warmth from his body. The touch of his thigh. The thrilling zingers. My pulse quickened and my breathing became shallower. It was a struggle to focus on the film.

Milo roared with laughter. I joined in, taking the opportunity to suck air into my lungs, because breathing properly was becoming a problem – to the point of feeling lightheaded.

Seriously flustered, I chucked the remainder of the brandy down my neck and tried to concentrate on the film.

A pistol-happy penguin was causing mayhem, while Gromit clung to a runaway train with Wallace's lampshade on his head. Wallace, meanwhile, was travelling at high speed on a parallel train track. He looked across at Gromit and begged for help. I identified with his inner panic. Whether it was the alcohol, the heat from Milo, or a genuine lack of oxygen, my emotions were spiralling out of control.

I wanted to tap Milo on the shoulder, tell him to forget all about the penguin and instead pucker up with the chick sitting beside him. Should I tell Milo that when a penguin found its mate, they stayed together for life? I wondered what he'd say if I asked him to be my penguin.

He'd think you'd lost the plot.

Cindy had opened her eyes and was staring at me. I met her gaze.

Go to sleep, I silently retorted.

I'm worried you're going to make a prize berk of yourself.

I ignored her. After all, it wasn't really my dog talking. It was my inner voice. The conscience. Or, well, something like that.

Meanwhile, how could I get Milo to think about me in the same way as his swipe-right ladies? Perhaps I could try chatting him up…

My name is Tilly, but you can call me *Tonight*.

Or…

I want to be your handbag, so I never leave your side.

Although Milo was male. He'd hardly have a handbag. Maybe a manbag? Or perhaps a briefcase? But then again, if a man took his briefcase everywhere, that would be a bit odd. Okay, Tilly. Forget the briefcase. What about…

You want to know who's the sexiest man on the planet? Let me repeat that first word!

Or… what about a *knock knock* joke?

Knock knock…

Who's there?

Tilly…

Tilly who?

Tilly who wants you to kiss you. Snog you. Ravish you…

I giggled tipsily to myself just as Milo laughed again at the penguin's antics. I caught a waft of his aftershave. Closed my eyes. Breathed it in. Mm. Heavenly.

Eyes tightly shut, I inhaled again. God it was divine. Just like him. Another deep breath. Such a divine man. And breathe. Divine thighs. Breathe again. Divine hotness. One more deep breath. Divine zingers.

I wriggled contentedly on the sofa. Sighed heavily. Took one more deep breath – only to have sleep unexpectedly claim me.

Chapter Fifty-Six

I awoke to grey light. I blinked blearily in the gloom and, for a moment, puzzled where I was.

This wasn't the bedroom I shared with my husband. Correction, ex-husband. Neither was I in Lisa's lounge. Nor was this the pullout bed in Milo's studio. And then I groaned.

Of course. Milo and I had been watching a funny film together. Well, until I'd flaked out. How very remiss of me. And where *was* Milo?

At the thought of him, I sat bolt upright and experienced a bit of a head rush. A cosy throw slid off my body. I made a cartoon arm and yanked it back over me. Evidently Milo had put it over me after I'd – how embarrassing – crashed out on his shoulder.

I had absolutely no recollection as to how he'd eased himself out from under my weight. Please God that I hadn't been snoring in his ear. Or dribbling on his shoulder.

I snuggled back under the throw again, grateful that he'd covered me up and – oh, God, had he undressed me too?

A quick peek under the cover revealed my attire. Scruffy pyjamas. Tatty dressing gown. Ah, yes. It was all coming back to me now. Upon my arrival at Starlight Cottage, I'd already been dressed for bed.

The wood burner had long gone out. Cindy was curled up in front of it, nose tightly tucked under her forearm as if to keep her muzzle warm. Rambo was lying on his back. He had all four paws in the air and was snoring his head off. For a little dog, he made quite a racket. He wriggled in his sleep, made a snuffling noise, then broke wind. Oh, *poo*, Rambo.

I flapped my blanket about, trying to waft away the putrid smell of eau-de-parp. As I did so, a yawning Milo came into the lounge.

Oh, terrific, Tilly. The room stinks and you're wafting the throw about as if you're the guilty party.

'Morning,' I gasped. I dropped the cover and scooted out of bed. Dashing over to the kitchen area, I threw open the window. 'It's very stuffy in here,' I gabbled as a gale force wind entered the room. The gusts ruffled a plant on the worktop, then swirled round my ankles. Under my dressing gown, a rash of goosebumps broke out on my skin.

'Stuffy?' Milo blinked at me owlishly. 'Shut the window, Tilly. I'm freezing my nuts off.'

At the mention of his nuts, my eyes automatically dropped to his groin. However, his privates were covered by a casual navy-blue dressing gown. He looked like a celebrity. An icon who'd invited a glossy magazine inside his home to photograph some behind-the-scenes moments.

And here we have superstar Milo Soren relaxing at home as he waits for personal assistant Tilly to make his morning coffee – freshly ground Italian beans, naturally, that epitomise the true essence of coffee culture. Milo wears his favourite Dolce and Gabbana robe accessorised with a pair of Versace leopard slippers to channel his inner tiger – grrrr! – while Tilly models vintage sleepwear with a fashionably distressed hemline and must-have hole to the left pocket.

Teeth chattering, I slammed the window shut. Hopefully the rush of air into the room had diffused Rambo's whiffy fart.

'I'm so sorry for falling asleep on your sofa,' I gibbered. 'Whatever must you think?'

'That you were exhausted,' he shrugged.

Milo gave a huge, noisy yawn, extending his arms high into the air. For a moment I was privy to a pair of waggling tonsils and a very pink tongue. The dressing gown lifted as he stretched. My eyes were immediately drawn to his lower legs. They were nicely muscled and covered in enough dark hair to make my sap unexpectedly rise.

Robin's legs had been at odds with the rest of his body. Almost hairless. Like a woman's. Too skinny. And too pale. Whereas Milo's were perfect. Muscular calves. Beautifully defined. Gorgeous biscuit-coloured skin. It had me wondering what the rest of his legs looked like. I had a sudden vision of strong thighs worthy of a professional footballer. Toned muscles. Lots of definition. And more dark hair. Nice.

My insides seemed to be melting. I leant back against the worktop. Casually flung my arms out – although in truth it was to keep me propped up. The thought of Milo's hairy legs was having a disastrous effect on me.

Milo finished stretching. As his arms flopped back to his sides, the robe gaped open revealing his chest. Holy Moly.

Just look at those pecs. And – I nearly groaned aloud – chest hair. Lovely. I was a total sucker for it. Especially when it was dark. No doubt it led all the way down his torso. Culminated in a sexy little snail trail. I could feel myself getting awfully hot, and it was nothing to do with being peri menopausal.

But wait. Milo was staring at me intently. And… yes… he was moving towards me. Oh wow, there was a definite *look* on his face. One that informed he was *a man on a mission.* As the distance between us closed, I gazed at him lustfully.

Omigod. What was he going to do? Scoop me into his arms? Lift me up and emulate that scene from *An Officer and a Gentleman*? Be my Richard Gere to his Debra Winger? And would he then stride manfully over to the sofa as Joe Cocker crooned the lyrics that every woman of a certain age knew by heart?

I shrank back against the worktop. Wow. My romantic life was about to take an upward turn. In that moment I knew exactly what Candace had meant in her puddly love note to Leslie.

I closed my eyes in anticipation of Milo's lips meeting mine, and mentally crossed my fingers that I had kitten breath rather than doggy halitosis.

My eyes pinged open again when Milo strode straight past me. Rather than his hands grabbing me, they were instead unlocking the backdoor. Once again, air swirled around my ankles as the man accomplished *his mission* and gave Cindy and Rambo their marching orders.

'Right you two. Wee wees.'

Chapter Fifty-Seven

The dogs shot out into the garden to do their business while Milo levered open a tin of dog food for Rambo and Cindy to share.

'What do you fancy?' he asked while spooning meaty chunks into two bowls.

You.

Picking up the discarded tin of dog food, I peered at the ingredients.

'Apologies, but meaty chunks isn't how I usually start the day.'

'Ha!' he gave a snort of laughter. 'Me neither. Whiffy or what?'

'Er, yes,' I said, my face flaming. I was still worried about Milo thinking Rambo's fart had been mine. 'Shall I make us some toast?'

'I'd prefer a fry up.'

'Oh,' I said, taken aback. I didn't usually start the day on such close terms with the stove, but no matter. The thought of a Full English made my tummy rumble. 'If that's what you want, sure.'

'But you're not cooking it.'

'Oh, wow,' I teased. 'Does this mean you're taking

charge of the frying pan? If so that's great cooking progress on your part.'

'You assume wrong,' he grinned, as one of the dogs scratched at the backdoor. 'I won't be cooking a meal any time soon.'

He let Cindy and Rambo in. The dogs sat at his feet; their eyes trained on the worktop. Milo picked up the bowls of meaty chunks, then set them down on the floor. They immediately tucked in.

'Get dressed,' he said. 'I'll take you to the Starlight Arms and treat you to sausage, bacon, egg, and a mountain of toast. We'll take the mutts with us. Afterwards, we can walk off our food babies with a hike. So, make sure you put on a sensible pair of walking shoes.' Milo paused. Gave me a questioning look. 'That was rather presumptuous of me. You might already have plans for today. In which case-'

'No, no,' I hastily interrupted. 'No plans.' Other than a trip to the supermarket, an appointment with the laundry basket, and then opening my laptop to look at more properties. But even if I *had* had an arrangement with anyone – Lisa for example – an excuse would have been given. Whether telling a fib about a twisted ankle, or claiming to have galloping dandruff, because nothing – *nothing!* – was going to stop me accepting this man's invitation to spend time with him.

'I was hoping you'd say that,' said Milo.

Hear that, Tilly? He was hoping I'd say yes to his breakfast invitation! And why? Because... well, because he likes your company. And you're great to talk to. Witty.

Interesting. Yes, absolutely. And… and… he also thinks you're attractive. And because – truth be told – he can't bear to let you out of his sight. Indeed. Because he's enthralled with you. Mad about you.

'Why were you hoping I'd say that?' I dared to shyly ask.

'Because I'm bloody starving,' he answered. 'And also, because it's nice to have someone to chat to over the condiments.'

Oka*yyy*. Milo wasn't *quite* on the same page as my fantasy daydream, but that was fine. There was plenty of time to wow him – but not in this naff nightwear.

'Let me get washed and changed,' I said, wondering what I could wear for this impromptu date.

Having wolfed down her breakfast, Cindy padded over. She gave me a look.

It's not a date, Mum.

Well, it could turn into one, I silently retorted.

My heart leapt with excitement. Yes, Tilly. It might indeed lead to a date. A *proper* date. So go and raid your capsule wardrobe. See what glamour you can muster. Obviously, you can't wear a dress. Or a skirt.

Could I possibly get away with jeans? When leaving the marital home, I'd donated much of my stuff to the charity shop. I now owned only two pairs of jeans. One in typical blue denim. The other, black. Both were a decent brand. They were jeans to dress up, rather than down. They might get ruined climbing over stiles with sharp nails poking out of warped wood. Not to mention mud. Ah, yes. Copious amounts of brown goo splattering up the legs.

The sensible thing to wear was my old joggers with fleecy lining. After all, we were still in freezing February. It wouldn't matter if they got snagged on nails or splashed with mud.

I sighed. Joggers and a sweater it would have to be. But with makeup. Yup. Soft kohl to enlarge the eyes. Something glossy for the lips.

Hey, Milo. Do you like my lipstick? It's called Colour Me Cupid.

It was true, I really did have a lipstick by that name. Although why the manufacturer couldn't stick to a sensibly named colour chart was beyond me. I mean, wasn't it easier to refer to the lipstick as *red*?

And perhaps Milo would take one look at my luscious ruby lips, clutch his chest, stagger sideways, and gasp that Cupid had shot him with an arrow, and that the pain could only be alleviated by a lover's kiss. Whereupon I'd launch myself at him and hungrily oblige.

'Back in a mo,' I said, tugging on the backdoor's handle. I nearly dislocated my shoulder in the process.

'Here,' said Milo, stepping forward. He turned the key. 'It helps if you unlock it first.'

Chapter Fifty-Eight

I fairly skipped out of Starlight Cottage. Cindy scampered alongside me. She picked up on my joyful mood and gave several yips of excitement.

Inside the studio, I stripped off my jammies and nightrobe. Dumping them on the sofa, I dashed off to the bathroom to relieve my burgeoning bladder.

Hurry, hurry, my brain chanted as I washed my face, then grabbed my toothbrush.

Ablutions complete, I raked a brush through my hair. Scooping it into a ponytail, I secured it with a scrunchie.

Right, joggers… joggers… where were my joggers? Damn and blast, they were languishing in the laundry basket. No matter. They were only going to get dirty again.

I pulled them out, wrinkling my nose at the smell of stale clothing.

Hurry, hurry. Back to the bathroom.

I plucked a cannister of deodorant from the shelf, then gave the trousers a liberal blast of *Summer Fragrance*. They might look like they'd previously had an encounter with a muddy puddle, but by heck they now smelt good. I gave the fabric a second blast, belatedly catching a hint of pine. Oh dear. That last scented note wasn't dissimilar to toilet cleaner.

Hopping about, I posted my legs into the trousers, found a clean t-shirt, then whipped a sweater over my head. When it came to winter walks, layers were the name of the game.

What next? Makeup. Red lipstick might be nice, but at this hour perhaps too vampish. Better to go for a soft pink. I slicked on some lippy, pressed my lips together, added mascara to my lashes – no time for the kohl – then pinched my cheeks for colour.

I stared at my forty-nine-year-old reflection in the mirror. A worn face gazed back, but overall, it was a huge improvement on yesterday. I wasn't quite so washed out, and the peepers were positively sparkling.

Now, then. What about earrings? I threaded some gold hoops through my ears. Big mistake. They didn't go with the rambler outfit. I quickly replaced them with some simple gold studs. I was just debating whether a necklace would be OTT when there was a knock at the door.

'Coming,' I warbled.

I grabbed Cindy's lead and my hiking boots. Oh Lord, they were plastered in mud. Best to put them on outside. I didn't want to mess up the studio's carpet. I snatched up my coat and Cindy's water bottle – I'd fill it at the pub.

There came a second knock. This time louder. Impatient. Oh, blimey. Mr Soren wasn't up for hanging around.

'Yes, yes, I'm right here,' I sang. 'Just a mo.'

Best to put on the hiking boots now. There was a vacuum in the cupboard. I'd clean up the mess when I was back. Milo wouldn't know. He'd never see it.

I stooped down, rammed my feet into the boots, then hastily began lacing. The panels of my coat kept obscuring my vision. Irked, I straightened up, yanked on the zipper, then bent down again to resume my lacing. Heavens, all this activity was making me terribly hot. It was one thing to be outside in the elements in fleece-lined tracksuit bottoms and quilted overcoat, but another to be indoors doing something of a workout. My body temperature was rising with every passing second.

There came another rap, then another, and then a succession that didn't stop. Blimey, how keen was this guy to see me?

I straightened up, back cracking alarmingly, just as a man's voice demanded that I open up and open up NOW!

I froze in my tracks. That wasn't Milo. With growing unease, I unlocked the door. Opened it a smidge. Peered cautiously through the gap. Then gasped aloud.

'Whatever are you doing here?' I demanded shrilly.

It was Robin.

Chapter Fifty-Nine

'Found you,' my ex-husband declared.

His tone suggested we'd merely been playing hide-and-seek, and that my hiding place had taken a little longer than usual to discover.

'How on earth–?' I began.

'Your ditzy mate,' Robin explained. 'Lisa finally told me where you were after I rang her phone a million times.'

Cheers, Lisa!

Robin glanced about.

'Why are you living in a garden shed in a back-of-beyond village?' He wrinkled his nose. His expression was akin to someone who'd parachuted into the jungle and didn't know how to find their way back to civilisation. 'Are you going to ask me in?' he said testily.

I stared at him in surprise, my mouth a perfect O.

'Er, no,' I said, finding my voice. 'I'm about to go out. With my dog,' I added.

'Woof,' said Cindy. She glared at Robin, hackles raised.

'Fine, fine,' he said, raking one hand through his hair. 'In which case, I'll come with you.'

I gaped at him. Why was my ex-husband in Milo's garden on a Saturday morning, and why was he suggesting we take a walk together?

'Just a moment,' I said irritably. 'First things first. Why are you here?'

'Isn't it obvious?' Robin's tone suggested I was thicker than my ex-mother-in-law's gravy. 'I've come to see you.'

'But why?' I said in bewilderment.

At that moment the backdoor to Starlight Cottage opened. Milo appeared. He had a phone clamped to one ear and was obviously in deep conversation with someone. He waved, and I waved back. Then he held up a hand indicating he'd be another five minutes. I nodded and gave him a thumbs up. He retreated and the backdoor closed again.

'Who was that?' Robin frowned.

'Milo Soren.'

'But who *is* he?' Robin's frown became a scowl.

I folded my arms across my chest.

'Who wants to know?'

'Well, me, obviously. Oh God' – Robin looked momentarily flabbergasted – 'don't tell me that you and Mr Handsome are an item.' His eyebrows promptly met his receding hairline.

I stared at my ex-husband's head in surprise. The chestnut hair was thinner than I remembered, and he was looking decidedly grey at the temples. There were fresh lines around his brown eyes, and the frown marks between his eyebrows had deepened. In fact, he looked rather haggard.

Perhaps his shenanigans with Sexy Samantha were starting to take their toll. Maybe it was a taddy exhausting keeping up with a younger woman.

I had a sudden mental picture of Samantha, sprawled over the dinner table. Announcing she was pudding. Tipping a jug of custard over her boobs. Ordering Robin to lick it all off.

Then the image shifted to my boss. Leslie. And Candace's note. Is that what she did? Chuck a packet of Tate & Lyle over her cleavage, then smirk at Leslie. "A whole new meaning to sugar tits, you lucky boy." And why was I even thinking such weird thoughts on a cold February morning? Had Friday's public shock sent me ever-so-slightly bonkers?

'Will you answer me?' Robin complained. 'Is that man your lover?'

Slack jawed, I glanced fleetingly at Starlight Cottage's backdoor. Please God, don't let Milo have overheard Robin's preposterous suggestion.

'Tilly!' Robin exhorted. 'Enough is enough. I demand you tell me what the hell is going on here. Frankly, I'm appalled. Do you hear me? *Appalled.* Not only is my wife living in a shed, but she's apparently paying her rent with sexual favours and–'

'How *dare* you,' I hissed. Cindy whined in protest. 'My private life is absolutely nothing to do with you. Do you understand?'

'So it's true.' Robin stared at me, his lips becoming a thin line. It was an expression I was familiar with, having been married to him for twenty years. But now it struck me how unattractive it made him look. Mean, even.

Suddenly all the fight seemed to go out of Robin. His body language shifted dramatically. His shoulders slumped.

When he next spoke, his voice was almost inaudible.

'Am I too late?' he whispered.

I gazed at him uncomprehendingly.

'Too late for *what*?'

'Isn't it obvious?' he shrugged. 'I want you back. And this time, I mean it. I really, *really* mean it.'

Chapter Sixty

'Robin...' I trailed off helplessly.

'Yes, darling,' he said. Like a light switch, his words flipped to endearment.

I shook my head, too flabbergasted to find words. But eventually I managed to spit a few out.

'Of course it's too late,' I spluttered. '*Way* too late.'

'But it doesn't have to be,' he quickly countered. 'We can start again. Properly. Move. A new county. A new *country*, if you'd prefer. And you can forget about work. Give it up. I'll sell my half of the business to my partner. Take early retirement. You can be a lady of leisure. Spend your days in, gosh, I don't know' – he spread his hands wide – 'Tuscany. Gazing at the vineyard beyond the kitchen window as you make fresh pasta. Or, if the lingo puts you off, we could go to America. Or, I know' – his face lit up – 'what about Australia? You'd like it there, wouldn't you! They have kangaroos and koala bears. You like fluffy creatures. You'd be in your element.'

I put my head on one side, like Cindy did when trying to work out if I'd said *Do you want a chew,* or *do you want a poo?*

'Robin, I don't want to emigrate–'

'Fine, fine,' Robin placated. 'We'll stay in the UK.'

'And as much as I like kangaroos and koalas, I already have a *fluffy.*'

'Do you?' said Robin in surprise. His gaze shifted to the interior of the studio, as if he might spot a wallaby in front of the television.

'I have a dog,' I pointed out.

'Oh, right. I see,' he nodded. 'It can always be rehomed.'

I scowled.

'My dog is not an *it,* and Cindy will *not* be rehomed-'

'Okay, not a problem.' He put up his hands by way of apology. 'The dog can stay-'

'Because' – this time it was my turn to interrupt – 'you and I are not getting back together.'

'Now don't be hasty, Tilly,' Robin soothed. 'You and I got along very well together. All we need to do is put an unfortunate episode behind us.'

'An unfortunate episode?' I repeated. 'Robin, we are divorced. We have the certificate to prove it – not to mention mutually depleted finances to pay for it. I think those circumstances go way beyond *an unfortunate episode.*'

'Listen,' he implored. 'We wouldn't be the first couple on this planet to remarry-'

'Remarry?' I cried. 'Flaming flipping Nora, Robin. What on earth has come over you?'

'Common sense,' he declared. 'That's what's come over me. And not before time. I think what happened was quite simply a mid-life crisis. Terrible. Awful. Hideous. Even so, I've worked my way through it and know now where my priorities lie. I want to marry you all over again. Please, sweetheart. Think of me as your very own Richard Burton. And you are my Elizabeth Taylor. Or I could be Don Johnson to your Melanie Griffith.'

'Melanie Griffith?' I frowned. 'Wasn't she married to Antonio Banderas?'

My thoughts immediately splintered off to another man who looked like Mr Banderas. A man who wasn't a million miles away either.

'Tilly, I implore you to listen to me – to listen to common sense. To give up this ridiculous' – Robin stumbled for the right word – '*dwelling…* and come home with me. Please. Let me help you pack your stuff. We'll do it together. Right now. I can't wait to have you home again. To hold you tight. I don't think I'll ever let you go again. In fact' – he took a step towards me – 'let me hold you now, Tilly.'

My hand shot up.

'Stop! For heaven's sake, Robin. I've had enough of this nonsense.'

'It is not nonsense,' he protested. 'I told you. It's common sense.'

I folded my arms across my chest.

'And where does Samantha figure in this apparent grand reunion?'

'She doesn't,' said Robin airily. 'She and I are no longer together. We weren't getting along.'

'So she dumped you.' I gave Robin a knowing look.

'It was a mutual decision,' he said, chin jutting. *A mutual decision.* Those famous words from my youth. 'And anyway'

– he continued – 'Samantha is now with someone else.'

'I'm sorry to hear that,' I said. Surprisingly, I felt genuinely sad for my ex-husband. He'd thrown away a twenty-year-old marriage, spent money buying me out, and paid a hefty legal bill. And all for what? To have a fling with a woman young enough to be his daughter. A woman who'd now cast Robin aside like a chewed up old slipper. 'I suppose she's met someone nearer her own age, eh?'

Robin looked momentarily mutinous.

'As it happens, no. She met someone older.'

'Older?' I gasped. 'What, a year or two older?'

He gave a thin smile.

'Try a decade or two. The guy came to me as a client. He was extremely wealthy. He took my tax advice, then he took my girlfriend.'

'Ouch,' I said.

Robin's chin jutted again.

'Good riddance,' he said belligerently. 'Good riddance to gold-digging rubbish. So, Tilly. You and me. Second time lucky, eh?'

Milo chose that moment to emerge from Starlight Cottage, Rambo at his feet.

'Sorry about that,' he said cheerfully, coming over to me and Robin. 'That was JJ checking in.' Milo suddenly noticed the strained look on my face – and the hostile one on Robin's. 'Hello,' he said politely to my ex-husband. Robin didn't deign to reply. 'Everything okay?' said Milo to me.

'Er–'

'My wife is perfectly okay, thank you,' said Robin

proprietarily. He then turned back to me. 'Have a think about what I said, Tilly. Then call me. Preferably when you're on your own,' he added, giving Milo a filthy look.

Without waiting for me to say anything further, Robin turned on his heel and stomped off. The garden gate slammed behind him.

Chapter Sixty-One

'What was all that about?' asked Milo, as the gate reverberated on its hinges.

I leant against the studio's doorframe feeling almost physically winded.

'I don't think you'd believe me,' I said, shaking my head.

'Try me,' said Milo. 'Tell you what, tell me on the way to the pub. Never mind a coffee, you look like you could do with a sharpener.'

'More brandy?' I gave him a wry look before whistling Cindy to heel. 'A fly on the wall might suggest alcohol is figuring too much in my life.' I locked the door, then turned to Milo. 'I'll stick to coffee, but don't let me stop you.'

'Coffee it is,' he grinned as we set off.

I was relieved to see that there was no sign of Robin's car and that he hadn't lingered. A part of me had been anxious about him following Milo and me. Well honestly! What a turn up for the books, and too ridiculous for words.

As we walked along the lane, I told Milo about Robin's proposal. Not just of getting back together, but also remarrying.

'And how do you feel?' said Milo carefully. He was gazing straight ahead.

'You really want to know?' I asked.

'Of course,' he nodded.

'Furious. That's how I feel. Just when I thought I'd moved on in my life, parted with eighty percent of my belongings, downsized to the point that I can fit everything that I own – apart from my car – into a garden studio, my ex-husband turns up and completely rocks my world.'

'Has he?' asked Milo cautiously.

I glanced at him, but he was still staring straight ahead.

'Has he what?' I frowned.

'Rocked your world,' said Milo. 'Such expression suggests you feel all over the place. In other words, not sure which way to turn.'

'I tell you exactly how I feel,' I said, feeling irritated all over again. 'Like a fish that's been happily swimming along, content with life in its pond, going about its fishy business, then suddenly finds itself being hauled out of the water, gasping for breath, before being thrown back again. It's like being completely' – I momentarily struggled to find the word – 'discombobulated.'

'I see,' said Milo. He opened his mouth to say something further, but I cut across him.

'Do you mind if we change the subject?'

'No, not at all,' he said.

'How's your son?' I asked abruptly.

'He's fine,' said Milo, suddenly pensive. 'Well, I think he's fine. He sounded a bit distracted. I suspect he and young Polly have had words.'

'Oh dear,' I sympathised. 'I thought their relationship

was all fresh and shiny and new.'

'Well, quite, but it's still early days,' said Milo hesitantly. 'JJ is now in Prague with a bunch of mates. It's meant to be a stag weekend. Apparently, Polly suggested JJ stay on in Prague after the stag do, and that she flies out on the Monday to join him. I think she was hoping they could enjoy a few days together and do some sightseeing. However, JJ blocked the idea. Unfortunately, Polly has translated it as something else entirely. In her head she believes it isn't a stag weekend. Rather a stag *week*. I guess she's imagining her boyfriend is having a raucous time with his mates, nursing hangovers in the morning and whooping it up at night. The fact that my son couldn't tell me precisely when he's coming home does suggest that he's not being entirely honest with Polly. However, it's not my relationship to comment upon.'

'Oh dear,' I said, secretly thinking that JJ seemed a bit of a lad. He sounded a little selfish not being upfront with Polly, even if they had only recently got together. 'Why are relationships so tricky?' I said gloomily.

'Because they require us to change and evolve,' said Milo. 'Each person has their own perspectives, beliefs, behaviours, and habits. So, sooner or later, any differences are going to get flagged up. Where there are disagreements, there needs to be compromise.'

'And honesty,' I pointed out. Surely splitting his time in Prague between his mates and his girlfriend would have been a perfect compromise.

Privately I agreed with Polly. That her chap was getting up to no good behind her back. Although maybe, after

Robin's infidelity, I was too jaundiced to think otherwise.

'Why are we having a heavy conversation so early in the morning?' Milo bantered, as the pub loomed into view.

'I blame Robin,' I said, flashing a rueful smile.

'Well, he's given you something to think about,' Milo pointed out, as we went through the pub door. 'So, it's appropriate you eat a hearty breakfast. I guess that's where that saying comes from – *food for thought.*'

Chapter Sixty-Two

The pub's breakfast was sublime. I forgot about Robin as I ordered sausage, bacon, egg, tomatoes, baked beans, mushrooms and toast.

Once again there was no sign of Polly. However, Cilla was a larger-than-life presence behind the bar.

Her platinum blonde hair was piled up on her head in a towering beehive. Gold hoops, like mini satellite dishes, dangled from her ears. Half a dozen bracelets jangled on her wrists. The false eyelashes were still in place, but today's lipstick had changed to a neon pink. It was so bright it possibly glowed in the dark. She was dressed in a clingy leopard print jumpsuit that emphasised her chunky figure. Somehow, she carried off the look. Possibly because she looked like she'd wandered straight out of *The Rovers Return*.

She approached our table with a plate in each hand.

'Blow on the sausages before giving them to your dogs,' she said, setting the plates down. 'They're piping hot. I don't want my four-legged visitors burning their tongues.' Cilla stooped to fuss Rambo and Cindy. Her bangles jingled as she stroked their heads. 'Gorgeous doggies,' she cooed. 'Have you heard the latest?' she asked, straightening up.

Milo suddenly looked wary. For one horrible moment I thought Cilla was going to blame Polly's absence on JJ. That she might tear Milo off a strip for not giving his son a stern talking to.

'Latest?' Milo frowned.

'About Starlight Hall,' said Cilla.

'Is that the hut next to the church?' I asked.

'It's a bit more than a hut, love,' Cilla sniffed. 'That's the village hall. It's been there since 1965. It's the centre of community life. It's where the village holds bi-annual fetes, and hosts gymkhanas. We even have a local dog show. It's also the perfect venue for weddings, parties, conferences and meetings.'

'Really?' I said doubtfully.

It reminded me of my schooldays and prefabricated classrooms. Whilst I could envisage it playing host to a local fete, I couldn't imagine anyone booking the place to celebrate their wedding. Not unless they were on a tight budget.

'There's been many a happy gathering at Starlight Hall,' said Cilla sharply. 'Last one was for Hugo and Linda Cartwright. They hired it to celebrate their Pearl wedding anniversary. There was a delicious buffet lunch and the whole village was invited to their bash. Have you met the Cartwrights?' Her tone suggested you were nobody if you hadn't.

'I've met Linda and her mother-in-law, Hetty,' I said timidly. I was very aware that I was a newcomer to Starlight Croft – a temporary one at that. My boss had once said that small villages had small minds. That you needed to go back three generations to truly belong. 'How lovely for Linda and Hugo,' I said, back-peddling to ingratiate myself. 'I can quite see how the hall' – I was careful not to say *hut* again – 'would be the perfect place for celebrations.' And as it was only a stone's throw from the pub, I could also see why Cilla was keen to promote events that might give a helping hand with a supply of booze.

'Indeed,' said Cilla, eyeing me speculatively. Obviously, I wasn't yet home and dry with her. 'The hall needs a bit of TLC, but that takes money. The local council won't splash out, so tomorrow there's a fundraising event. I hope you'll both go along and be supportive. Hetty and her cronies in high places are organising a craft fayre.'

'We will be sure to attend,' said Milo.

Pleasure rippled through me. He'd said *we*. Oh, goody! Another day with Milo. Robin aside, this weekend was turning into a fabulous one.

'Thanks for telling us,' I beamed.

'Oh, but that's not what I wanted to tell you both. Craft fayre aside, there's a rumour circulating that the local council are putting Starlight Hall on the market. Even worse, a builder is after it.'

'How incredible,' I breathed.

My mind galloped ahead. Wow. That building was sitting on a huge plot of land. If a builder demolished Starlight Hall, maybe ten, or even twenty, houses could be built. And Yours Truly would be the first in line for putting down her deposit.

'Incredible?' Cilla's eyes narrowed.

'I-I mean, it's incredible that... that the Council have the *gall* to think of selling part of the village's heritage.' My cheeks flamed with embarrassment at the faux pas. 'Outrageous,' I added in a peeved voice.

'You can say that again,' Cilla agreed, misconstruing my rosy cheeks as *pink with indignation*. 'So, we all need to keep our eyes – and ears – peeled. No builder is getting his paws on our hall, right?'

'Indeed,' I said stoutly, but my mind was already elsewhere.

First thing Monday morning, I'd be telephoning the local council. There were some discreet enquiries to be made. About planning applications for starters.

Chapter Sixty-Three

Milo and I left the pub with sated appetites. We set off for our walk taking a route that encompassed swathes of fields dotted with sheep.

I kept Cindy on her lead just in case she gave chase. The last thing I wanted was my dog being responsible for distressed sheep. Several woolly faces peered at us curiously. There were a few enquiring bleats, but mostly the sheep were immersed in a busy grazing schedule.

Rambo gamely trotted along at Milo's heels but, after a couple of miles, he ran out of steam. Milo resorted to carrying him. Cindy, a bigger dog with longer legs, gamely kept going. After some six miles, she too began to flag. To be honest, I wasn't far behind her. My calf muscles were aching.

'Home?' Milo suggested.

'I think that's a good idea,' I agreed.

Eventually we made it back to Starlight Lane. Rambo wriggled in Milo's arms, then whined to be back on the ground. As he trotted alongside Cindy, Milo jerked his head at the dogs.

'These two will sleep well tonight,' he said.

'I think we all will,' I laughed.

Frankly I couldn't wait to get back to the studio, kick off

my hiking boots, and collapse on the sofa with some trash telly viewing.

'Er, Tilly,' said Milo, as we entered the cottage garden. 'I need to go to Bluewater and buy a new shirt. I was thinking…'

'Yes?' I prompted.

'Well, if you're not too tired after our long walk, I wondered if you'd like to come with me. We could grab a coffee and be naughty. *Really* naughty. I'm thinking-'

I immediately went a bit googly-eyed. Be naughty with Milo? *Really* naughty? As in… him trying on a shirt, inviting me into the dressing cubicle, seeing him half naked, then Milo shrugging helplessly. "I know a changing room isn't the most romantic of places, but can I kiss you?" Or maybe a different store all together. A bed shop. "I need to buy a new bed. Fancy testing the mattress with me?" And then being overcome with lust and grabbing me–

In the window display? Cindy interrupted. *In front of passing shoppers? I KNEW you had a crush on this man, but your fantasies are becoming ridiculous.*

I ignored her and instead focussed on what Milo was saying.

'I'm thinking … chocolate cake.'

Chocolate cake? Ah, well. That was nice enough. Not as nice as Milo, but a sweet alternative.

'Also' – he continued – 'I'd appreciate your guidance on which shirt to buy. I'm not a great follower of fashion and don't want JJ later laughing at me.'

'I can't say I'm a great follower of fashion either,' I said wryly. 'But I'm happy to give my opinion.'

I thought you were knackered? said Cindy slyly.

Tired? Me?

'Terrific,' said Milo. 'In which case, that's a date.'

Omigod. A date. This time we really were going on a date!

You really aren't.

He said *it's a date.* Help! What shall I wear?

Cindy didn't deign to answer.

'Shall we rendezvous in' – Milo checked his wristwatch – 'half an hour?'

'Perfect,' I beamed.

'Good,' he smiled. 'That gives me time to put on a clean pair of jeans and tidy myself up.'

'Right-oh,' I trilled, trying to tone down my euphoria. 'See you in a little while.'

Milo gave me a small wave before heading off to his cottage. I fairly bounced into the studio. Shutting the door, I turned to Cindy, eyes shining.

'*Eeeeep*,' I squeaked. 'I'm going out with Milo. *Eeeeep*!' I squealed again, jumping about like Tigger.

Mum, it's just a shopping trip.

'I know, but even so!' I gave a twirl of happiness. 'Meanwhile' – I looked at Cindy's paws in dismay – 'you're muddy. Let me find a towel and clean you up.'

Five minutes later, muddy towel in the laundry basket – I really must do some washing – I headed off to the shower. Time to freshen up. Everywhere. I gave a smutty laugh. After all, who knew if this *naughtiness* – Milo's word – might lead to another naughtiness. And if it did, I wanted to be prepared.

It's amazing, when put to the test, what can be achieved. In record time, my ponytail had been replaced by a smooth sheet of blonde hair. My makeup had been refreshed and my eyes were now smoky with kohl. My face – thanks to luminous skin foundation – was flawless, and my lips were now cherry red. I was also wearing a sheer, slightly plunging, clingy black sweater. Thanks to my recent divorce diet, matching jeans showcased a trim figure. As I stood in front of the mirror assessing the *overall effect*, Cindy padded over.

Are you going to a funeral?

'No,' I answered snippily. 'I know I'm wearing black with black' – I withdrew some ankle boots from the wardrobe, and yes, black – 'but it sets off my blonde hair. Also, I'm wearing red lipstick. Do you think I need more colour?'

Add some costume jewellery.

'Good idea.' I reached into a drawer, removed a string of brightly coloured beads, and slipped them over my head. 'Ta da!'

That's better.

'Glad you approve,' I beamed, just as Milo knocked on the door.

Chapter Sixty-Four

'Goodness,' said Milo, unable to hide his surprise. 'I mean … you look nice. In fact… you look stunning.'

'Thanks,' I said, thrilled to bits. 'You look pretty tasty yourself,' I said carelessly.

Milo looked astonished, as well he might.

Mum, he's not a cookie, said Cindy.

Shit! Never mind the sodding biscuit. I've basically told the guy he's sexually desirable and that I fancy him something rotten. *Noooo*! What am I going to do?

Compliment him on his aftershave.

Brilliant idea.

'Y-Yes, that aftershave you're wearing is… also very tasty.'

'Is it?' said Milo looking bemused.

'Mmmmm.' I sniffed the air theatrically. 'Er, tasty.'

Stop saying that word! Cindy implored.

I can't – it's got lodged in my brain.

'You're reminding me of that old advert,' said Milo. 'The one where kids smell the air and discover gravy. So long as I don't smell like a stock cube.'

'You really don't,' I said, flustered. I grabbed my bag and housekeys. 'Shall we go? After all, I can't wait to be naughty.' Feckity-feck. Stop it, Tilly. 'The cake,' I gasped. 'Naughty with the cake.'

'Er, quite,' said Milo, his mouth twitching.

Was it my imagination, or did he just wink? Mortified, I followed Milo through the garden gate and over to his car.

During the ride to Bluewater, I tried to settle down. However, I felt on edge and jittery. That stupid *tasty* word had changed the energy between us.

Up until now we'd been relaxed together – albeit with me having zingers whenever Milo's hand had brushed mine – whereas now everything seemed highly charged. Or was it just me experiencing this?

Discreetly, I turned my head a fraction. Enough to squint sideways at Milo. He was staring straight ahead. Eyes on the road. Oblivious to the effect he was having on me. And he really was having an effect. His thigh was inches from mine. My fingers twitched in my lap. They longed to walk the short space between us. Land on his thigh. And why stop there? It would be the work of a moment to walk them up to his fly. Yank down the zipper and–

'Okay?' said Milo, glancing at me. He caught me gawping at him.

I flushed guiltily and hoped my expression hadn't given my thoughts away. After all, they'd been incredibly lustful. Was Milo privately thinking, *Oh no! Why did I tell Tilly she looked stunning? She's now got the wrong end of the stick. Cringe...*

'Tilly?' he prompted.

'I'm fine,' I squeaked.

'Really? You sound like you've been mainlining on

helium.'

'Ah ha ha ha!' I brayed.

Oh no, this was awful. I needed to get my head straight. Either that or emigrate.

The rest of the journey passed in awkward silence. Well, awkward on my part. I wasn't sure whether it was the same for Milo. And no way was I doing another sneaky peek in case he caught me out a second time.

When we finally arrived at Bluewater, happily the place wasn't rammed with shoppers. I casually scanned the mall, attempting nonchalance.

'Where would you like to start?' I asked.

'I'd like to start with being naughty,' said Milo mischievously.

Was he flirting? Or was I *hoping* he was flirting?

I gave him a curious look. There was a gleam in his eye. Or was it my imagination? I no longer knew. My flirt radar had stopped working long ago. Perhaps Milo's twinkling irises were nothing more than bright lights bouncing off his eyeballs. His body language didn't indicate anything other than slight boredom. After all, what was exciting about traipsing around shops? Yes, perhaps his flirty tone had merely been an attempt to alleviate shopping tedium.

'The cake,' Milo reminded.

'Oh, the *cake*,' I enunciated, as if I'd forgotten all about that. 'That sounds-'

'Tasty?' he said innocently.

My face instantly reddened.

'Most agreeable,' I muttered.

Chapter Sixty-Five

We spent a happy thirty minutes hoovering up cappuccino and the stickiest ginger cake I'd ever tasted.

'Mmm,' I said, closing my eyes and sucking one sugary thumb.

'Tasty?' Milo deadpanned.

I instantly dropped the lascivious licking. What sort of signals was I sending out? Likely emulating dirty birdy Nigella Lawson. She wasn't averse to slurping the life out of her syrupy fingers. Or talking about her *slut* red raspberries, *the length* of a vanilla pod, or – as the camera zoomed to stove – *turning up the heat*.

'Delicious,' I said, determined not to repeat the *tasty* word.

'Good,' said Milo, draining his cup. 'In which case, are you fit?'

You certainly are, I privately thought.

'Yes, ready,' I trilled, grabbing my bag and standing up. 'Lead the way.'

We went into several shops. Browsed the shirts. To me, every single one looked the same. The only obvious difference was the colour or fabric. I mean, the checked shirts hanging by the denims was visibly different to those plain jobbies by the men's suits. But other than that, I was stumped.

Milo was now considering some shirts in an arty-farty arrangement on a glass table. Overhead spotlights flagged up those that were slim fit and… what? Fat fit? Wasn't that a bit, you know, non-PC? And, dear Lord, since when did a shirt cost two hundred pounds? But then again, this store wasn't the same as where *I'd* recently bought a work shirt. *George* at Asda.

A sharp-eyed assistant was tracking Milo. A tape measure was slung artfully around broad shoulders. The assistant's physique screamed *yes, I'm a gym bunny, and yes you can admire me*. He was drop-dead gorgeous. However, the limp wrist informed any female admirer that her interest wouldn't be reciprocated.

As Milo continued to study shirts, the assistant pounced.

'Can I help you, sir?'

'Maybe,' said Milo, looking perplexed. 'I'm going out tonight. I want to wear something smart, but casual. Fashionable, but classic. Something that can be worn socially, but also at work.' He gave the assistant an apologetic look. 'The truth is, I simply want to wear a nice shirt tonight.'

Milo looked at me as he said that last word. *Tonight*. I straightened up. Suddenly, my internal antenna was on red alert.

Tonight was… wowzer… *Saturday* night. And what did most couples do on a Saturday night? They went out, that's what! I stifled a squeal. Omigod, was Milo going to ask me to go out with him tonight? Was he looking for a new shirt because he... yes!... he wanted to dress to impress!

Suddenly, I was very interested in his potential purchase. After all, if he was going to ramp up his style, then I might have to do likewise, and nip off to Zara.

The assistant clapped his hands together in delight. Evidently, he was thrilled that Milo needed help, and that *he,* style icon extraordinaire, would be the one to steer this customer into a whole new experience with shirts. He leant in. Plucked a shirt from the arty-farty pile. Fingered the fabric. Stroked the buttonholes.

'This, sir, is an Oxford button-down shirt. It's *incredibly* versatile. It can be used in both social and professional settings and will give a flawlessly put-together vibe.'

I blinked. Were we still talking English?

'Now, traditionally, it comes in lighter blues and whites. But might I cautiously suggest, if you ever want to wear it to an office event, that you go a teensy bit darker.' Suddenly his tape measure was around Milo's neck. 'As I thought. In which case' – he grabbed another shirt – 'consider this one. The weight and thickness of the fabric means it's perfect for varying temperature changes. This affords both coolness and confidence all year long.'

'Really?' said Milo eagerly. He took the shirt and held it reverently. As well he might at that price. If I were him, I'd never wear it. It would be put on an altar and worshipped.

'I think it's very you, sir,' said the assistant. 'I can see you now' – he closed his eyes and assumed a dreamy expression – 'looking hip at a rooftop party. Obviously, you would have accessorised the shirt with some well-tailored trousers.' He opened his eyes again. 'The latter is an essential staple for every gent's wardrobe. You'd be the star of the gathering, showing off your chest, looking all manly and sexy.' He fluttered his eyelashes at Milo. 'The modern man needs *this* shirt in his closet, whether going out or… *coming out.*' He gave Milo a speculative look.

Milo looked momentarily startled.

'Um, definitely *going* out.' He nodded his head vigorously.

Yes, Milo. You tell 'im! "Back off, gym bunny. My heart belongs to the woman by my side. And we're *going out*! On *Saturday night*. The two of us!"

I wanted to rub my hands together and cackle with glee. This weekend was going from strength to strength. Getting better and better. I wondered where Milo would take me. Somewhere with lots of candlelight. Ambience. Staff that served wine – no champagne! – in hushed tones with lots of bowing and scraping. Bring it on!

'Ah, sir wants to impress a girl, eh?' said the assistant, unoffended by Milo's gentle rebuff. He gave a meaningful look in my direction. 'You want to impress a lady, yes?'

'I do,' Milo confirmed.

I knew it! The anticipation of what lay ahead was sending my breathing haywire. I could see us both now. Full of champagne bubbles. And boldness. My lungs did a chuggy gasp as I visualised Milo boldly going where no man had gone before. Well, not for a while, anyway. I stifled a snort of anticipation. Careful, Tilly. Patience. You don't want to start whinnying and pawing the ground.

'In which case' – said the assistant – 'the blue shirt is the one for you. Can I also suggest, sir, that in addition to the tailored trousers, you also consider some shoes. It's important to get the right footwear to complete the overall look.'

'Okay,' Milo agreed. 'That's the shirt sorted. Now for the trousers and shoes.'

The assistant steered Milo into a changing room. He wiggled back and forth with various trousers. Several pairs of shoes followed. By the time Milo was finished, over an hour had passed. By this point I was anxious about having enough time to buy something for me. No matter. I could always dress up my existing outfit. Change the costume jewellery. Swap the boots for high heels.

'Thank you so much for your help,' said Milo, as the assistant bagged everything up at the till.

'Yes, thank you,' I gushed. 'He's going to look amazing for his date.'

Milo gave me a sheepish grin. I returned it with a megawatt smile of my own. Forget all the earlier embarrassment. The horror over the *tasty* word. It had been worth it. We were now back on track with each other. Easy going. Friendly. Flirty even. Bring on some more zingers!

As we left the shop together, I felt so fizzy, I nearly grabbed hold of Milo's hand.

No, Tilly. Stop. Let Milo be the one to take your hand.

We paused for a moment, while Milo popped the receipt into the folds of his wallet. Seconds later it had been tucked inside a pocket. He looked at me.

'Thank you,' he said simply.

'I'm so… happy,' I said shyly.

'Impressed?' he asked.

'Definitely,' I nodded.

'Good.' He heaved a sigh of relief. 'I hope Sarah will be too.'

I froze. Who?

The sounds within the mall – shoppers talking, children crying – suddenly became a roar. The noise rose up, rushed into my ears, then screamed through my brain like a highspeed train.

'S-Sarah?' I stuttered.

'I haven't actually met her,' Milo confided. 'But she matched with me.' He noticed my look of confusion. 'On the dating app,' he explained. 'I wasn't going to bother with it anymore,' he shrugged. 'You see, I recently met someone and thought she was available. But it then transpired that she wasn't.' He shrugged again. 'So, I ended up making a last-minute arrangement for this evening.'

'With Sarah,' I muttered.

'With Sarah,' he confirmed.

Omigod. How could I have got it so wrong? Been so naïve? Sarah was one of the swipe right ladies. Personally, I'd like to grab Milo's phone and send Sarah a private message. One that invited her to sod off.

My shoulders drooped. Oh, forget it, Tilly. Even if Milo wasn't going out on a date with Sarah, even if there never had been a dating app, you still wouldn't feature on his romantic radar. After all, he's just told you that he was interested in someone else. Someone he'd thought available, but apparently wasn't, but – who knew – might become available in the future. Talk about getting the wrong end of the stick.

'Did you want to do any shopping?' asked Milo.

'Um, no,' I shook my head.

'Sure?'

'A hundred per cent,' I said, forcing myself to act normally. To speak fluidly. Currently my words sounded jerky. Robotic. Unexpectedly, I felt on the verge of tears.

'In which case' – he said – 'shall we go?'

I kept my head down. Did some rapid blinking.

'Yes,' I agreed. 'Let's go home.'

We moved off, heading towards the exit point that lead to the carpark. As I walked alongside Milo, I thanked the universe for one small blessing. That I'd not grabbed Milo's hand as we'd left that shop.

Chapter Sixty-Six

Once home, Cindy greeted me ecstatically, then rushed outside to relieve herself. Seconds later, Rambo had joined Cindy.

The dogs wagged their tails at each other, then checked flowerbeds together, looking for precise places to sprinkle their tinkle. I patiently waited at the door for Cindy to finish.

'Tilly?' Milo called from his own backdoor.

'Yes?'

He began to walk along the garden pathway. As he headed over, I saw he was holding something in his hand. A key.

'This is a duplicate for the backdoor. Can I be cheeky and ask if you would let Rambo out later? I'm not sure what time I'll be home.' Unspoken words hung in the air. *If at all.* 'I'd be very grateful.'

'Tell you what, let Rambo stay with me and Cindy. That way you can take as long as you like.' I stopped myself from adding *all bloody night if need be.*

'Well, if you're sure,' said Milo hesitatingly. 'I don't want to take advantage.' *If I end up shagging the living daylights out of Sarah,* was what he surely meant.

'I'm sure,' I nodded. *Yup, totally sure that you will be a swipe-right tart and bonk Sarah's brains out.*

'We're meant to be watching a movie at her place,' he said.

'Nice,' I said. *I really couldn't care less what you do together.*

'And she said she'd cook me her signature dish. Something with chicken. The dinner, not the movie,' he explained unnecessarily.

'Well, quite,' I agreed. 'I don't know any movie about, you know, chickens.'

'I do,' said Milo brightly. 'Chicken Run. Remember? With our favourite movie stars, Wallace and Gromit.'

'Ah, yes. The plot chickens,' I joked weakly.

I felt a sharp pang of sorrow as I remembered the two of us laughing together. Sitting side by side. On the sofa. In front of the telly. Me falling asleep on his shoulder. Bittersweet. For me, a case of *so near and yet so far*. But not for Sarah. Bitch!

I had a sudden mental picture of a sultry brunette with Milo. There they were. Together. Consuming their chicken dinners. Curling up on the sofa. Watching a movie that featured chickens. Then pecking each other with kisses. If they went all the way, what might Sarah say as she orgasmed? Not, *oh-oh-oh* but *cluck-cluck-cluck?* But maybe they'd watch a pirate movie instead. In which case, would Sarah's climax be an *arr*gasm? Or, if they instead cosied up in front of a nature programme featuring ants, might Sarah suffer an *ant*iclimax?

'Tilly?'

I zoned back in.

'Yes?'

'Will you be all right?'

'Yes, of course,' I assured. 'You go and get yourself ready. I'll feed Rambo. He can have some of Cindy's food.'

'Okay.' He paused. Hesitated a moment. 'What are you doing tonight? Talking to Robin?'

'Robin?' I said vaguely. Who was he? Oh, yes, the man who'd been dumped by his youthful mistress. The guy who'd asked not just for a reconciliation, but also remarriage. Geez, what a prat. My life with Robin suddenly seemed so very long ago. Why was that?

'Your ex-husband,' Milo prompted. 'You spoke of getting married again.'

'Oh, that,' I shrugged. 'I'll give him a call.'

'Right,' Milo nodded. 'Well, good luck to you and Robin.'

'Thanks,' I said. 'And, um, good luck to you and Sarah.'

'Er, yes. Thank you.'

Suddenly there didn't seem much else to say. Milo turned on his heel, taking the duplicate key to the cottage's backdoor with him.

I whistled Rambo and Cindy to heel. Yes, I'd give Robin a call. I'd speak to him. But only to tell him to never darken my door again.

The dogs trotted into the studio. I shut the door after them. And, with it, I shut out all my previous hopes and dreams for Saturday night.

Chapter Sixty-Seven

I fed the dogs, had a shower, pulled on my scruffy pyjamas, then decided to watch some telly. Briefly, I channel hopped. Oh, *Chicken Run*. What a coincidence.

Outside came the sound of Milo's car starting up. I resisted the urge to rush to the window, press my nose up to the glass, and see if I could catch a glimpse of him. No doubt he looked scrumptious in his new shirt, tailored trousers and shiny shoes.

Impulsively, I switched off the TV. Instead, I found myself watching the reflection of his car's taillights in the television's blank screen. I inclined my head. Listened to the throaty hum of the engine. A few seconds later and the sound receded as his vehicle disappeared into the night.

Restless, I stood up and finally moved over to the window. Stared at the darkness beyond. My head felt like it was full of angry, buzzing bees. I rubbed my temples viciously then rested my forehead against the cold glass. Why was life sometimes so… frustrating?

Unable to face cooking, I made myself a sandwich. Picking up the remote control, I once again settled down in front of the telly. Okay, *Chicken Run* it was – even if it did remind me of Milo. Cindy and Rambo jumped up beside me.

'Hi, guys,' I said.

Hello, Mum.

Hey, Tilly.

'So tonight I'm having imaginary conversations with not one, but two dogs. How amazing is that?' I cranked up a smile.

Oooh, chickens, said Rambo as a brood of hens stampeded across the screen, hellbent on taking out the baddies.

I sat morosely for a bit. Munched on my sandwich. Debated whether I could be bothered to make myself a cup of tea or remain sitting in a heap with the dogs. Just when I was about to rouse myself, my mobile pinged. A text. For one insane moment, hope flood through me. Could it be a message from Milo?

Sarah is a nightmare. Please, Tilly. Rescue me. Now!

PS – I have a confession. My heart belongs to you xxxxxxxxx

I reached for the phone and, as I did so, hope ebbed away. Robin.

Well? I'm waiting for your response.

Gosh, how romantic, Robin. Your loving words blow me away! Why couldn't he be bothered to pick up the phone and have a proper conversation? What a plank. Sighing, I tapped out my reply.

There was a man called Robin
He had a secretary that he was knobbing
His wife caught him out

311

And was left in no doubt
That Robin was a–

I paused. Robin was a what?

Hm. What was an appropriate word that rhymed with my ex-husband's name. Dobbin? Like a farm horse? Rather unkind to horses. Goblin? Unkind to fairy folk.

I returned to the screen and resumed typing.

That Robin was a bellend.

It didn't rhyme, but it was appropriate, so would do. I pressed the send button, then flopped back against the cushions. Seconds later my phone pinged with another text.

Does that mean no?

My goodness, this man caught on quick. I tapped my phone's screen. Searched for the emoji I wanted. Seconds later, a pair of clapping hands whooshed off into Cyber Space.

Barely a second had passed when my phone burst into life. Its merry tinkle was at odds to my plummeting mood. On the television screen, animated chickens were running amok and squawking with anger. I knew exactly how they felt. Perhaps I should follow their example. Let loose with a few squawks of my own. Scowling, and without bothering to look at the screen, I snatched up the phone.

'Now you listen here, Robin. Enough is enough. You can take your marriage proposal, and shove it right up your-'

'Er, hello?' The voice was familiar but, in the middle of a red mist moment, took me a moment to place.

'I'm so sorry,' I apologised. 'I thought you were Robin.'

Who the heck was I talking to? I quickly moved the

phone away from my ear so I could see the caller's id. And then I gasped aloud. It was Jake.

Chapter Sixty-Eight

'Jake,' I wheezed. 'I'm so embarrassed. Whatever must you think of me greeting you like that?'

I inwardly cringed. I'd only just been reunited with my son. The last thing I wanted was him running for the hills believing his biological mother was a fruit loop.

Let's be honest, Mum. A pair of brown eyes looked over at me. *Sometimes you make fruit loops seem sane.*

Is your mum not quite all there? Rambo gave Cindy a worried look.

'I was berating my ex-husband,' I gabbled, well and truly in a fluster. 'He is... was... being a bit of a nuisance.'

'No worries,' said Jake. He sounded very laid back. Like dealing with scatty women was something he regularly took in his stride. 'Look, can you talk?'

I pointed the remote control at the telly. Instantly, a screen full of chickens and flying feathers disappeared into black nothingness.

'Yes, I can talk. It's just me and the dogs. I'm on my own. How are you?' I asked, recovering my equilibrium. 'It's lovely to hear from you,' I added. And I truly meant it. The joy of hearing Jake's voice had cancelled out my bad mood over Robin's text – and even some of the despair about Milo being with Swipe Right Sarah.

'I'm fine,' said Jake. I sensed a smile in his voice. 'I'm truly fine.'

'That's good,' I said, relaxing against the cushions again. Rambo climbed onto my lap. He gave a sigh of contentment. I leant over to Cindy, and rubbed her ears, so she didn't get jealous.

'Look, I'm going to get straight to the point,' said Jake.

'Okay,' I said cautiously. *Please don't dump me, Jake. Please don't tell me you now want me out of your life. Not when you've only just come back into it.*

'The thing is' – I sensed him picking his words carefully – 'I don't want to make you feel weird or anything, but…'

'Go on,' I prompted.

His next words tumbled out in a rush.

'Can I call you *Mum*?'

I instantly burst into tears.

'Oh, Jake,' I sniffed.

I knew he'd saved my contact details under the same name, but to hear him ask to call me that was everything. Just… everything.

'Sorry, sorry,' he said, sounding distressed. 'I didn't mean to make you cry. It's just that you *are* my biological mother, and I don't want to call you Tilly. It doesn't sit right with me. But equally, it doesn't mean I'm expecting anything from you,' he gibbered. 'It's simply-'

'I would *love* you to call me Mum,' I interrupted, wiping the tears from my face. 'And listen, Jake. I would love to be your mum in every sense of the word, but I will go along with whatever pace you want to set.'

'Really?' he said in astonishment. 'That's… that's… phenomenal,' he said, his voice catching. 'I'm really grateful.'

'Jake, *I'm* the one that's grateful,' I whispered. 'More than words can say.'

'Then I guess' – I sensed him gulping – 'that the feeling is mutual.'

'Good,' I quavered. I cleared my throat. A regrouping gesture. 'When I last saw you, you mentioned catching a plane. Are you back home again or' – I had no idea where he was in the world – 'still overseas?'

'I'm in Crete,' he said.

'Oh, wow. How lovely. I've never been there, but it's meant to be a pretty island.'

'It is. But there was a reason behind the trip. Listen, Mum' – I glowed at his immediate use of the name – 'I hope what I tell you isn't upsetting, but I've been discovering my roots and… well, we're in this together, right?'

'Absolutely,' I said, my heart picking up pace. *Finding my roots* rather suggested seeking out relatives. Or, in Jake's case, his father. 'Does that mean' – I closed my eyes for a second – 'that you've found… Nicholas?'

'Yes,' he said simply.

For a moment, the sofa rocked. I clung on to Rambo and steadied myself.

'And… how did it go?' I asked calmly.

'Dad agreed to meet me. Initially it was just the two of us. He told me he was married. His wife is called Eleni.'

Jake paused. I sensed he was waiting for my response.

'That's... good,' I said, exhaling gustily. I hadn't realised that I'd been holding my breath until then. Right. So, Nicholas was married. And why not? After all, I'd gone on to marry Robin. Two schoolkids had finally grown up and, as adults, married other adults. That was generally the way things were done.

'However' – Jake continued – 'Eleni knew nothing of Dad's, er, *history,* if you catch my drift. So, Dad and I initially met for a coffee without her knowledge. Our meeting went well. It was... emotional. On both sides.'

'I'm sure,' I whispered. 'And... does your dad have a family?' I asked lightly.

'He does,' Jake confirmed.

I blew out my cheeks. Another release of tension. Okay, so Nicholas wasn't just father to Jake, he was also father to...

'How many children does he have?' I asked, my curiosity piqued.

'Four.'

'*Four!*' I exclaimed. Blimey, he'd not had any issues about sowing his seed. Oh, stop it, Tilly. Don't start getting bitter.

'Can you believe I have four half-sisters,' Jake declared. He sounded delighted. 'They're called Konstantina, Dimitra, Lyra and Phoebe. And just to backtrack slightly, Dad went home and spoke to Eleni about me. She was initially taken aback but took the news well. She then personally invited me to the family home where I met my sisters.' Jake paused for a moment. I sensed him reining in his emotions. 'They welcomed me, Mum. They welcomed me with open arms.

Eleni was so kind, and her daughters were lovely. Phoebe was particularly sweet. She said, "Do you know, I've always felt like I had a brother." And then she touched her heart and said, "I felt it here." She's a very gentle soul.'

'Jake, I'm so happy that you're happy.'

'Thanks,' he said quietly. 'And I told Dad that I was in contact with you. He asked me to send his very best wishes.'

'L-Likewise,' I stammered. I was so pleased for Jake. Delighted, in fact. But all this unearthing meant, well, where did it end? Would I, too, be expected to contact Nicholas? Or him me? Were Nicholas, Eleni and their four daughters to be added to my Christmas card list? And vice versa? Or did we leave the past in the past?

I think, Mum, this is about Jake reestablishing family ties. It's not about you.

Of course.

'Anyway' – Jake continued – 'they've invited me to stay with them for a few days, and I've accepted.'

'That's amazing, darling.' The endearment slipped out before I could stop it. But it had felt so natural. 'And how are you feeling now?' I asked tentatively.

I had a flashback. Jake telling me how his ex-girlfriend's wish to have a baby had caused him to fall apart. To subsequently find out who he truly was.

'Mum, I can't begin to describe how I feel.' I sensed the joy in my son's voice. 'I feel whole again. *Complete.*'

Chapter Sixty-Nine

I awoke on Sunday morning with a glow. The conversation with Jake had ended on such a positive note.

We could never recapture those lost decades, but we could be there for each other in the years to come.

At some point I needed a conversation with my parents. I felt sure they would want to meet their grandson, just as Jake would wish to meet his grandparents. But, for now, he just needed to do what he was doing. Embracing the discovery of who he was, and then balancing all these new emotions with his heart. And head. And feeling complete.

I sighed and turned my thoughts to the more pressing matter of the dogs and our respective bladders. Throwing off the covers, I swung my legs out of bed.

Seconds later, both dogs were out in the garden, sniffing around, choosing the perfect place to tinkle. Rambo cocked his leg against some shrubs, but Cindy had yet to decide which patch of grass should be treated to her waterworks. The emerging brown circles on Milo's lawn were not lost on me.

I glanced at Starlight Cottage. The place looked deserted. But then again, Milo could be having a lie-in. After all, it was Sunday. In which case, had he brought Swipe Right Sarah home with him?

I retreated into the studio. Peered through the rear window to the area where we parked our vehicles. There was Octavia. Milo's car was missing. Ok*ayyy*. So, he hadn't brought Swipe Right Sarah home. Instead, he'd stayed over at her place.

My mouth gave an involuntary twist, the sides turning down like an upside-down smile. I wandered into the bathroom and caught sight of myself in the mirror. Oooh, Tilly. Change that expression now! You look like a right old miserable cow. Or, as Lisa would say, showing off my *resting bitch face.*

I reached for my toothbrush and set about getting ready for the day. As toothpaste frothed around my mouth, I tried not to think about Milo. Or the new woman in his life. Or the rampant sex they'd had last night.

Outside, the day was damp and cold, but it wasn't raining. Pulling on layers of clothing, I fed the dogs, munched my way through a piece of toast, then snapped a spare lead onto Rambo's collar. Minutes later, the three of us were heading along the lane.

An hour or so later, Rambo was tired. I picked him up and walked, with Cindy, for another mile or two. Eventually, going full circle, I stood on a footpath and surveyed Starlight Cottage in the distance. The space beside Octavia remained resolutely empty.

Turning away, I took another path and decided to walk a few more miles. Cindy still had plenty of energy. Rambo, having rested, wriggled to be put down again. I felt perilously close to tears and chided myself not to be ridiculous. I had so much to be joyful for. Cheating Robin was out of my life. My fabulous son was back in it. I'd also found yet another property online that looked promising. Meanwhile I had a roof over my head and was living alongside a kind man who'd become a friend. The fact that I'd hoped for more was disappointing, but so what? That's how life sometimes went. Get over it. Get over it and get on with it. Yes, absolutely.

Peptalk over, I took another path, this time turning into the wind. The cold on my face was surprisingly pleasant. I enjoyed the feeling as it lifted my hair, roared into my ears, and uplifted my soul. That's more like it, Tilly! Get some optimism seeping back into your bones. And straighten that spine while you're at it.

Marching now, the three of us picked our way through the mud and puddles. My goodness, we'd all sleep well tonight. Maybe this evening I'd properly watch a movie – but not anything that reminded me of Milo – and I'd settle down in front of the box with some piping hot comfort food. Yes, good idea, Tilly. I'd make a chilli con carne. In fact, I'd head to the Strawberry Shed right now. Buy some locally sourced minced beef. All the vegetables to go with it. Bung everything in the slow cooker, and Bob would be my uncle.

Maybe I'd pick up a bottle of wine, too. The Cartwrights had a small range of organic wines. Perhaps I'd buy two bottles. Get macrobiotically sozzled. That way I'd stop thinking about Swipe Right Sarah. The way she'd kissed Milo's lips. And other parts of his body. Don't go there, Tilly.

By the time the three of us got to the Strawberry Shed, Rambo was back in my arms and Cindy was drooping. I felt tired myself now, not to mention starving hungry.

I was delighted to spot Hetty Cartwright. She was perched on a stool so she could chat to her daughter-in-law between customers. Linda gave me a friendly wave before turning to serve someone. I went over.

'Hello, stranger,' said Hetty, her face wreathed in smiles.

'Hi, Hetty,' I grinned, genuinely delighted to see her.

'How are you?' she asked.

My smile wobbled.

'Oh, you know' – I made a see-saw motion with one hand – 'good. I'm good. Just been dealing with… the winds of change.' My tangled hair and windswept appearance backed up that statement.

She nodded.

'I can see from your aura that you've had some recent challenges.' Her blue eyes danced with merriment. 'But remember those silver linings I told you about, Tilly? They're still there. Even more so now that you're secret is out.'

Startled, I gazed at her in astonishment. How could she possibly know about Jake?

'I don't know what your secret is, dear,' she chuckled. 'Don't look so worried. I just know that the cat, so to speak, is out of the bag – but in the loveliest possible way.'

'Yes,' I said cautiously. 'Yes, you're right.'

'And it's going to get better, dear.' She nodded her head. 'You mark my words.'

'Good to hear,' I said politely.

'I told you that I saw you living at Starlight Cottage.'

'You did,' I agreed. 'Although living in the studio at the bottom of the garden wasn't quite what I'd envisaged,' I laughed.

'Those winds of change' – Hetty leant forward and lowered her voice – 'they haven't stopped blowing, you know.'

'What do you mean?'

'You *will* live at Starlight Cottage.' She gave me a knowing look. 'Of that there is no doubt.' She waggled a finger at me. 'I'm never wrong.'

'I'm delighted to hear that,' I said, deciding to humour her.

Hetty shifted off her stool. She gathered up her belongings, then yodelled to Linda.

'I'm off now. Got to do my bit for the village.'

'Okay, see you later,' said Linda cheerfully.

Hetty's daughter-in-law had finished serving and was now on the other side of the shop setting out fresh stock. Linda caught my eye. She gave me a discreet wink accompanied with an imperceptible shake of the head. Her meaning couldn't have been clearer.

Take what my mother-in-law says with a pinch of salt.

I didn't like to pry and ask Hetty what it was that she had to do for the village. Whilst her eyes held an intense inner radiance, was it possible that their brilliant blue shade also held a touch of madness?

Chapter Seventy

Once back at the studio with the shopping, there was still no sign of Milo. Wow, Swipe Right Sarah must have thought she'd won the lottery having a handsome man turn up on her doorstep, whisk her off for a romantic meal, then take her home and deliver some action between the sheets. Lucky cow.

I had a sudden mental picture of her and Milo in bed, earlier this morning. A white bedroom. Floor-to-ceiling windows. Bright light pouring in. Sarah wafting into the bedroom with coffee and croissants on eau-de-nil porcelain. A wisp of a dressing gown covering her naked body. Hair swept into an updo. Loose tendrils tumbling artfully over her shoulders. Milo propped up against the pillows. Hair sexily tousled. Eyes lighting up as his new love stood before him and huskily declared, "What do you want first? The croissants or me?" A slow smile spreading over his face. Him declaring, "You, of course."

Oh, stop tormenting yourself, Tilly. Why imagine the scene as a perfect one? Why not have him reaching for the tie on her robe and inadvertently knocking the breakfast tray out of her hands? Yes, brilliant idea. And in a flash, she'd have transformed from seductive Sarah to screaming Sarah.

Snarling at Milo. Ranting that her pale carpet was *ruined*, the white bed linen *wrecked* and that he was nothing more than a clumsy prat. Even better, he would yell back at her. "Never mind the sodding soft furnishings. That coffee landed on my privates. My pubic hair has turned *au*-burn."

I dumped my shopping on the kitchenette's worktop, and frowned. Was that what I wanted? To have the man I was lusting after to be scalded. To have him *injured*. How horrible of me. What sort of person was I turning into? A dour one. And grumpy with it.

'Alexa,' I commanded. 'Play some cheerful music.'

As Vivaldi's *Spring* from Four Seasons filled the studio, I set to work chopping onions and crushing garlic. The frying pan sizzled and spat as the sound of violins joyfully announced the return of spring – which was now only a few weeks away.

Adding the minced beef, I stirred with one hand. With the other, I conducted an imaginary orchestra. The violins. Violas. Cellos. Double basses. A lone harpsichord.

The beef began to brown. My free hand urged the violinists to announce the arrival of birds. To celebrate the return of sunshine... blue skies... daffodils bursting from winter's dark soil.

I sprinkled a stock cube over the meat, added water, turned up the heat – oh, hello, Nigella – then closed my eyes. The stirring spoon had morphed into a baton. The music became menacing. Thunderstorms had arrived, along with April showers that could drench one faster than driving through a carwash with the window down.

I stopped conducting and turned my attention to prepping the veg. Chopping and slicing. Stirring and mixing. Then – just as the music was coming to an almighty crescendo – transferred everything from pan to hotpot. I'd leave it all to slow-cook while opening one of the Strawberry Shed's bottles of wine.

It was time to let my hair down, alcoholically speaking. To sip a few bubbles. Get fizzy. A bit dizzy. To mentally declare *sod you, Swipe-Right-Sarah*. And *stuff you too, Milo*. Well, I'd like to stuff him. Unfortunately, he was currently busy stuffing Sarah.

That's crude, Tilly. Too crude. But as more golden liquid glug-glugged into a wine flute, I realised I didn't care.

In no time at all, I was on my third glass and feeling nicely fuzzy. Cindy gave me a mournful look.

Do we have to listen to this racket?

Even Rambo looked pained. Suddenly, he threw back his head and began to howl.

'Woooooo,' he declared. 'Woo-woo-wooooo.'

'Really?' I said, squinting at him. 'Is that meant to be your idea of singing?'

'Oooooooh,' he replied.

Howling is in our genetic code, Cindy explained. *It's a form of communication. Wolves howl to rally the pack, ward off danger, or locate a lost pack member. Actually, I might give it a try myself.*

And with that she flung back her head, shut her eyes, and began to duet with Rambo.

Alexa had since moved on to Beethoven's *Choral* Ninth

Symphony. I flopped down on the sofa. As an outpouring of triumphant music rang around the room, I decided to join in with Cindy and Rambo. Copying them, I closed my eyes, tossed back my head – along with the wine – and let rip.

Blimey. It was unexpectedly rather good. Very liberating. Eyes shut, I yodelled up a storm, joining in with the cacophony of noise. Certainly, I was oblivious to a tapping on the studio door. Likewise, when the knocking became heavy rapping. Nor was I aware of the door flying open, and a tall figure blocking out the light.

It was only when the dogs went silent, the music abruptly stopped, and it was just me wailing into a wine glass, that I realised I had company.

Chapter Seventy-One

The yowling died on my lips. My eyes snapped open.

'Milo,' I said hoarsely. My ears rang in the ensuing silence. I shook my head. Were there bells on my earlobes? Still sprawled on the sofa, I squinted up at him.

'Forgive me for barging in,' he apologised. 'I did knock, but there was no response. Given that the three of you sounded like you were being murdered, I took it upon myself to use my key.'

'Oh,' I stared at him. God, he was handsome.

He sniffed the air.

'Something smells good.'

'It's shilli.'

'Silly, eh?' He eyed me beadily. 'Are you a bit tipsy?'

I waved a hand expansively.

'Poss'bly.'

He took in the glass, the wine bottle and our dogs looking put out at their jamming session being short-lived.

'Are you celebrating something?'

I frowned. What could I be celebrating? Well, being me, I suppose. Being amazing. Being stoical. Being grownup over Milo falling for Swipe Right Sarah. Even though I'd fallen for Milo. I gulped as the realisation fully hit me. Yes, I'd fallen for him, all right. I'd fallen head over heels in love with him.

'Want a drink?' I invited, waving the bottle.

Milo paused for a moment, then went to the sideboard. He helped himself to a glass.

'I came to collect Rambo,' he said, taking the bottle from me and pouring himself a drink. 'Also, I, er, wanted to talk to you.'

I caught the hesitation in his voice.

'Really?' I frowned.

He sat down alongside me. Looked at me gravely. And in that moment, I knew what he wanted to talk about. Sarah. How it was love at first sight. That he couldn't wait to see her again. And, actually, it was all rather embarrassing, but could I possibly move out? You see, Sarah would be moving into the cottage, and he didn't want to conduct his affair in front of his son. So, if I could be on my merry way, then JJ would be able to live at the studio.

'Go on,' I prompted. 'You want to tell me about Swipe Right Sarah, yes?'

'Swipe Right...?' Milo's lips twitched. 'Um, no. I don't want to talk about Sarah.' He took a sip of wine, and then his eyes locked on mine. 'I spent the whole of yesterday evening thinking about someone else.'

'Ahh,' I nodded sagely. 'The lady that you recently met, and thought was available. But it transpired she wasn't.'

'That lady' – Milo's eyes were now pinning me to the wall – 'is you.'

I stared at him. Suddenly I felt sober. Very, *very* sober.

'Did I hear you correctly?' I whispered.

'You heard me correctly,' he nodded.

'B-But' – I stuttered – 'I'm available.' Careful, Tilly. Don't make it sound like you're the local bike that's always up for a ride. 'I-I mean… I'm not seeing anyone.'

'What about Robin?'

'What about him?'

'Your reunion. Isn't that what *this* is all about?' He indicated the wine bottle. 'Celebrating your reconciliation. Your remarriage.'

I nearly dropped my wine glass.

'You must be joking,' I spluttered. 'There was never going to be any reunion. Whatever made you think that?'

'Because the guy turned up here,' Milo explained. 'And you looked absolutely dazed. Indeed, you said you felt *discombobulated.* I took that to mean you were confused about what to do for the best. You also said his appearance had *rocked your world* which I construed as being serious about giving it another shot.'

'Never in a million years,' I gasped, shaking my head. 'If you must know, I was drinking to drown my sorrows.'

Suddenly there was a highly charged silence. Milo was the first to break it.

'And why should you feel the need to drown your sorrows?' he asked quietly.

'Because of you going off with Swipe Right Sarah.' There. I'd said it. 'And having rampant sex.' Might as well say that too.

His lips twitched again, and suddenly there was a light in

his eyes. He grabbed my hand, and I nearly shot off the sofa as a zinger tasered my arm.

'I spent the whole of my date with Sarah unable to think about anyone other than you,' he confessed.

'Really?' I said uncertainly.

'Really,' he nodded. 'Yesterday was magical. I was aghast when your ex turned up and ruined it all. Thought I'd lost my chance. So, I met up with Sarah.'

'And had a night of rampant sex,' I pointed out wryly. 'After all, you didn't come home.'

'No, I didn't come home,' he agreed. 'But there was no rampant sex. I can swear to that on my son's life,' he said earnestly. 'It was a disastrous night. At the restaurant, Sarah burbled on and on about her ex. Got totally pissed. I waited with her for her taxi. But when the driver saw she was paralytic, he declined the fare. Wise man. Because when I said I'd take her home, she instead threw up in my car.'

'Oh no!' I clamped a hand over my mouth.

'Oh yes. Anyway, we finally got to her place. I helped her inside, whereupon she threw up in the hallway. I managed to get her upstairs, into the bathroom, and left her to sort herself out while I cleaned up downstairs as best I could. Afterwards, when Sarah was in her pyjamas, she wouldn't stop crying. She kept bleating on and on about the mess she'd made of her life, and what was the point of being here. That last sentence made me twitchy. I didn't want her doing something stupid in a drunken moment.' Milo sighed. 'I felt unable to leave her. Eventually, she fell asleep in the armchair, and I nodded off on the sofa. This morning, she awoke with a stonking hangover and a hazy memory of what had happened. She was appalled. Majorly embarrassed. She then assured me she was fine and gave me my marching orders. I think I can safely say that the woman was mortified and never wants our paths to cross again. I then drove home, knocked on the studio door, but there was no sign of you, so I drove off again. Went to Meopham. Costa to be precise. I holed up with several black coffees and the newspaper. So where did you go?'

'For a walk.'

'More like a trek,' he said. 'You were gone for hours.'

'Yes,' I agreed. 'The dogs are exhausted.'

Milo glanced at Cindy and Rambo.

'So it would seem. I've never seen dogs with bags under their eyes.' His face grew serious again.

'I thought you'd gone to Robin's to talk about your reunion and taken Rambo and Cindy with you.'

'I *told* you,' I said, rolling my eyes. 'Never in a month of Sundays. So, what did you do next?'

He sighed and squeezed my hand.

'I had a quick shower followed by a belated breakfast, then went and had the car professionally valeted to remove, er, all reminders of Sarah.'

'And did they do a good job?' I asked, shifting in my seat.

'They were very thorough. The car now smells like a dentist's surgery. A blend of antiseptic and clove oil.'

'Good,' I nodded. 'So...'

'So' – his eyes locked on mine again – 'I'm not seeing

anyone. And neither are you.'

'Correct,' I said, smiling shyly.

'In which case' – he moved closer to me – 'can *I* see you?'

'You can,' I whispered, as Milo leant in. I turned my body to face him. 'But there's one condition.'

'Oh?'

'You have to see *all* of me,' I said softly. 'And I have to see *all* of you.'

'I think we can both manage that,' he whispered, as his lips finally met mine.

Rambo, I heard Cindy say. *Look away now.*

Chapter Seventy-Two

Much later, sated, but not exhausted, Milo turned to me with a lazy smile. He kissed me again, then suddenly looked horrified.

'What?' I said in alarm.

'I nearly forgot,' he said.

'Forgot what?'

'Our date!'

'What date?' I said, now thoroughly confused.

'Come on,' he said, getting up from the sofa bed. 'Get dressed.' He hopped about, putting on his boxers back to front and nearly overbalancing as he hastily posted his legs into his jeans. 'We're meant to be supporting the Starlight Croft mini mafia. Remember? The village hall.' I gazed at him blankly. 'The craft fayre,' he reminded. 'Yesterday, Cilla said Starlight Hall needed TLC but readies were required, especially as the local council aren't keen to splash out. So, there's a fundraising event. Cilla is expecting our support.'

'Is Hetty part of the Starlight mafia?' I asked tentatively.

'Absolutely,' said Milo. He briefly disappeared inside his shirt – which was still buttoned up – before reappearing again.

'Ah,' I said as realisation dawned. 'That's what Hetty

meant when I saw her earlier. She said something about going somewhere to support her village.'

'That will be it,' Milo nodded, tucking shirttails into his denims.

At that moment, my stomach growled noisily.

'Good heavens,' Milo laughed. 'Are you hungry?'

'I haven't eaten since breakfast,' I confessed, hauling myself upright. 'And that was some time ago.'

'In which case' – Milo pulled me towards him and kissed me on the nose – 'let's quickly have a bowl of that delicious grub that's simmering in the hotpot, and *then* we'll head off to the hall.'

A little later, stomachs full and coats on, we set off along the lane, but this time without the dogs. Rambo had flashed me an appalled look.

Have you noted the length of my legs? They're still aching from being out earlier.

The craft fayre was synonymous with that of every village fete. From homemade cakes, jams and chutneys to local artwork and bric-a-brac. A competition was going on for who had grown the biggest marrow. Hugo Cartwright, owner of the Strawberry Shed, was favourite to win. And no fete would be complete without its very own inhouse fortune teller.

Hetty was stationed at one end of the hall. She looked rather incongruous with a jewelled turban on her head. Her wrists jangled with cheap bracelets and her fingers sported huge rings. Their fake diamonds glittered and sparkled under the hall's lights. She was seated before a small table.

Centrepiece was a crystal ball and a small sign. This informed members of the public that *Oracle Hetty* gave accurate readings for the modest sum of thirty pounds.

Milo immediately got waylaid by Cilla. Uh oh, young Polly was here too. As she spotted Milo, her face looked strained. She made towards him, no doubt keen to hear if Milo had heard anything from JJ – her gallivanting boyfriend.

I drifted away to give Polly her some privacy, and found myself gravitating towards Hetty.

'Hello, again, my dear,' she beamed.

'Hetty,' I smiled warmly. 'You look… incredible.'

She inclined her head graciously.

'And so do you.' She patted the empty chair opposite the crystal ball. 'Come and sit down.'

Goodbye thirty quid, I inwardly sighed. *Ah well, it's for a good cause.*

I parked my bottom, then regarded her. Those eyes! That vivid blue. So strange. Even in this light they seemed unusually intense. If I was being fanciful, I'd even say… *supernaturally* bright.

'Your aura is radiant, Tilly,' Hetty began. 'Positively *radiant.*'

'Is it?' I said innocently.

Hmm. That would be the sex. The post-coital glow. And no wonder. Milo had certainly put me through my paces. He was an exceptional lover. And I couldn't wait to go home and do it all over again.

'Since I saw you this morning, another silver lining has been revealed.'

Yup. Milo's boxer shorts. They'd revealed something rather wonderful. My eyes glazed at the memory.

'A romance,' said Hetty, giving me a knowing look. 'A new man.'

'Oh?' I said, feigning innocence.

'You've already met him.' Her eyes slid past me and landed on Milo. 'I see the M word.'

Nooo! Could that be… M for Milo? I stifled a giggle and endeavoured to take her seriously.

'That's M for *marriage*,' she said, wiping the smile off my face.

'Oh, I don't think so, Hetty,' I asserted. 'Been there, done that, as they say.'

'Your ex-husband was never The One,' she countered. 'And you need to tell your friend at work that the man from overseas isn't The One either.'

'Juan?' I gasped.

'Tell your friend to see me. I'll put her straight. But back to you.' She patted my hand. Gave it an encouraging squeeze. 'It's all good, my dear. Marry your new man. This time it's for keeps. One big happy family,' she assured.

I gulped. Crikey. I hadn't even thought about that side of things. We'd only just got together, and I dared not presume too much. It was too early. Too soon. Too brand new and shiny. And as for referring to *one big happy family,* well, I hadn't even got around to telling my parents about Jake – never mind Milo. What would he think when I crept up behind him, put my hands over his eyes and trilled, "Surprise! Turn around now and meet your new stepson!"

And then there was the matter of Milo's son. Fingers crossed – when we eventually met – that we'd get along. Right now, I still had him down as a good-time guy who put his jollies and mates before his sweet girlfriend.

'It will all come good,' Hetty assured, as if she'd been privy to a video of my thoughts. 'You'll see.'

Chapter Seventy-Three

While at the craft fayre, Milo bought jam, chutney and marmalade, also a homemade quiche and chocolate cake. He insisted we scoff it the moment we were home.

'I don't know about you' – he murmured in my ear – 'but all that sex has made me hungry again.'

'I'm hungry for you,' I giggled.

Oh, cringe, Tilly. That was such an uncool statement.

But then I thought *sod it,* because it was true. I *was* hungry for him. I couldn't wait to be alone with Milo again.

We then paused to browse at another stallholder's table. *Happy Days Designer Jewellery* was displaying gorgeous handmade silver and copper treasures. I admired a lapis lazuli pendant with matching earrings. Milo promptly bought the set, causing me to squeak with delight.

'I'm going to wear them now,' I declared, threading the beautiful earrings through my lobes. 'Can you help me with the pendant's clasp?'

'You're like a little girl at Christmas,' said Milo in amusement.

'I *feel* like it's Christmas,' I said honestly.

And it was true. There were all sorts of emotions cascading through me, and they were all good. Happiness.

Joy. Gratitude. Not to mention a huge sense of anticipation – just like when you're about to open a present that gives you all you've ever wanted.

'Oh wow,' I said, bobbing down in front of the stallholder's mirror. I admired the blue stones with their bright threads of gold. 'Stunning.'

'Like you,' murmured Milo, as he fastened the pendant's clasp.

We finally left the fayre walking hand in hand, which didn't go unnoticed by Hetty. As we walked past her, she gave me an almost imperceptible nod. I beamed at her by way of response. *Oracle Hetty* may claim never to be wrong about her predictions, but I didn't quite have the nerve to reveal what she'd said when Milo enquired about the reading.

'Oh, you know,' I answered vaguely. 'This and that.'

As we headed back to Starlight Cottage, Milo squeezed my hand. I glanced up at him.

'Tilly, how do you feel…' he trailed off.

'Go on,' I prompted.

'How do you feel about staying the night with me at Starlight Cottage?'

I'd grinned up at him.

'I'd like that,' I said honestly.

'Good,' he said, squeezing my hand again. 'And how about we enjoy our quiche and chocolate cake in front of the telly.'

'Sounds good. A film?'

'I fancy a scary one this time.'

'Oooh,' I said. 'I'm not a big fan of horror films. They frighten the living daylights out of me.'

'Don't worry,' Milo assured. 'If you get nervous, I'll hold you tight. I know the perfect movie.'

'Right,' I said, hoping he wasn't going to suggest *The Exorcist* or something. 'What have you got in mind?'

He grinned mischievously.

'*The Curse of the Were-Rabbit* starring Wallace and Gromit.'

I playfully cuffed him on the arm.

'You had me going there.'

He regarded me with wide innocent eyes.

'But it's true,' he protested. 'You haven't seen the decimation those bunnies cause. *And* they're threatening the annual giant vegetable contest. The Starlight Mafia would have a field day if that happened here. They'd be ringing up the local council demanding they do something.'

'Surely Oracle Hetty would tune in to the ether and come up with a humane solution,' I bantered.

'Now there's a thought,' said Milo, suddenly looking serious. 'Do you know, I have a mate who is a bit like Hetty. But unlike her, Jack claims he can communicate with vegetables.'

'Vegetables?' I frowned.

'Straight up,' said Milo. 'Jack and the beans talk.'

I burst out laughing.

'That's bad, Milo. *Really* bad.'

'Made you laugh though, didn't it!' he said, as we swung through the garden gate. 'I'll go and pop this quiche in the oven. You fetch the dogs. Oh, and don't forget' – he waggled his eyebrows – 'bring your toothbrush.'

And so the scene was set. Me and Cindy, Milo and Rambo. But it wasn't just Sunday night we all spent together. Somehow, me and Cindy were there again on Monday evening. And Tuesday. And Wednesday. In fact, the whole week.

At work, Lisa was delighted for me. She'd been the first to notice the shift in my – as Hetty would say – *aura.*

And who knew how long things would have continued like this if Milo's son hadn't turned up just as we were canoodling on the sofa.

Milo's arm was around me. The only light in the room was that from the muted television. Just as Milo leant in to kiss me full on the mouth, the front door banged. Suddenly, the overhead light flooded the room. A bug-eyed Milo and I were staring at a young man who looked back at us in both surprise and shock.

'Pops?' he gasped, before staring at me. 'And whatever are you doing here… Mum?'

Epilogue

I'd always known that at some point I'd meet Milo's son. However, I'd never anticipated that – at the same time – he would meet mine.

For a moment the three of us had regarded each other in stunned silence. Milo had been the first to move. He'd reached for the remote and switched off the telly. For a moment, everyone had tried speaking at once. It had been quite a commotion.

Bit by bit – and with the aid of a stiff sharpener – the three of us had pieced together everything that had led up to this moment.

Jacob Joshua Soren – *Jake* to his friends, and fondly named *JJ* by Milo – had not been on a mate's stag do. Nor had he partaken in any laddish gallivanting. That story had been contrived. A cover so as not to hurt his Pop's feelings about what he was really doing.

Jake had taken himself off to Crete to meet his biological father – my first boyfriend, Nicholas – and discover his genetic roots.

Jake hadn't wanted to complicate things by taking Polly along. He'd gone on to explain that, much as he felt Polly was the girl for him, he *had* to find out his roots before committing to her.

Now Jake had that knowledge and his heart was complete. He apologised to Milo for not confiding in him but said it had been something he'd had to do for himself.

Milo had blown out his cheeks and looked flabbergasted. But he wasn't the only one.

'Sorry,' I said eventually, my brows knitting together. 'Call me dense, but I'm not joining all the dots.' I looked at Milo in confusion. 'You told me that you and your ex-wife never had children.'

'Correct,' Milo nodded. 'Martha and I adopted JJ when his parents died. His parents were Jerad and Sue. Jerad was my brother. You remember me telling you he was much older than me. Well, my deceased brother and sister-in-law were JJ's parents.'

'But' – I shook my head in confusion – 'Sue *can't* have been JJ's… Jake's… mother because *I* am Jake's mother.'

'Tilly, there's obviously one key thing I forgot to mention about my late brother and his wife.'

'Omigod,' I paled as realisation dawned. 'Your brother and sister-in-law *adopted* Jake.'

Milo's face softened.

'Yes, they did. They couldn't have kids, and made the decision to adopt. They got lucky. *Very* lucky. After several false starts and lots of heartache, they adopted a baby boy. I was so happy for them.' Milo's face lit up at the memory. 'They couldn't wait to show off Jacob Joshua Soren, and I couldn't wait to be a doting uncle. And I was. Fate can play some amazing cards. It can also play some terrible ones. A few years later, I lost Jerad and Sue.' Milo's eyes briefly swam. When he next spoke his voice was hoarse. 'But I gained a son. Fate has played a hand in your life too. You lost your son, but now you've found him again.'

It was at that point the three of us gave way to tears. So many emotions. So many scenarios. But only one ending. A happy one.

In the months that followed, I mused at Hetty Cartwright's knack of making predictions that somehow came true. Not forgetting another time. The day I'd stood with my dog and intoned to the universe all my hopes and dreams. Namely, to live in the village of Starlight Croft. Or, more specifically, a cottage named after the diamonds that glittered in a midnight sky.

It was strange how life sometimes delivered what we wanted but not in the way we'd expected.

Meanwhile, Jake's relationship with Polly had gone from strength to strength. They'd initially moved into the garden studio while house hunting. I'd been delighted to have my precious son literally on the doorstep. Milo and I had been even more thrilled when Polly had revealed she was pregnant.

'Dear God,' Milo proclaimed in mock horror. 'I'm sleeping with a grandma.'

I'd gulped back tears when Polly and Jake had broken the news to us. In a few months' time, I'd be holding a newborn in my arms, but *this* time I'd have the joy of watching that child grow up.

My parents were delighted that I'd found happiness with

Milo and were stunned about Jake. It had stirred up the past. But, as we'd all agreed, you couldn't change the past, but you could do something about the future.

Mum and Dad had eventually met their grandson. Many tears had been shed, but tears of joy. They'd both agreed that they couldn't wait to be great-grandparents.

Meanwhile, at Home and Hearth, and true to *Oracle Hetty's* prediction, Lisa's relationship with Juan collapsed. Nor did colleague Candace's secret fling with Leslie, our boss, work out.

Candace was infuriated that Leslie wouldn't leave his wife for her. She abruptly left Home and Hearth to work for a competitor.

However, it transpired that Leslie's wife was having her own illicit romance – with the gardener no less. Leslie apparently walked in on them both in the greenhouse. He claimed that there were scattered seeds and upturned flower trays everywhere. He later said that the difference between Miracle Gro and sex in a greenhouse was *not mulch*.

Leslie, aware that Lisa was nursing a broken heart, issued an impromptu invitation asking if she fancied going out to dinner. Strangely love went on to blossom between a most unlikely couple. Lisa made it clear to Leslie that she could never be his supplier of sugar tits, although she does sometimes surprise him with a homemade Victoria sponge. Leslie told Lisa that was fine, because *life is what you cake of it*.

And finally, just when I thought things couldn't get any better, Milo went down on one knee in the Starlight Arms.

Landlady Cilla was overjoyed when I accepted Milo's proposal. She wants us to have our wedding reception at Starlight Hall ensuring her pub supplies all the celebratory champagne.

However, rumours prevail about the village hall's future – the main one being that it's going up for sale on the open market. This, in turn, has attracted the attention of a builder who, according to Cilla, is *sex on legs*.

But that's another story…

THE END

A Letter from Debbie

I've given you a little teaser about what's coming next. The *Starlight Series* centres around the village of Starlight Croft.

My next novel – God willing – will be called *Saving Starlight Hall*. I gave a few hints in *Starting Over at Starlight Cottage* about the village's community hall coming under threat by greedy bureaucrats wanting to sell it for a small fortune to a local builder.

The novel has been outlined and I can't wait to introduce you to sexy builder Liam who upsets both the locals and my next leading lady. Sparks fly when they lock horns over the bulldozer. Watch this space!

Meanwhile, you may remember that, at the craft fayre, Milo bought Tilly a lapis lazuli pendant and matching earrings from *Happy Days Designer Jewellery*. This amazing small business really does exist. Check out the super-talented Sarah's work on Instagram or take a peek at her website www.happydaysjewellery.co.uk for all things stunning!

I love to mention my furry family in my novels. It will come as no surprise to discover that Tilly's dog, Cindy, is based on my own mongrel, Molly Muddles. Just like Tilly, I have imaginary conversations with my pooch all day long. Naturally, Molly Muddles understands every word I say!

In the last couple of years, real life dramas seem to vie with my fictional dramas. Currently, my father is ill in hospital with kidney issues related to bladder cancer. Lurching from one crisis to another currently seems to be the way. This morning, I gave in to a good cry. I then sat down to write this letter armed with a bottle of moisturising eyedrops and a strong black coffee. More than ever, writing has become a therapeutic haven.

Starting Over at Starlight Cottage is my twenty-first romantic novel. I love to write books that provide escapism and make a reader occasionally giggle. You will also find some drama, and sometimes that can be uncomfortable. Trying to once please a critical reader who said I only wrote *froth* and *fluff*, the next book saw me responding with a *take this* chapter which – yes! – horrified another reader who complained about having all her trigger buttons pressed. Can't win! So now I let my characters decide how the story is going to unfold. Best to buckle up, just in case there's a tense moment!

There are several people involved in getting a book "out there" and I want to thank them from the bottom of my heart.

Firstly, the brilliant Rebecca Emin of *Gingersnap Books*, who knows exactly what to do with machine code and is a formatting genius.

Secondly, the fabulous Cathy Helms of *Avalon Graphics* for working her magic in transforming a rough sketch to a gorgeous book cover. Cathy always delivers exactly what I want and is a joy to work with.

Thirdly, the amazing Rachel Gilbey of *Rachel's Random Resources*, blog tour organiser extraordinaire. Immense gratitude also goes to each of the fantastic bloggers who took the time to read and review *Starting Over at Starlight Cottage*. They are:

@teaandbooks90; Splashes Into Books; Little Miss Book Lover 87; Tealeavesandbookleaves; Tizi's Book Review; Frugal Freelancer; Jenny Lou's Book Reviews; Sapphyria's Books; It Girl World; jen_loves_reading; Pause the Frame; mjporterauthor.blog; Books, Life and Everything; Kirsty_Reviews_Books; The Intrepid Reader and Baker; Eatwell2015; Staceywh_17; annette_reads_daily; Novel Kicks; Against the Flow; and The Eclectic Review.

Fourthly, the lovely Jo Fleming for her sharp eyes when it comes to typos, missing words, and the like.

Finally, I want to thank you, my reader. Without you, there is no book. If you enjoyed reading *Starting Over at Starlight Cottage,* I'd be over the moon if you wrote a review – just a quick one liner – on Amazon. It makes such a difference helping new readers discover one of my books for the first time.

Love Debbie xx

Enjoyed *Starting Over at Starlight Cottage*?
Then you might also like *Lottie's Little Secret.*
Check out the first three chapters on the next page!

Chapter One

'So, when am I going to meet this new man of yours?' my bestie demanded. 'It's high time Stu and I made up a foursome with the pair of you.'

We were seated in my tiny cottage kitchen on a sunny, but cold, November morning. The weekend stretched ahead, and I knew Jen was hinting at doing something this evening. In her opinion, a Saturday night was wasted if it didn't involve company and plenty of wine.

'Soon,' I soothed.

'You said that last month.'

Jen folded her arms across her chest. Uh-oh. Her chin had thrust forward. Body language. Bad signs. Right now, I could read my mate like a book. She didn't believe my story about me having a new man in my life. Indeed, suspicion was oozing from her very pores.

Jen had every right to suspect my fella was fictitious. After all, I'd pretended before. Not that I usually told porkies. But at the time I'd been going through an arid patch in my love life. I'd been fed up with Jen bossing me about, banging on about a popular dating app. She'd joined and consequently met Stu. Naturally he was her soulmate. She'd almost ended up with Repetitive Strain Injury from so much swiping right.

'Well?' she prompted.

'It's tricky,' I said, making a see-saw motion with one hand.

'Lottie, you're repeating yourself.'

'Oh, for goodness' sake,' I huffed, pushing back my chair. I stood up. 'Do you want another coffee?'

Jen's eyes tracked me as I picked up the kettle.

'If you're having one,' she sniffed. She unfolded one arm and made a show of studying her fingernails.

'Yes, I am.'

'Okay, in which case I'll also have another doughnut,' she added.

'I thought you were on a diet and calorie counting.'

'No. *You're* the one who said she was on a diet. Instead, *I'll* count the calories that I'm saving *you* from eating.'

'You're such a thoughtful friend,' I said, giving her a smile as sweet as the sugary doughnuts we'd been tucking into.

'Anyway,' said Jen. 'Regarding this boyfriend of yours.' Her eyes swivelled back to my face. They were her most expressive feature and gave away exactly what she was thinking. Currently they reminded me of two hazel-coloured searchlights. They almost pinned me to the cupboard as I reached for the coffee jar within. As she tucked a strand of dark hair behind one ear, I pretended not to notice her scrutiny.

'What about my boyfriend?' I said casually, spooning coffee into mugs.

Jen narrowed her eyes.

'I smell a rat.'

'What do you mean?' I said, playing for time. Slowly, I poured boiling water over the granules.

'I don't think this boyfriend of yours really exists. You're trying to fob me off again, aren't you?'

Flipping heck, I *knew* I'd been right about her thinking that.

'No, no!' I hastily assured. 'He's real. Promise.'

'So what's the problem about us going on a double date?'

I stirred milk and sugar into the mugs but didn't reply.

'Oh God,' Jen groaned. 'Please don't tell me you're embroiled with a married man.'

I picked up the mugs and set them down on the table, alongside the plate of remaining doughnuts.

'Ryan is *not* married,' I said emphatically.

'Hm.' Jen picked up a doughnut, all the while eyeballing me suspiciously. 'Are you certain? After all, you said he's sixty years old. No man gets to that age without some sort of track record. He must have history. Unless he's been a monk. A celibate one at that.'

'All *right*,' I snapped. I snatched up my coffee, slopping hot liquid over my jeans in the process. 'Bugger,' I muttered. Grabbing a nearby roll of kitchen towel, I tore off a strip and mopped ineffectually with one hand. 'Ryan is single, but this status is quite recent.'

'You mean it's not that long ago he was a married man. I knew it,' Jen crowed.

'He's *single*,' I said tetchily. I swapped the kitchen towel for a dishcloth, patting away at my denims. Typical. Clean on this morning. Worn for barely three hours. Now I'd have to wash them again. It was either that or smell like a Costa Coffee shop. 'Anyway' – I pointed out – 'there's nothing wrong with being newly single. Remember, we've both been married too.'

'Ah, but we only have one ex-husband apiece,' Jen pointed out. 'How many ex-wives does Relic Ryan have?'

'Don't call him that,' I tutted, ignoring the question. 'Anyway, these days, sixty isn't that old.'

'It isn't that young either,' Jen muttered.

'Sixty is the new thirty,' I said airily.

'Where did you read that twaddle?' Jen snorted. 'Probably in one of those trashy magazines you secretly read – yes, don't deny it. I extracted one from behind a cushion the other week. It was full of nonsense about Prince Harry taking up painting to supplement his income.'

'Would that make him the artist formerly known as Prince?' I said dryly.

'Ha bloody ha. And don't think I haven't spotted your attempt to evade answering my question.'

'You think Ryan is too old for me.'

'Put it this way. If you live your life all over again, you'll be ninety-six. Whereas the six for Ryan will be in relation to him being six feet under.'

'There's only a twelve-year age gap between us,' I protested.

'Never mind that for now. Spill the beans about his marital history.'

'Oh, okay,' I sighed, tossing the tea towel to one side. I

leant back in my chair. 'He was married to someone called Heather for about thirty years. Prior to that, there were a couple of partners he lived with – not at the same time, obviously. Anyway, co-habitations can't be included when reviewing a potential partner's history.'

'Of course they can,' Jen scoffed. 'He might not have exchanged wedding bands with the women concerned, but they were still relationships.'

'Well they didn't last very long. Only a few months apiece.'

'That's a poor track record-'

'That can be put down to youth and inexperience,' I interrupted. 'His subsequent three decades of marriage with Heather demonstrates – to me – some serious staying power.'

'Hmm.' Jen looked down her nose. 'Who left who?'

'I don't know,' I said, trying to still the fluttering that had started in my stomach. I didn't want to tell Jen that, despite Ryan being single, he was still living with his ex-wife. Something about not yet finding suitable alternative accommodation. It was time to smartly move this conversation forward. 'Anyway, we've only been dating for a couple of months. I haven't, you know, felt able to ask any pertinent questions. Reading between the lines, I think they just got bored with each other. Ryan did divulge-'

'Oooh, yes?' said Jen, leaning forward. 'I sense juicy gossip. Don't tell me. Heather went off with the postman, and Ryan had a deep flirtation with a neighbour?'

'Nothing like that.' I shook my head. 'More... Heather being annoyed at always finding the loo seat up. Or... Ryan being irked by Heather's long hair bunging up the bathroom drains.'

'Fascinating,' said Jen, rolling her eyes. 'So, when are you next seeing him? Presumably tonight.' That was another thing about Jen. It wasn't just plenty of wine she wanted at the weekend. She expected lots of sex too. 'After all, it's Saturday. That's when lovers get together.'

'Maybe,' I shrugged. 'Ryan said he'd be in touch. Mind you, we seem to spend more time on the phone to each other than having one-to-one dates, what with the demands of his son-'

'Who must surely be grown up?' said Jen incredulously.

'Y-e-s,' I agreed. 'But unfortunately, he's still-'

'In nappies?'

'No,' I shook my head again. 'He's at school.'

'Ryan is sixty years old and has a child at primary school?'

'Of course not,' I said, doing my own eyeroll. 'Joshua is at secondary school. He's studying for his A Levels, but he seems very…' I paused, trying to find the right word. 'Needy,' I said eventually. 'He's always buttonholing Ryan to do things with him.'

'Like what?' Jen's eyebrows shot up. 'Fly kites at the local park? Go to London and visit museums for the day? Surely, if Joshua is a teenager, he's a bit beyond all that?'

I'd privately thought the same. Sally, my own daughter, had almost disowned me when she'd been a teenager. She'd found herself several jobs to pay for her social life – from babysitting to waitressing to shelf stacking – and had accordingly spent her earnings in clubs with mates or on days out with friends. The only time she'd ever freely wanted to hang out with her old mum was if I'd suggested shopping and offered to pick up the tab.

These days, I didn't see my girl as often as I'd have liked. Sally was miles away at Bristol university, in digs. Our contact was mostly confined to FaceTime or text messages. A bit like my relationship with Ryan, now I came to think of it.

'Perhaps' – my tone took on a defensive edge – 'Joshua is just a thoroughly nice boy who loves his dad's company.'

I had a sinking feeling that meeting Ryan's son was an event that wouldn't be happening any time soon. I also had a nagging suspicion that Joshua was hellbent on getting his parents back together again. I even suspected that Heather might be in cahoots with their son.

Jen would not approve of Ryan's domestic setup – no matter if it was temporary – or a woman who continued to treat her ex-husband like a spouse. Heather ensured Ryan was always at her beck and call. From putting up a shelf here. A new picture there. Changing a flat tyre. Assembling a new lawnmower. From what Ryan had let slip, such occasions involved Joshua and Heather too, whether passing a screwdriver or just idly looking on. Whenever a job was finished, they always seemed to get in the family car and take off to some local eatery or other. I'd discovered this after looking Heather up on Instagram and having a snoop. There were always lots of pictures. The three of them. Beaming away. Shoulder to shoulder. Sometimes at McDonalds. Other times, a five-star bistro. Yes, hands up, I couldn't deny it. I'd been a bit of a stalker.

My insides briefly curdled with jealousy. And why was it that whenever Ryan and I *did* manage to meet up, we'd get interrupted? Whether going for a walk together or grabbing a snatched coffee, invariably his mobile would ring. It would either be Heather or Joshua, but the outcome was always the same. Ryan being summoned to return home and attend some contrived urgent matter.

'So exactly how much time *do* the two of you spend together?' Jen now asked as she licked jam from her fingers.

'Not a lot,' I said miserably.

She gave me a curious look.

'You have slept with him, haven't you?'

I picked up a doughnut and took a huge bite, rendering speech impossible.

'Lottie?' she urged.

My jaw rotated as I eyed her silently.

'I do not believe it,' she shrieked. 'You haven't done the deed?' She rolled her eyes dramatically. 'Why ever not?'

'There never seems to be the right moment,' I said in despair.

'Don't be so ridiculous.'

'It's true,' I protested.

After all, I could hardly go back to Ryan's place. Not with Heather and Joshua in situ. I could imagine the scene now. Ryan yodelling, "It's only me. Lottie's here too. We're going to have a quick bonk, then we'll all bond together over a nice cup of tea."

Ryan had been to my place a couple of times now, but nothing had happened. On one occasion Sally had been home from uni – and no *way* was I having a romantic night with my daughter on the other side of a paper-thin wall. On another occasion, we'd just got up close and personal when, embarrassingly, I'd been caught short by a dodgy prawn from the curry we'd had earlier.

'There just hasn't been the right moment,' I despaired. 'There's always been an interruption. The last time we almost got to first base. However, Ryan's widowed mother telephoned at a crucial moment. She insisted he get in his car and drive over to her *immediately* because she'd lost her dentures. Apparently, she was fed up eating strawberry creams instead of chocolate toffees. Our intimate moments always seem to descend into a fiasco.'

'If I were you, I'd dump Ryan. You need to find someone who is properly available.'

'That's a bit harsh.'

'No it isn't. You want a guy who prioritises you.'

'Ryan is trying.'

'Ryan sounds very trying,' Jen muttered.

'Actually' – I folded my arms across my chest, a defensive gesture – 'he's suggested we go away for a weekend.' I gave Jen a coy smile. 'To *properly* get to know each other.' I followed that statement up with a meaningful look. 'Without any interruptions.'

'Then make sure it happens,' she said sternly. 'It's about time you had someone reliable in your life. Someone who gives you happiness instead of turdy nonsense. After all the hoo-ha with our respective exes, we now deserve to be cherished. Stu is coming up trumps, and I want someone in your life who does the same for you. After all, the last thing you need is another prat like that husband of yours.'

'Ex-husband,' I quickly corrected. 'Anyway, let's not talk about Rick.'

Geez, if Jen got me on to the subject of the disastrous life I'd shared with Sally's father, then I'd be exchanging the coffee and jam doughnuts for a stiff gin and tonic.

Chapter Two

After Jen had left, I went to the sink. On autopilot, I washed the dirty cups and plates.

As I stood there, swishing soapsuds about, I gazed blankly through the window at the view beyond. My eyes took in the bleakness of the narrow country lane that ran alongside my cottage.

A thorny hedgerow bordered the road. In summer months, its thorny stems were loaded with blackberries. Now winter was just around the corner and the hedge was an exploding froth of Old Man's Beard. On the other side of this rustic fence, grazing land stretched almost as far as the eye could see. A large group of shaggy cows were huddled together, as if silently communing.

I'd moved to Little Waterlow not long after the collapse of my marriage. Jen had lived in the village for the last couple of years. She'd urged me to bring Sally and live with her, kindly putting a roof over our heads while I'd sorted out my personal circumstances.

I'd been so grateful for the offer of this lifeline and taken Jen up on it. During this period, I'd overseen all manner of jobs to cover our keep and outgoings.

Despite experiencing the fallout of my disastrous marriage, Sally had somehow managed to pass her exams and secure a place at uni. She now lived away in halls.

And then – just down the road from Jen – a house had come up for rental. I'd leapt at the chance of leasing it. Much as I loved my mate, she needed her own space, as did I.

Catkin Cottage had been offered to the market for a six-month letting. It was the perfect stopgap as I continued to pick up the reins of my new life.

I'd already discovered that tittle-tattle was a national pastime in villages like this one. Rumour had it that Sophie Fairfax, the owner of Catkin Cottage, had fallen in love with another man while on her honeymoon. There was also some gossip about the man Sophie had been briefly married to. According to someone called Mabel Plaistow – an ancient pensioner who made other villager's lives her subject of special interest – Sophie's husband had been cheating all along with the wife of an old schoolfriend. Mabel had also shared chit-chat about the bridegroom having a false leg that had fallen off at a most inopportune moment.

I'd dismissed the stories. They were of no interest to me. I had enough of my own *stuff* to contend with. Nor did I want Mabel Plaistow getting wind of my personal life and spreading tall tales. After all, everyone has secrets. Some bigger than others. And my secret was a whopper.

I picked up the scourer and removed some lipstick from one of the cup's rims. A secret was only a secret if you kept it to yourself. And up until now, I had. However, just like a nasty boil that needs lancing, this secret had started to reach epic proportions. If it ever erupted, there would be a ghastly mess. One that would be entirely of my own making.

If Jen found out, she'd probably whip off one of her size sevens and whack me over the head. If Sally ever got wind… well, it didn't bear thinking about. And what of Ryan? That would be an altogether different scenario. Bye-bye Ryan. The end of a relationship before it had even properly begun.

My hands continued to whisk through the soapy water as memory after memory started to unfurl. The latter ones were far from happy. Thank goodness for Jen. She'd been such a rock. A shoulder to cry on. Due to her own failed marriage, she'd been sympathetic about mine. She'd understood my anguish.

Jen's marriage had unravelled in the unhappiest of circumstances. A woman had unexpectedly turned up on Jen's doorstep. The woman hadn't been alone either. In her arms she'd cradled a bonny baby boy. A smiley-faced gurgling bundle. The stranger had coolly announced that Simon – Jen's hubby – had been living a double life. The baby was his. Jen had been beside herself.

'The BASTARD,' she'd later shrieked. Her cheeks had been raw from crying so many salty tears. 'It was awful discovering there was another woman, but discovering she'd had Simon's child was the absolute pits.'

Despite numerous attempts to get pregnant throughout her marriage, Jen's ovaries had refused to co-operate. There had been many fertility investigations. The results had concluded that nothing was wrong. There had then been several attempts at IVF. These had been both costly and unsuccessful.

For Jen, trying to get pregnant had been all-consuming.

Eventually, it had taken its toll on her. For a little while, she'd understandably lost her marbles. It was during this period that Simon – nursing his own sorrows – had taken solace in another woman's arms. This woman was younger than Jen, and seemingly more fertile than the local farmer's fields.

Being careless with condoms had resulted in pregnancy. Simon, morally weak, but also terrified of Jen finding out, had instead tried to juggle things. This had led to him living a double life. For a while he'd succeeded – until the other woman had discreetly followed Simon home. Armed with her lover's address, she'd later returned to spill the infidelity beans.

Just like Jen, my marriage had ended on my doorstep – except my visitor had been very different.

Chapter Three

Rick Lucas had been everything my twenty-seven-year-old heart had ever desired – which just goes to show what a rotten judge of character one's heart can be.

Instead of listening to my heart, I should have paid attention to my brain. At the time, my grey matter had been screaming louder than the defunct smoke alarm in my flat.

Rick had been the drop-dead-gorgeous electrician who'd answered my emergency telephone call. He'd also been the one to come out and fix it.

'Thank goodness that racket has finally stopped,' I'd said gratefully, taking my fingers out of my ears.

'It's a common complaint with this particular brand,' Rick had said. He'd tossed the faulty alarm to one side and then set about collapsing his stepladder. 'If any dust or dirt lands on the photocell, the sensor gets triggered.' He'd paused. Glanced around my light and airy apartment. 'This is a nice place.' His eyes had rested briefly on the view beyond the lounge window. The River Thames had glistened like a strip of silver steel. 'Have you lived here long?' he asked conversationally.

'About a month.'

'Lucky you. Your hubby must earn well to have bought one of these.'

I'd reddened. Partly out of indignation at this guy's assumption that I needed a man to pay for the roof over my head. Also, partly from the insinuation that I had a husband who was loaded.

'There is no husband and I bought this myself,' I'd retorted frostily.

'Ah, in which case you're either a high-flier' – his eyes had mocked me – 'a lottery winner or, let me guess, you've blown an inheritance.' At those last words, he'd caught the look of surprise on my face. 'Bingo. Wow, lucky you. So, who snuffed it? Don't tell me. Your ancient great-aunt Matilda? The one who had a penchant for blue rinses, lavender perfume and loved to suck – careful, Rick – the occasional pear drop?' He'd given me an impish grin. No doubt he'd believed himself to be a cheeky chappie, instead of an outspoken Cockney with a glaring lack of tact.

My eyes had momentarily brimmed. Furiously, I'd blinked back the tears, aware of two pink spots staining my cheeks.

'Actually, it was my parents who – as you so eloquently put it – *snuffed it*. One from cancer. The other from a heart attack six months later. I'd much prefer to have them back in this world with me, instead of living in this lap of waterside luxury. Money doesn't buy happiness, you know.'

There'd been a horrible, tense silence.

'I'm so sorry,' he'd eventually said. 'I've offended you.' He'd put down the ladder. 'Sorry,' he'd repeated. For a moment he'd held his arms wide, then let them drop back at his sides. A gesture of helplessness. 'My mates are always saying I speak without thinking. Please accept my condolences too.'

'Okay,' I'd said stiffly. 'Meanwhile, how much do I owe you?'

He'd backed away, hands gesturing wildly.

'Nothing.'

'Don't be silly,' I'd protested. 'You responded to an emergency callout.'

'Yes, but it's not like it was the middle of the night, or a weekend and out of hours. Anyway, as I said, I'm mortified for putting my foot in it over your parents.' He'd made to pick up the ladder. 'So, no charge.'

'Look, we all have a living to earn. Despite you thinking I'm some sort of rich bitch, I *do* go to work. After all, bills don't pay themselves. So could we please park that previous conversation to one side, and you tell me what I owe?'

'Let me see.' He'd leaned on the ladder and pretended to consider. 'It's half past six on a Friday. This is a very civilised time to be caught out by a faulty smoke alarm. It means you're my last client of the day. Ordinarily I would now slip off my overalls and enjoy a drink, like at that trendy place just around the corner.'

'Good for you. So can I now settle your invoice before you head off?'

'Well, if you're absolutely adamant-'

'I am.'

'Then my fee is' – he'd stroked his chin thoughtfully – 'half a lager.'

'Pardon?' I'd frowned.

'You heard. Buy me a drink. But there's one condition. You must have a drink with me too.' He'd winked. 'That's the fee.'

And that was how it had started.

Also by Debbie Viggiano

Maggie in the Middle
Lottie's Little Secret
Wendy's Winter Gift
Sadie's Spring Surprise
Annie's Autumn Escape
Daisy's Dilemma
The Watchful Neighbour (debut psychological thriller)
Cappuccino and Chick-Chat (memoir)
Willow's Wedding Vows
Lucy's Last Straw
What Holly's Husband Did
The Man You Meet In Heaven
Stockings and Cellulite
Lipstick and Lies
Flings and Arrows
The Perfect Marriage
Secrets
The Corner Shop of Whispers
The Woman Who Knew Everything
Mixed Emotions (short stories)
The Ex Factor (a family drama)
Lily's Pink Cloud ~ a child's fairytale
100 ~ the Author's experience of Chronic Myeloid Leukaemia

Printed in Great Britain
by Amazon